Grey Griffins

Grey Griffins

The Clockwork Chronicles | Book 3

THE
PARAGON
PRISON

DEREK BENZ & J. S. LEWIS

Ⓛ Ⓑ

LITTLE, BROWN AND COMPANY

New York Boston

Copyright © 2012 by Grey Griffin Industries, LLC
www.greygriffins.com

Little, Brown and Company

Hachette Book Group
237 Park Avenue, New York, NY 10017
Visit our website at www.lb-kids.com

Little, Brown and Company is a division of Hachette Book Group, Inc.
The Little, Brown name and logo are trademarks of Hachette Book Group, Inc.

The publisher is not responsible for websites (or their content) that are not owned by the publisher.

First Edition: May 2012

Library of Congress Cataloging-in-Publication Data

Benz, Derek.
  The Paragon prison / by Derek Benz and J.S. Lewis. — 1st ed.
    p. cm. — (Grey Griffins. The clockwork chronicles ; bk. 3)
  Summary: Transported to an alternate reality, the Grey Griffins must battle arch enemy Otto Von Strife in order to find a portal back to their dimension.
  ISBN 978-0-316-04525-4
  [1. Friendship—Fiction. 2. Magic—Fiction. 3. Adventure and adventurers—Fiction. 4. Good and evil—Fiction. 5. Fairies—Fiction.]
I. Lewis, J. S. (Jon S.) II. Title.
PZ7.B44795Par 2012
[Fic]—dc23

                                                          2011035295

10 9 8 7 6 5 4 3 2 1

RRD-C

Printed in the United States of America

DEDICATION

Derek:

To Ioulia & Noah, as ever, forever, with love.

To Bryanna and Gabrielle: I'm so proud of you. Smart. Beautiful.
And so very cool!
To the Burkes. The House of Pure Talent. You're the best.

Jon:

To Benjamin Jacob Grimm, the pride and joy of Yancy Street.

And to Thomas Oscar Morrow, creator of my favorite android.

CONT

PART ONE: THE OTHER SIDE

1	**Born Again**	3
2	**Discoveries**	12
3	**Interrogation**	22
4	**Reunion**	32
5	**The Party**	40
6	**Back to School**	55
7	**Back from the Grave**	65
8	**Von Strife**	74
9	**Scarecrow**	82
10	**Out of the Blue**	96
11	**Eavesdropping**	102
12	**The Replacement**	109
13	**Killer Fog**	118

ENTS

PART TWO: THE PLAN

14 **The Machine** 127
15 **Raven** 138
16 **The Plan** 142
17 **The Break-In** 150
18 **Busted** 158
19 **Epiphany Jones** 166
20 **The Big Day** 177
21 **The Game's Afoot** 184
22 **The Fish** 190
23 **Stirling Rising** 195
24 **Theft** 200
25 **An Inside Job** 208
26 **The Party** 217
27 **The Return of Yellow Eyes** 221
28 **Sic 'Em** 229
29 **An Unexpected Invitation** 234

PART THREE: THE OMEGA OPTION

30 Brooke's Story   241

31 Answers   247

32 The Exploding Sandwich   252

33 Another Earth   259

34 The Werewolf   263

35 Invaders   273

36 The Lost Souls   285

37 Into the Impossible   292

38 Clockwork Jungle   299

39 The Fire Girl   307

40 The Paragon Engine   311

41 Where It All Unravels   321

42 Good-Bye   337

43 Reflections   341

THE LEADER: Max Sumner

After his grandfather's mysterious death, Max learned that his billionaire family was a part of the secret Templar society. He became the Guardian of the *Codex Spiritus*, an enchanted book that holds monsters, evil faeries, and other dangerous creatures captive within its magical pages. The *Codex* can change shapes, from a book to a ring to a gauntlet capable of channeling Max's family power: Skyfire!

THE INVENTOR: Harley Davidson Eisenstein

Built like a linebacker and incredibly smart, Harley is a technological prodigy who designs gadgets critical to any successful monster hunt. Unlike Max's wealthy family, Harley and his mother are barely getting by. But he's not bothered; he knows that happiness isn't measured by how much money you have in your bank account.

THE SLEUTH: Natalia Romanov

Fearless, fiery, and intensely smart, Natalia uses her keen observational skills and her analytical mind to solve any mystery. As a part of her sleuthing kit, Natalia carries a Phantasmoscope, which allows her to see into the faerie spectrum. Since a close friend betrayed her, Natalia has had a hard time trusting other girls, but she's trying to befriend girls again. She feels more at home with the Griffins than with anyone else.

THE CHANGELING: Ernie Tweeny

Ernie became a changeling after a transfusion of faerie blood, which gave him super speed, rapid healing, and enhanced eyesight. But there's a catch: whenever Ernie uses his powers, he becomes more faerie and less human. Despite that risk, he has vowed to fight evil as his superhero alter ego, Agent Thunderbolt.

THE KNIGHTS TEMPLAR

The Knights Templar is an ancient society that has sworn to protect mankind against unseen dangers like monster invasions and zombie uprisings. Recently, the Templar were nearly exterminated by an army of werewolves called the Black Wolf Society. They are slowly rebuilding their strength.

MAX RACED THROUGH A DARK FOREST, HIS HAIR slick from the pelting rain. Lightning flashed. A blood-curdling howl cut the night. The hounds. They were still on his trail and getting closer.

Max plunged into the thickets. If he could just make it into Avalon, he could get help. Call the cops. Logan. Anyone.

His lungs rattled as he pushed ahead. His sneakers were mud-caked, his laces tattered. His face burned from the thorns that entangled his every turn.

Another howl, closer still.

Max burst out onto a stretch of black highway. A road sign loomed over him: AVALON: ½ MILE. Max gulped down a breath of misty air and took off.

As he ascended a small hill, he heard the familiar sound of a car engine idling. He smelled the exhaust. Those were taillights up ahead. A police car.

Max glanced back to see three shadows emerge from the woods. A man in a broad-brimmed hat holding the leashes of two snarling dogs. Another lightning flash gave Max a horrific realization. Those weren't dogs.

"Slayers," Max said. His wide eyes took in the monsters: black, tight skin stretched over unbreakable bones and lean muscles. Their claws were chipped and bloody, their jaws were lined with rows of teeth, and there was that unmistakable glare from the empty eye sockets that saw everything and nothing at all.

The Slayers broke their leashes and leaped toward Max, who raced away desperately. The police car was his only chance. Max slid to a stop in front of the driver-side window. He hammered on it.

"Help! Sir, you have to help me. They're coming!"

The window was fogged, and though he could see a figure inside, the officer didn't seem to be able to hear him. Max yanked at the door handle. Locked!

The Slayers were getting close, their iron claws sending up sparks as they bounded over the hill. Why wasn't the policeman answering?

Max pounded on the window, his sweaty hands sweeping away the fog in frantic streaks. Max looked inside as he yelled for help. The officer, suddenly aware of Max, unlocked the back door. Max threw himself inside.

"You've got to get out of here!"

"Relax," said the officer. "Everything is under control."

"No, you don't understand. We have to go. Now!"

"It won't be necessary. We've been waiting for you."

"Waiting? But how…"

At that moment, the officer turned toward Max, and as he did, the dashboard light illuminated a face not of flesh, but of metal. And behind those sunglasses were two flickering red diodes. In a whirl of spinning gears, the clockwork officer's arm shot back over the seat and latched onto Max's throat. Squeezing. Tearing.

Max beat uselessly at the machine. He gasped. He choked. Everything flashed white and then faded to black. It was over in seconds.

PART ONE

THE
OTHER SIDE

BORN AGAIN

Max Sumner awoke to a blaze of swirling light. Everything around him spun like the inside of a fiery cosmic drain. He tried to get his bearings, wondering if this was only another dream or if this was real. All he knew was that moments before, Max and the Grey Griffins had been staring at the Paragon Engine, wondering how to blow up the inter-dimensional gateway, before Otto Von Strife's clockworks stopped them. It hadn't worked out as planned. Now they were seemingly tumbling across a kaleidoscope of dimensions. Lights flashed. Worlds swept by. And always the humming of the wormhole that funneled them to some unknown destination. It smelled of bleach.

Then the walls of the wormhole collapsed. Max saw—or thought he saw—a massive ringlike structure ahead. Another Paragon Engine? But as it neared, something else seemed to catch hold of him and pull him away. The lights blurred as he moved sideways through several doors of light.

With a flash, he was tossed out of the wormhole and onto wet grass. He heard shouting, and before he could roll out of the way, the other three Griffins tumbled on top of him. There was another flash, and the wormhole disappeared.

They were in a midnight forest so suffocated with shadows that the only sounds they could hear, besides their own breathing, was the soft patter of rain overhead.

"Did we screw that up or what?" Harley Eisenstein groaned. "One second, we're about to blow up the Paragon Engine, and the next, someone throws a switch and we're sucked into the very machine we were supposed to destroy. I bet Von Strife planned it all along."

"I don't care what he planned," said Max anxiously. "We left Logan back there, with Brooke and Raven. If we don't get back fast, the clockworks will finish them off."

"Well, at least we're alive. I don't suppose anyone thought to be thankful for that," Natalia Romanov said, fixing her braids and cleaning her sweater of leaves. Her summer glow had long since faded, along with her freckles, thanks to a cold winter fighting monsters. She looked through the lens of her Phantasmoscope, an ornate cousin of the magnifying glass, but instead of magnifying words, it made the invisible world visible. Not even the fingerprint of a pixie could escape her notice. "Wherever here is. Say, this place looks awfully familiar."

Ernie—the half faerie, teen super speedster known as Agent Thunderbolt—took off his helmet, slid his goggles up on his forehead, and scanned the dense woods. "You're right. It's like we're back in Avalon. These are the Old Woods. But why would the Paragon Engine send us back home? I thought we were going to another world."

"The trees are taller here," said Max, squinting up in the darkness. "Anyway, wasn't Von Strife going to use the Paragon Engine to invade the Shadowlands? Maybe that's where we ended up." Max hoped he was wrong. The Shadowlands was a wild, magical world controlled by the dark king Oberon, who had an unfortunate and ugly grudge against Max. Meeting him this way, in his own world and on his own terms, would probably result in the Griffins' being hand-fed to a nest of dragons.

Harley's pocket flashed twice. He pulled out his communicator. "Wherever we are, they've got phone service. Full bars!" The Griffins sighed in relief.

Natalia took the phone from Harley and flipped through the screens as he protested. "If you have reception, that means you have GPS. Let's figure out where we are!" The Griffins gathered around the communicator and watched it zoom in on a familiar map. A moment later, Max backed away.

5

"If this is correct," Max said, "my grandma's house is right over there." He pointed through the trees. "What I don't get is, what happened to all the snow? Look at the trees. Some of them have leaves already. What's going on?"

Natalia looked at the phone again. "Midnight of March twenty-first."

"We were stuck in the Paragon Engine for a month?" asked Ernie, turning pale. His thoughts returned to Raven, the changeling girl who he'd come to think was the prettiest and scariest girl in the world. "What if Raven's dead? Do you think...? Oh, no. And she was just starting to like me."

"She's a tough girl," said Harley, patting his skinny friend on the back. "I'm sure she's fine. And when we see her again, you can tell her what it was like to go through a Paragon Engine." Ernie brightened at the thought. It would certainly be nice to have something to brag about.

"We need to take a look around," Max said, who wasn't as optimistic as Harley on the topic of their friends' survival. For now, he had to focus. He turned to Ernie. "How's your super speed, Agent Thunderbolt? Working?"

Ernie replaced his goggles and helmet, then zipped across the forest floor in a blur. He went faster and faster until, with a flash, he disappeared completely. A moment later, he was back with a bug-smeared grin. "Holycowthisissoawesomelyawesome. NotonlyamIworking, butI'm-fasterthanever!"

"How fast?" asked Natalia. "And try to slow down, okay?"

Ernie took a breath and began again. "The whole world freezes. It's sick fast." Ernie wiped away the bugs from his goggles and grinned. His teeth were a traffic pileup of insect fatalities. "I think I need a windshield."

Natalia blanched at the sight. "Or a mouth guard."

"So what did you see?" asked Max.

"Let's just say that your grandma's house is there, all right. So is Avalon. Although it looks kind of weird. But it's night, so who knows?"

Max grabbed his backpack.

"Where do you think you are going, Grayson Maximillian Sumner?" Natalia exclaimed. "We need to be careful. Ernie's super speed may not be the only changes around here."

"Well, we're not sleeping out here," said Max, wiping a slick of mud from his knees. "Let's head to the red barn. At least it will be dry."

The others agreed, and they quickly slipped out of the woods, trudged along the cold and barren rows of corn in the neighbor's field, and rounded the murky old pond. They soon opened the barn's back door and stepped into the darkness. Harley switched on his flashlight.

"Sure looks the same," he whispered.

"Smells the same, too," complained Ernie. He covered his nose as he stepped over a pile of fresh horse manure.

They were in the main section, which was broad and dirt-floored. To their left were the tack rooms and the horse stalls. To their right was a door leading into the milk room, which was filled with all the usual junk: lawn mowers, bicycles, tin cans, jam jars, and chain saws. Confident they were alone, Max circled back to the main room and led the way up into the loft.

"Oh, hey, Mouser!" Max whispered, after nearly stepping on the familiar black cat. It sniffed Max's outstretched fingers, then coiled back into a hiss. With a yelp, it disappeared behind a crate and howled. The rest of the barn cats fled the loft like rats leaving a sinking ship.

"That was weird," said Natalia.

"Mouser's always been weird."

The Griffins piled onto the mountain of hay bales, making sure their flashlights couldn't be seen through the loose sideboards. "Well, so far so good," Harley said.

"And we're dry," Natalia added, wiping her wet hands on her jeans. She took off her shoes and wiggled her toes. "Or we will be. My socks feel like oatmeal. Anyone bring an extra pair?"

Ernie dug through his pack, then whimpered.

"What's wrong?"

"I only have one candy bar left. Agh! What was I thinking? It's times like these I hate being a changeling. I mean, I love eating. But why does it have to be every second?" He wasn't exaggerating. Ernie's faerie metabolism burned through calories. And if he didn't get enough calories, he passed out.

"Not that I mind carrying you," Harley said, "but you don't always smell so good."

"Hardy har har." Ernie snorted. "And it's my changeling medicine that smells bad, not me. Speaking of which, I didn't bring any dragon dung tea with me, Natalia...."

Natalia looked over at Max with concern. Hunger was one thing, but this was serious. If Ernie didn't have his special tea, his changeling blood would start to take over. Good-bye Ernie, hello monster—or whatever it was he might become. Nobody would know for sure until it actually happened. "We'll get you some more. Don't you worry, Ernest."

"Fine. But I'm still starving. First chance I get, I'm raiding his grandma's refrigerator."

"Oh no, you're not," Max said.

Natalia stretched her damp toes. "You know what bothers me about this whole thing? Paragon Engines only work in pairs. The one we went through in our world had to be connected to one in another world. But instead, we were dumped off in the woods like a sack of unwanted kittens. It doesn't make any sense."

"The Paragon Engine is just a big clockwork computer, and computers have glitches," said Harley, an engineering genius. There wasn't anything he couldn't learn or couldn't build. He sure didn't look the boy-scientist part, though. A head taller than most boys his age, he fit the action-hero description much better than Ernie did.

"A glitch?" asked Natalia. "A glitch just wiped out a month of our lives? Is that what you call a glitch?"

"A month is better than dead," said Max bleakly. "Which is what Logan, Brooke, and Raven might be." He sighed. "I feel horrible. Like somehow it's my fault they were left behind." He stood up and paced the floor. "Don't you guys ever think about it? I mean, what we are and what we do? Nothing's simple anymore. And no one is safe. Don't you just ever wish we could go back before everything got so crazy? Before we met the Templar? Before I found the *Codex*?" He paused, his voice growing quiet. "Before Dad left..."

The Griffins regarded Max silently. He was a great leader. The bravest of the brave, and the truest of the true. They'd been through thick and thin together. Each of the Griffins had had these same thoughts. They knew. They understood in a way that only the very best of friends could.

"Max," said Natalia, placing a hand on his shoulder, "we were trying to save the world. And if you haven't noticed, the world's still here. That means that somehow, whatever it was we did, it worked. There's every chance in the world they are alive. Just wait and see. In the morning, everything will look different. I promise."

Max nodded. He was exhausted. Too tired to think. They all were. Maybe Natalia was right. Maybe things would be better after all. They turned off their flashlights, and the Grey Griffins went to sleep one by one.

DISCOVERIES

Max awoke to the sound of a car engine rumbling to life. He rolled off the bale of hay, nearly kicking Ernie in the head, and sprang to look out. It was Grandma Caliburn. He caught just a glimpse as she pulled out of the white gravel driveway.

"Did you see her?" asked Natalia as she joined Max.

"Sure looked like her," he replied with a smile. He never realized how relieved this fact would make him feel. And what if things had turned out just fine for everyone? Maybe Logan was out there somewhere, tuning up his Ferrari's engine. Maybe Brooke was curled up in a chair with her favorite book. Maybe everything had worked out after all. Then Max spotted Ernie popping a hard-boiled egg into his mouth.

"Hey, where'd you get that?"

"From your grandma's kitchen—where do you think? She should really lock her door. It's not safe."

"Ernie! I told you not to do that. What if someone saw you?"

Ernie brought out a tray of carrot sticks and gnawed away. "I don't think so. I'm pretty fast. You should try your Skyfire, Max. I bet you are all powered up, too."

Max looked down at his magical ring—the *Codex Spiritus*. A little more awake now, he could definitely sense something had changed. Was it the enchanted Skyfire that coursed through his veins? Or perhaps his shape-shifting ring, which could turn into a gauntlet of power or a magical book? Max would have to figure it out. "So inside the house—it's all the same?" he asked.

"Looked the same to me. Man, I love the way your grandma always keeps the carrots so crispy in the water tray." He munched a dozen sticks in rapid succession. "I was only in the kitchen. Want me to go back? There's a pecan pie on the counter I had my eye on." Before Max could answer, Ernie disappeared...and reappeared again. His careless smile had vanished, and his hands were behind his back.

"What's the matter?" asked Harley. "What have you got there?"

Ernie squirmed. "I, ah...here!" He thrust a photograph

into Harley's hand. In it, Harley saw himself, standing next to his mother. Beside them stood a man Harley had never seen before. "Check the writing on the back," Ernie prompted meekly.

The Eisensteins. Summer at Lake Waconia.
Harley, Candi, and Henry.

"Holy smokes, Harley!" Max gasped. "That's your missing dad! You look just like him."

Harley said nothing. His finger traced the figures. He'd never known his father. Never even seen a picture.

"Henry," Natalia read aloud. "That's a really nice name." She studied Harley closely and saw a frown forming.

"What sort of sick joke is this?" Harley growled.

"Guys," Ernie said, "that's not all." He pulled out a newspaper clipping. It was a picture of all four Griffins standing together on the grounds of Iron Bridge Academy. They were dressed in their monster-hunting gear and looked very grim. More grim, however, was the headline: Missing Teens Pronounced Dead.

"Dead?" exclaimed Max.

"Well, I certainly don't remember this picture being taken," said Natalia. "Even if it was, how do you explain the earrings in that picture? My ears aren't even pierced!"

"Keep reading," Ernie said.

Harley Davidson Eisenstein, Natalia Felicia Anastasia Romanov, Grayson Maximillian Sumner III, and Ernest Bartholomew Tweeny—the intrepid Agent Thunderbolt— have been declared dead by the Avalon crimes unit. The four teens went missing on December 24 last year while on assignment with the Templar. An anonymous tip led investigators to Sumner's bodyguard, a man known only by the name Logan. The man was questioned, but he denied involvement, then injured several officers—including Sheriff Wilfred Oxley— in his escape. At this time, the bodyguard is still at large and considered extremely dangerous.

Ernie sat down and sighed. "I feel so weird. Is this what it's supposed to feel like when you're dead? Why would Logan kill me? Do you think he was mad because we left them behind?"

"Wait," said Max. "I don't get it. December twenty-fourth? Is this the future, or the past?"

Natalia scanned the clipping again. "Neither. You're totally missing the point."

"What do you mean?"

"The photo. It was taken in front of Iron Bridge Academy, right? But this is the Avalon newspaper. Last I knew, no one in Avalon knew Iron Bridge existed, except us. They aren't supposed to know about the Templar, about monster-hunting, and they certainly shouldn't know Ernie is called Agent Thunderbolt."

Max's and Natalia's eyes locked. They spoke at the same time: "This isn't our world!"

"You mean the Paragon Engine worked?" asked Ernie.

Natalia looked up from the newspaper clipping. "It gets weirder. This paper calls itself the *New Avalon Times*. And look, there're advertisements on the other side for dwarf-made furniture and pixie-dust elixirs. I don't know what weird, parallel world we just discovered, but magic isn't a secret here. It's as normal as a box of Cheerios." Natalia quietly scribbled some notes into her *Book of Clues*—her pink detective notebook that had been with her on every mission.

"Once Grandma discovers the missing food," said Max, "she'll call the cops. We need to find someplace else to hide until we figure this out."

"Do you have a place in mind?" asked Harley.

"If the Griffins here are dead, no one will be looking for us in our old tree fort, right?"

"Maybe we should take a look around town first," said Ernie. "Just to see how much has changed. I can do it. No one will see me."

"We can't take any chances on getting caught, Ernie," said Natalia. "We should stay together, at least until we know more."

They agreed, and after Ernie gathered up enough food for all of them, they crept out of the loft and through the back door, and tromped down an old, familiar path back to the Old Woods, where they'd hide out until dark. This was the very path that the other Griffins might once have taken. They were dead now. As Max regarded the well-worn footprints, he shivered. If the other Griffins could be killed, then so could they.

When the sun went down, the Griffins snuck out of their hiding place in the Old Woods and took the dusty road leading toward the outskirts of town.

"I still don't understand why we're taking the long way around the woods," said Ernie. "There's a shortcut to the tree house from your grandma's. It'll only take twenty minutes."

Natalia sighed. "Like I've told you already, Ernest, there's no telling what's lurking in those woods at night. With your speed, maybe you'd be all right. But the rest of us are safer walking *around* the woods. Trust me."

They soon crossed a pungent field of alfalfa and struck the road leading past Max's house. They hadn't meant to come this way. But Max found his footsteps pulling him along. He wanted to see his house. He wanted to see who lived there.

"Into the ditch!" Max hissed. A moment later, a strange car swept by, a mechanical horse and carriage that floated on a field of blue energy. The driver wore a topcoat and top hat, while the passengers inside were hidden by smoky glass.

As the Griffins clambered out of the ditch, Max smiled. "I'd expect something like that in New Victoria.

But in Avalon? This world is going to take some getting used to." Even as he spoke, the stars disappeared behind a slow, hulking shadow overhead: a zeppelin! It had overtaken them without a sound.

"It's the *Graf Zeppelin*!" Harley exclaimed with a smile. "Monti's zeppelin." It was the very same airship that had carried the Griffins across the world and back only a few months before. "Wait a second. Are those deck cannons? And missile launchers? Holy smokes! He's turned her into a battleship!"

The Griffins ascended a familiar hill framed by iron lampposts that flickered with gaslight. To their left sprawled the Victorian mansion where Brooke lived. If this was a completely different world after all, then there were no guarantees that the Brooke back in their world had survived. Max's eyes dimmed.

"There's your house, Max," Natalia said as they reached the top of the hill. The Sumner mansion, just one of several luxurious homes on the lakeshore, stood forth in its castlelike majesty. A warm, cheery glow shimmered from inside. But Max's own home hadn't been cheery in years.

"How do you do it, Harley?" asked Max.

"What do you mean?"

"After seeing your dad. Don't you want to meet him? Look at him, at least? You haven't said anything about him since you saw the photograph."

Harley shrugged. "I guess I do. But...I've spent my whole life thinking he left Mom and me behind. What would I say to this guy?"

"How about 'hello'?" said Natalia. "You have to be curious to meet him."

"I like my life just fine the way it is."

Max turned toward the Sumner mansion. "Well, I need to find out. I'm going to take a look."

"Max!" Natalia protested. "There are security cameras everywhere in this neighborhood. What if you get caught?"

"Let me go for you," Ernie suggested. With Agent Thunderbolt's speed, he'd be there and back again faster than Max could blink.

"I'm sorry, but I have to do this," said Max. "You guys will understand when you see your own houses." He took in a breath of courage and set off. Moving from bush to bush, he made his way to the living room window. Inside, he could hear the blare of a television. His heart pounding, Max peered through the window.

In Max's home back in his world, the living room had been a sterile cube fit only for blobby white sculptures made in Barcelona that cost as much as a yacht. Max wasn't even allowed in the room. But in this world, there was a wraparound leather couch, a wall-sized television, and a floor covered with toys. Unfortunately, the couch faced away from him, obscuring its occupants. Max moved to another window.

As he peeked through the lowest pane, his jaw dropped. There sat his mom with his little sister, Hannah. His father sat next to them, laughing and absently playing with his wife's hair. A bowl of popcorn rested on his lap. He certainly didn't look like the scoundrel and traitor who'd nearly taken over the world.

Max slid to the ground, his heart racing. This wasn't the shattered home he'd left behind. This was his old family. The one before the divorce and before his father had revealed himself as the iron-fisted leader of the armies of the Black Wolf Society. Lord Sumner's werewolves had nearly exterminated the Knights Templar on his quest for global annihilation. The man was a military genius. A business icon. And an actor capable of fooling those who loved him the most. Max hated him. Sometimes. Max decided on one more look, just to be sure.

There it was again: the perfect family picture. And his father, the most loving of them all. Max tried to clear his head. He scanned the room for other familiar objects, and his eyes stopped on a picture frame: a photo of Max looked back at him. A small candle burned nearby. A memory candle. Pictures of Max covered the room—on the shelves, on the hearth, on the walls. And each of them had black silk ribbons wrapped around the corners. Max turned to leave, wondering if he'd just seen something he shouldn't have.

As Max tried to make sense of everything he'd just seen, he heard a slight rustle of grass behind him. Max turned in time to see a black bag thrown over his head. It smelled strange. Before he could cry out, he wobbled, fell to the ground, and closed his eyes.

INTERROGATION

"Who are you?"

Max slowly regained consciousness as he felt two strong hands shake him. Max's brain tried to reassemble a jumble of memories. He tried to stand up, but he couldn't find the strength. His mind cleared after a moment. Ropes secured him to his seat, and a bag covered his head.

"Who are you and where did you come from? Fast," the voice pressed. Max's mind slowly turned the question over and over, unsure how to answer. "Don't make me repeat myself, boy."

Max knew he wouldn't be held captive for long. Not once he activated his *Codex* ring. But as he felt for it, his stomach dropped. It had been taken! But if his abductor knew what the ring could do, then he must have also known who Max was. There would be no point in lying. He replied slowly, his tongue thick and slow, "Max. Where are my friends?"

"They're not your concern. I am. Now, how did you come here?" The voice was being deliberately disguised. But the way the words came out seemed familiar to Max.

Max paused to consider his answer. "A portal," he said finally. True enough. He didn't have to blurt out that it had been the Paragon Engine. After all, it could very well be Von Strife questioning him.

"Where from?"

Max fell silent. "I, uh, I don't remember."

"Who do you think you're foolin'?" Max heard the man growl. A very familiar growl.

The head covering lifted. Staring back at Max was the face of his old friend Logan. But this Logan looked older and wore a patch over his eye. He took hold of Max's collar and pulled him close. "Look, kid, I don't know what you're playing at, but you ain't Max. The real Max wouldn't be skulking about the Sumner place, peering in windows. You say you popped out of a portal? Fine. How long ago?"

"Midnight, last night."

"Has anyone else seen you? Talked to you?"

"No."

Logan looked long and hard at Max. "Seems to me there's only one way to prove your story. Only the real Max Sumner could wield the *Codex* ring."

"Then give it back to me."

"Right. I don't think I'll be doing that." He held up Max's ring. "My scanner readings put this little darlin's power off the charts. But it doesn't mean it's the *Codex*."

Max remembered his Skyfire. He didn't want to use that magical flame on Logan, especially without the *Codex* to keep it under control. But maybe just a show. Maybe that would be enough to prove who he really was. Yet, after several frustrating moments of concentration, his eyes opened again in desperation. "What did you do to me?"

"You're wired to a neural inhibitor," said Logan. "And I'm not about to take it off.".

"I've already told you everything."

"Not nearly enough," the Scotsman said. As he spoke, Max noticed a hovering clockwork emerge from the shadows behind Logan. As it moved toward Max, its gears whirring and ticking, he could see in its claw a syringe of bubbling blue liquid with a very long, very frightening needle. Max's jaw dropped. "Now, kid," said Logan, "suppose we start from the beginning. My way."

24

Max rolled over and blinked up at the early morning sun. He slowly raised himself up. His muscles were stiff; his mouth tasted chalky. Then he remembered Logan and the clockwork interrogation probe.

"Good morning, sunshine," greeted Harley. The other Griffins were sitting nearby, eating the rest of Grandma Caliburn's hard-boiled eggs. Overhead hung a thick cloud of trees. Max knew these trees well. They were in a small park across from his house. "Logan got the drop on all of us."

Max rubbed his neck and winced. "Man, he's good. I never saw him coming."

"No one did," said Natalia with a disgusted sigh. "You'd think Agent Thunderbolt, with his fantabulous powers, might have seen him coming."

"I told you, it's not my fault," Ernie said as he pulled a tiny metal gadget from his pocket and tossed it over to Max in annoyance. "It's a changeling inhibitor. He shot this into my neck with a blowgun. Can you believe that? Man, I hate these things." Ernie threw the inhibitor on the ground and stomped on it a few times.

"At least you got your powers back," said Max. "Logan still has my ring."

"Well, you aren't dead," Natalia said. "And goodness

knows he had the chance to kill you. Anyway, none of us can remember much—it's all blurry. How about you?"

"I'm not sure." Max sighed as he peeled an egg. "Oh, boy, was I stupid visiting my house or what?"

"Look, if Logan knew we'd be at your house, then ten-to-one he was already following us. This is Logan, after all. We never stood a chance."

Max shook his head. "Well, if he didn't kill us, maybe he didn't kill the other Griffins, either." Max shoved his hands into his pockets and heard a squeak. Something warm and furry had been sleeping inside. An instant later, the face of a baby chipmunk blinked up at him. It stretched its paws, then cleaned its whiskers.

"Oh my gosh, it's the cutest thing!" exclaimed Natalia. "Can I pet it?"

The chipmunk cast a withering glare at Natalia. With a shimmer, the brown fur became a coat of jagged needles. "Do not touch!"

"Sprig!" Max exclaimed as the shape-shifting spriggan changed into a tiny dragon. Bounder Faeries like Sprig were inseparable from their masters, though Sprig liked to stretch the limits from time to time. There were only a handful of students at Iron Bridge with Bounders, and none were like Sprig. How she'd followed him here was nothing short of a miracle. She flew to Max's shoulder and melted into her true form: a catlike creature with gleaming teeth, spiky dark fur, and mesmerizing, long-lashed eyes. Her leathery tail swished back and forth across Max's back.

Natalia shook her head at Max, warning him that this might not be his Sprig. But the spriggan yawned and said, "Max shouldn't have left us behind. But Sprig followed. Sprig knows the way to many worlds."

"But...how did you get here?" asked Max.

Sprig batted at a moth lazily. "Sprig is a Bounder. Wherever Max goes, Sprig goes."

"If you're so smart," Natalia said, "then maybe you can tell us exactly where here is?"

"You are in the same place you were. Only different."

"Oh, could you be any more useless?" Natalia sighed.

Sprig changed forms into a figure that looked exactly like Natalia. "Now," said Sprig. "Now Sprig is more useless." Her eyes suddenly darted to the foliage. Someone was coming. Sprig changed into a bat and disappeared.

"Well, well, well. Looky what we've got here." The Griffins turned to find a man in an officer's uniform and a Stetson. His thin, craggy face presented a push-broom mustache that concealed his mouth. On either side of him stood two broad-shouldered clockworks, both with badges. Despite the humor in the man's voice, he didn't look amused. "Now aren't the four of you supposed to be dead?"

As the Griffins rode in the sheriff's car, they peered out at the town. It was Avalon, all right—the Lutheran church, the town hall. But it was as if the town had somehow blended with the strange Victorian qualities of Iron Bridge Academy. The streetlights were gas lamps, the roads were cobblestone, and people were walking down wide thoroughfares with parasols and top hats. As the squad car drove around the square, Max noticed that the buildings, all the ones he remembered, were stretched thin and tall, and loomed out over the sidewalk like rows of giants hunched with age.

The Griffins were quickly sat down in Sheriff Oxley's office. He closed the door, locked it, and sat back in his chair. He put his feet up on the desk, one boot at a time. This was the same sheriff mentioned in the newspaper clipping. The one whom Logan injured in his escape. Max could see a fresh but slight scar on the man's jaw. But he didn't look much like the Chief Constable Oxley from their own world. Max wondered who else might look different.

"Now, let's get started. Where in the blazes have you been? You put the town, not to mention your parents, through the wringer." As he spoke, he didn't look sad and he didn't look relieved. He looked suspicious. Max had seen that same look in Logan's eyes the night before.

Max shared the story he told Logan, careful to leave out the Scotsman. The sheriff said nothing, then kicked back and picked up the handset of an old rotary phone.

"Jane? Where is that file I told you to bring me? Of course the one on the Griffins—who else do you...oh,

28

all right. That's fine. Oh, and get me a coffee while you're over there. No. Black. See that it's hot. There's a good girl."

"Well, now." The sheriff set down the phone and stood up. "There's a few people who will be very interested to ask you a few questions. So don't you go nowhere." He tipped his hat to them, then stepped out of the office, locking the door behind him.

"Well, aren't we a nice little catch?" Natalia sighed in annoyance. "We didn't last a day in this world without getting caught. How embarrassing. And can somebody tell me what a sheriff is doing working with clockworks?"

"Von Strife's clockworks," added Ernie. "I saw a stamp on their arms. This is too crazy. It's nuts! Maybe this is all just a bad dream."

"Okay, then whose dream is it?" asked Natalia.

"Shhh…" warned Harley, pointing at the sheriff's telephone, which wasn't quite hung up.

Just then, the Griffins heard a great commotion outside, and the door burst open. There, her face as white as chalk, stood Ms. Merical, their homeroom teacher. They were quickly scooped into loving arms. "Oh, it's true. I couldn't believe it!"

"Now wait just a minute, ma'am," the sheriff protested as he pushed his way past her. "You can't just barge in here. We've got an investigation on our hands. We've got a process to follow."

Ms. Merical smiled back at him with a glittering glow

in her eyes. "What you have here is a miracle." As their gazes met, the sheriff's own eyes glazed over. He reached for his chair and sat down. To Max, it appeared the man's brain had just fallen into a cloud. A cozy cloud. But a cloud, nonetheless.

"Well, then," Ms. Merical continued as she put her arm around Natalia, "your mom and dad are going to be over the moon to see you!"

The sheriff suddenly roused himself, his eyes refocusing. "Listen here, I don't know how you found out about these kids, but this is as far as this information goes." He tried to stand, but his heel broke on his cowboy boot. He sank back into his chair with a thud.

"I'm afraid it's a little late for secrets, Sheriff," Ms. Merical replied. "Their parents are already on their way."

"What?"

"Well, I called them, naturally." Her eyes intensified. "I am sure they will be especially thankful to you, Sheriff, for bringing these families back together. You're a hero. Something you've always wanted to be. And towns don't forget their heroes." She smiled warmly at him. He smiled back dreamily.

"Well, I . . ." He paused. Then his eyes took on a similar glow as Ms. Merical's. "How can I help?"

"By doing a little dusting and cleaning," she replied, looking around the office thoughtfully. "It probably hasn't had a thorough going-over in years. Not your fault, of course. You're a busy man. But there's no better time to begin than right now. After all, we're about to have guests." She turned to the Griffins. "I think it's time for the four of you to get ready!"

"Ready for what?" asked Max.

"A welcome-home party like you've never seen!"

REUNION

Within five minutes, Ms. Merical had taken over the police station, assigning each Griffin to a private office as plans were made, while Sheriff Oxley took on the role of hero as if it had been his idea all along. Then the media swept in, setting up their wooden box cameras and snapping photos of everything, from Ernie's flashy goggles to Max's missing ring.

"Where's the *Codex*, son?" asked a photographer. "Hate for that beauty to go missing. And what's with the strange getup?" Max looked at him quizzically. "Your clothes, son. What do you call those?"

Max looked down. "Um, blue jeans and a polo shirt?"

Judging by the clothes of everyone else in the room, Max concluded that what he considered normal was anything but. It was all about top hats, trousers, and waxed mustaches.

"So you've been playing polo while you were away, eh?" The man whistled, lifting his bowler hat and scratching his head. "I don't go in for the sport myself. Silly hats. Well, we're all glad you're back. And, if your obituary helped our circulation, just wait'll your resurrection hits the presses."

Max sat in the sheriff's office, his legs dangling over the leather chair. He wrung his hands anxiously. He was about to see his family—the family he always wished he'd had. Yet now that they were on their way, he desperately wanted to disappear. What would they be like? Kind? Loving? Or stern and suspicious? After all, Max was a fraud, posing as their dead son. He was a rat, and he knew it.

He drummed his fingers on the desk. Not much longer now. He heard the station door burst open outside and heard the shouts of Ernie's parents. His mom wept with joy, and Max's worry that Ernie would blow the whole thing was unfounded. His friend played it all off as a big misunderstanding. The Griffins hadn't had much time to rehearse their story, but it seemed to be working.

The doors opened again, and there were the sounds of Natalia's parents and sister. More cries of joy and sobbing hugs. Soon, Harley's parents arrived. Max peeked out the door to look at Harley's dad. He looked like a kind man and as strong and handsome as Max's own father, but in a more rugged-linebacker sort of way. He threw open the door to Harley's room and wrapped a viselike hug around his son.

Max shuffled back to the chair and sat down. He swiveled it around twice and drummed his fingers again. Were his parents even coming?

"Max?" called a soft voice, startling him. Annika Sumner stood in the doorway. Dark mascara ran down her face as she looked at him in disbelief. She moved slowly toward him, then reached out and ran her hand through his hair so carefully it seemed as if she was afraid he might suddenly disappear.

"It's okay, Mom. I'm, uh, sorry I gave you a scare," he told her, readying his speech. But the words didn't come. This wasn't the mother he'd left behind, the cold, businesslike woman who knew entirely too much about pearls and not enough about jelly sandwiches.

As he looked up, he spotted Lord Sumner standing nearby. Max's eyes met his father's, and he felt an instant connection. His dad nodded at Max and smiled. Max knew what it meant: "Good to see you, champ. I never had a doubt."

Sniffing and wiping her eyes, Annika stepped away. "Well, let me take a look at you." Max did his best to straighten up and stick his chest out, but she only giggled. Smile lines appeared, unlike the grim frown lines his own mother had.

"I can explain everything," Max offered.

Lord Sumner shook his head. "Ms. Merical told us enough and warned us not to rush you. You've been through a lot."

"Not as much as you," Max replied honestly. "Where is Hannah?" He quickly bit his tongue. What if his sister's name wasn't Hannah?

Annika took him by the hand and led him out of the office. "She's with your grandmother. We had to be sure. It would have just broken her heart if you weren't... well, you." Max swallowed a lump.

Max climbed into the Land Rover. His mother sat in the back with him, not letting him out of her sight. She held his hand the entire way home. And Max liked it.

The ride back to the house was surreal, both in the way his parents were talking to him and in the landmarks they passed. It wasn't only because the town had wrapped itself in brass, stone, and steam. The land itself was different. The streets were broader. The trees were taller. The hills rolled more. Then there was the lake. Before, a lazy rowboat could slide across Lake Avalon in twenty minutes. This new lake seemed to just stretch on and on.

And the island, where Iron Bridge Academy lay, was now connected to land by an expansive stone bridge lined with ornate lamps. There was a city on its misty summit, and over its skies were dozens of airships, floating freighters, and strange dragon-sized birds. Yet, in the car, everything seemed normal enough. The air-conditioning hummed. The satellite radio played. In the cup holder next to him was a Big Gulp.

This world would take some getting used to.

They pulled into the driveway, and Max hopped out. His mother's hand was on his shoulder all the way through the door into the house. Then she knelt down in front of him and looked him over, as if he might disappear at any moment. "Your grandfather's dog tags from the war," she said, looking at his throat in sudden disappointment. "The ones he gave you before he died. Did you lose them?" Max instinctively felt for the absent necklace, then tried to give a convincing nod. "That's too bad. I know how much they mean to you. And to me." She took in a resigned breath and offered a weary smile. "I'm sorry... I'm probably over-mothering you. I bet you'd like some time to yourself. Go on upstairs. Your room is just the way you left it. Rosa will call you for dinner."

With an awkward good-bye, Max made his way up the stairs. The stairs even squeaked in the same place as back home.

He closed the door to his room and threw himself

onto the bed, noting that the pillow smelled the same and had the same lumps in it he knew so well. For a long while, he just stared at the ceiling. Then he realized he was smiling. He sprang up and walked over to the mirror—his mirror! There was his smile, looking back at him.

"I'm happy," he said quietly. Max couldn't remember the last time he felt like this. Every cell in his body seemed to be jumping with joy. It had been so long since he'd had a family—a normal family.

He scanned his room, a near twin of his own. There were different posters on the wall. Same comics, though. Same aquarium—different fish. Then Max walked over to the computer. It wasn't his home computer. It was a DE Tablet from Iron Bridge, a clockwork computer so elegant and refined it could have been hung on a museum wall.

"I wonder if we use the same password...." Max fired up the computer and typed in his password. It worked!

You have four hundred thirty-six unread messages.

Max cringed. Probably the friends of the dead Max...

Then a chat window popped up. It was Natalia.

Natalia: What in the world took you so long?
Max: Sry. Just got home. R ur parents cool?
Natalia: OMG, you wouldn't believe it. Everything has changed. The house. The cars. Thankfully my room is still pink. But more on that later. You have to know something. My dad.

He's some sort of expert on magical relics. And he works for you know who....

Max: Von Strife?

Natalia: Surprise, huh? By the way, VS is also the director of our school. NOT the Baron. How's that for a shocker?

Max: O…M…G

Natalia: You can bet VS knows we're here already. Anyway, how did it go with your dad?

Max: weird. Is your chat session encrypted?

Natalia: duh…

Max: Well, my dad asked about the Codex. He knows I lost it.

Natalia: What did you tell him?

Max: I said Sprig was looking for it. ;-)

Natalia: Good cover. And maybe she will. Lord knows she could stand to do some work around here. So anyway, Rosa just called my mom. Your folks are throwing a big party for all of us. Tomorrow night. I guess keeping a low profile is a little out of the question now.

Max: what are you going to do in the meantime?

Natalia: Detective work. To get the lay of the land. You should, too.

Max: k. I will.

Natalia: gotta go. L8er g8er.

Max: k. Good luck.

That evening, Max sat on the same couch he had looked at the night before. His parents were with him, eating buttered popcorn as they watched one of Max's favorite movies. As Max sat there quietly, he felt a tingle on the back of his neck. He turned quickly and looked out the window. Someone had been there. Maybe the person wasn't visible, but Max could sense someone. Even without his magic ring, he wasn't completely without talent. He got up and walked over to the glass. He couldn't see anyone. But he knew. He knew who had been watching him.

And Logan knew he knew.

THE PARTY

Max rolled out of bed the next morning and was halfway to the bathroom when he remembered that this wasn't his house. He stood quietly, his hands on the banister, and looked out over the expansive marble foyer below. Even though it looked nearly identical to his house, this one actually felt like a home.

"Hey, Max," called his father from downstairs. "How do you want your pancakes?"

A simple question. Even this could be Max's undoing. "Oh, uh, the usual, I guess."

"Paper-thin pancakes coming up!"

Max quickly disappeared into the bathroom. Paper-thin? Max had no idea what that meant, and it didn't sound good. He brushed his teeth and studied his face closely. Then he considered something else: scars. Max had several on his arm. Chances were that the other Max had scars in different places. Annika would know. A little camouflage would do the trick. Max returned to the bedroom and pulled on a long-sleeve shirt. Sprig was waiting for him, peering out of the sock drawer nervously.

"Where have you been?" asked Max.

Sprig wrung her paws. "Max is in danger. Max is being followed. Something. It moves fast. But Sprig is clever. Sprig will find it. Sprig will make it stop. Do not worry."

"Who? A monster? A person?" Max looked out the window. Everything seemed bright and cheery. Kids were skateboarding down the street and laughing. "You don't mean Logan, do you?"

Sprig hissed. "No. Something else. Something with yellow eyes..."

Yellow eyes? Suddenly, Sprig fled out the window. As he watched her go, Max felt a creeping tingle on the back of his neck. He turned in time to see a swirl of smoke near his aquarium. As he moved toward it, it faded from view. There was no smell of smoke, no sign of fire. Max rubbed his eyes. "Man, I need to get some sleep." He grabbed his ball cap and ran downstairs.

"Hey, sport," Max's dad called as he wound up for another pitch later that afternoon. "How's that old glove of yours feel? Just like old times?" Max grinned and smacked the baseball glove with his left hand. His lucky glove.

Max hadn't played catch with his own father in two years. Or was it three? As they passed the ball back and forth, Max found himself wondering about the difference between this Lord Sumner and his own father. They were the same man. They talked the same. Threw the same knuckleball. They'd gone to the same schools, married the same woman, bought the same house, and had the same kids. But somewhere along the line, his own father had made a different choice.

When Max returned to his bedroom, he flipped on the DE Tablet. Natalia was already there.

> **Natalia:** Where have u been?
>
> **Max:** Finding out what my life would have been like if my dad hadn't screwed it up. How is your family?
>
> **Natalia:** I can't believe I finally have COOL parents. My sister's still a BR@T, but what do you expect? They're giving me space and all that. Which is fine because it's weird, and I'm afraid

I might say something stupid. Anyway, more about that later. Are u alone? I've been a busy bee.

Max: YES. Tell me.

Natalia: First things first. The Templar are a superpower in this world. They've practically eliminated war, hunger…everything is hunky-dory. And they are all dripping with money. Oh, and as for Iron Bridge Academy—it's only the most famous school in the world. It's like Harvard for kids with swords.

Max: Well, at least we don't have to keep who we are a secret anymore.

Natalia: You're missing the point. You're a Templar. All the Griffins are. Your life may look and feel the same because you were already rich. But you should see my house. Brick drive. Dad drives a Jaguar. A carriage house with an actual carriage! Not to mention the horses. Everything! U can bet Harley's not living in a trailer anymore.

Max: Have you talked to him?

Natalia: No. But Ernie's going to visit him later this afternoon.

Max: What else did you find out?

Natalia: Well, Iron Bridge, for one. The kids there are already planning parties for our big return. Which, BTW, is Monday. Get ready. I wonder if Von Strife will show up, or if he plans to kill us before Monday. I hope not.

Max: Good point.

Natalia: And one more for the papers. Natalia Romanov is among the ADMIRED and FASHIONABLE, thank you very much. In this world, I was never a geek. I was cool. Cool! I can't stand it. So bizarre. All those girls I always hated in school for being witless, inane, and self-absorbed? They're my buddies now—HA—well, not all of them. Can u just imagine me as one of the popular girls? Chattering on the phone like crazy chickens? Wow. Blows my mind. Oh. My sister is banging on my door. What a pest! Why couldn't I have had a sensitive, older sister in this world. AGH! L8er.

"Welcome home!" the crowd cheered.

The Sumner mansion was decorated from floor to chandelier, and the party soon spilled out onto the back patio. For nearly an hour, Max was paraded up and down a line of people he'd never seen before. He'd never been hugged so much in his life.

His old friends from King's Elementary were there,

as was his favorite aunt, Audrey, who had died of cancer back in his world. Max felt like he was walking through a dream. There were some other shockers, too, like Ray Fisher. Apparently, the evil creep had never turned into a monster with blue skin, horns, and a taste for the end of the world. In fact, the worst this Ray had done was slip a frog into someone's soup at the state fair.

As for Ms. Merical, she'd personally planned the whole party, enlisting the help of Sheriff Oxley. Apparently the suspicious sheriff had slipped and hit his head shortly after the Grey Griffins left the police station. His memory of the whole day was erased. Now he was just one more smiling face at the party. Lucky break for Max—a little too lucky. He wondered if Ms. Merical has something to do with it.

Max had been especially excited to see one particular guest: the Griffins' mentor and adopted grandfather, Olaf Iverson. In their world, Iver had been killed by Max's father. In this world, however, he was still very much alive. Unfortunately, he couldn't make it to the party.

"He's on some sort of Templar mission," Natalia whispered to Max after an hour of plying her new girl-friends for information. She seemed to have a core of three or four best friends and at least a dozen admirers. "No one knows when Iver will be back. But he still runs the Shoppe of Antiquities, and he's still our mentor—I think. The Baron never was…" Before she could finish, a crush of boys swarmed them, patting their backs and hooting and howling. Ross and Todd Toad were there, grinning like gophers, along with Kenji Sato, a friend from Max's Bounder Care class. All around, some even flying overhead, were the changelings: Denton the lion boy, Yi Lu the fire elemental, Laini the pink-haired pixie girl, and many others. Then Max caught sight of some of the changelings who had been kidnapped by Von Strife, including Hale and Becca. Max felt chills when he shook their hands. He wanted to be happy. And on the surface, he was. He'd missed them, and their captures had horrified the Griffins. But these weren't the same kids Max had known. They might have looked the same, but they were nothing more than copies. Then again, maybe Max's world was the copy, and this was the real one.

Ernie, however, was an unstoppable hand-shaking machine. He'd missed his friends. Some of these kids had been members of his superhero team, the Agents of Justice. Of course, they didn't know anything about the team and its failed mission to take down Von Strife's forces, but Ernie was just happy to see them, especially those who had gone missing. He felt like his family was back from the dead.

"Whoa, take it easy with the hugs," complained Hale, pushing Ernie away. "I'm glad to see you, but let's not get carried away."

Everyone was dressed in the industrial Victorian way

that the Griffins had become used to at Iron Bridge. It wasn't just the students, though. The men from Avalon wore top hats and monocles as they escorted ladies dressed in velvet corsets with elegant cameo jewelry. There were handlebar mustaches, brassy bits of gadgetry on belts, and leather—lots of leather.

"Man, what a party, Maxie," said Todd Toad, adjusting his polarized goggles as he stood next to his fluffy-haired brother. Todd pulled on his suspenders proudly. "Totally awesome. Great food, too. Glad to have you back. How about you? Feeling the rush? Of course you are. Bet you miss Round Table, because Round Table misses you. Did you kill any cool monsters—maybe a Bull Troll or a sixty-foot squid? Knew you would. Knew you would, killer. Didn't I tell you he's a killer, Ross?" Ross Toad bobbed his head in agreement. "Maxie is the man! The *man*! Back from the dead. You don't look dead. Are you sure you were? Hey, is that chocolate pudding over there? Excuse me." The Toads headed quickly to the buffet. Max watched them go with a breathless smile. At least the Toad brothers hadn't changed.

"So what was it like being trapped inside a portal for so long?" asked Denton. While Agent Thunderbolt's superpower didn't make him look any different, Denton was known as the lion boy, with his sharp teeth, swishing tail, and manelike hair, which was gelled into a great pompadour.

Ernie crossed his arms smugly. "Dude. A portal? That's so last year. I'm talking the king of all portals. A Paragon En—hey!"

Harley cut Ernie off by putting him in a headlock. "Hey, Denton! How's the mane?" Ernie talked way too much.

Denton grinned and slicked back his hair. "It's hard to be this handsome. But you know how it is. Hey, have you seen Raven yet?"

Ernie squirmed out of Harley's hold and zoomed to the other side of Denton. "Raven's coming?"

"Of course. But I got to tell you. She was pretty messed up about you."

"Messed up? About me?"

Denton grinned. "You're such a clown, Thunderbolt. Messing with Harley like that..."

"Harley?"

Denton put his paw on Harley's shoulder. "Raven hasn't been the same since you disappeared." His face grew serious. "Have you seen her yet? No? Well, you better get on that. She was pretty torn up about you dying and stuff."

"What? Harley?" Ernie nearly fell over. What was wrong with this world? He was the one who liked Raven, not Harley!

Meanwhile, Harley choked on the news. A girlfriend hadn't exactly been part of his plan. Especially not one whom Ernie had had his eye on. He watched his friend sulk back toward the buffet. There'd be a very uncomfortable conversation later.

Max saw his father approaching with a broad smile. "Hey, Max. Your grandma just arrived. And you-know-who is with her."

"Hannah?"

"Your sister is dying to see you, Max."

"Max!" called Grandma Caliburn as he arrived at the front door. She was dressed in all black, from her high-buttoned shoes to her broad-brimmed hat. She grabbed him in a tight embrace. "I knew you'd be back. You're too much like your grandfather to let anything like this stop you." If she was crying, Max couldn't tell. She was the sort of person who cried only when no one was around.

"Now, Max, there is someone who has been waiting to say hello to you...." She slowly let him go and stepped aside to reveal a young girl, in spiraling curls, wringing her hands and squirming in her shoes. His sister, Hannah.

Max knelt down. He smiled gently as he reached out to her. "Hey, there. Thanks for coming to see me."

She looked at him closely and then stepped back, horrified. Her eyes began to water. "You're not my brother!" she cried, and ran into the kitchen. Max felt like he'd been kicked in the gut.

"Give her some time, Max," his grandmother said soothingly. "She's been through a lot."

First Logan. Now his sister. Who else knew Max was a fraud?

When the party ended, the four Griffins sat on the back patio under the stars. It had been an exhausting day. So far, no earth-shattering mistakes had been made.

"You should have seen the way Hannah looked at me," Max said.

"I wish my sister was afraid of me," replied Natalia tersely. "Kat's even more annoying than before. While she thought I was dead, she took almost all my stuff. My unicorn collection! And I found one of my diaries in her room this morning! I am so going to kill her."

"You mean the other's Natalia's diary?" asked Max.

"What's the difference? Private is private."

"Anything interesting in the diary?" asked Harley.

"I'm a detective, not a snoop. What kind of creep reads another person's diary? Honestly. Even if she is me and I'm her. I can't believe you'd even think that." Natalia paused. A guilty blush rose in her cheeks. She cleared her throat and moved on to another topic. "So, Ernie, how different is your house?"

"Same house. Which is good. But not so good for the neighbors. Apparently the other Ernie was running some laps around the house when he accidentally created a tornado. There's not much left of the block except a couple of trees. No one seems to want to move back."

"Go figure. So how about your changeling buddies?

What did you think when you saw Hale and the others? Make you want to put the Agents of Justice back together?"

Ernie sighed, recalling the superhero changeling team with mixed emotions. He missed the team, but he didn't miss the arguing and stupid decisions that had nearly gotten all of them killed. "And make a mess of things again? Maybe I'm not cut out for leading a superhero team. I don't know. But even if I did, what's the use? Who would we fight if Von Strife is a good guy these days?"

"You could start with bad breath," said Harley. Ernie rolled his eyes.

Natalia turned to Harley. "And what about you? How's the new dad? I heard you don't live in a trailer anymore."

Harley shrugged. "I hate the house. Too clean. I'm constantly afraid of breaking something. Man, Max, how do you do it?" Instead of a dented trailer near the swamp, the Eisensteins' home was now a glass-and-steel, zero-energy marvel on the top of a hill. Harley's father, Henry Eisenstein, had designed some of the most famous houses in the world. Mostly for the Templar rich and famous.

"Well, at least you know where you got your brains."

"Maybe. I don't really talk to Henry, or Candi. It's too creepy."

"Creepy? But you've always wanted to know who your dad was."

"He isn't my dad," Harley snapped. "And the people you're living with aren't your parents. Wake up! We're trapped in some creepy mirror world. We don't belong. Don't you get it?"

"Geez, fine." Natalia shook her head. "Be that way. But I say, if we're stuck here, we might as well enjoy ourselves. Speaking of enjoying ourselves...when were you going to tell me about Raven? I didn't know you liked her."

"What?" Harley snorted. "Come on."

"I wonder why she didn't show. I mean, if you guys are such an item."

"We are not an item," Harley said. "Anyway, knowing her, she'll probably pop out of thin air and scare the bejesus out of us. She's a lurker."

"What are you saying?" said Ernie.

"She lurks. She just hides in the shadows and eavesdrops. Then she appears and drops a bomb on everyone, walking off like she's Queen High and Mighty. Come on. You know it's true."

"We need to be careful, though," said Natalia. "If Max's sister knows Max isn't the real Max, then there are others out there who probably can figure it out, too. Like that yellow-eyed thing following Max. The one Sprig warned him about. Do you think it's some sort of faerie assassin?"

Max's shoulders slumped. He'd been hunted by assassins before. If Yellow Eyes was an assassin, Sprig was in over her head. And Max was in deep trouble.

"Maybe it works for Von Strife," said Harley. "I mean, he has to know the truth about us, right?"

"The question is," said Max, "is he the Von Strife from our world, or from this one?"

Natalia pulled out her *Book of Clues* and flipped through the pages thoughtfully. "It's a good question. But maybe it doesn't matter. I've been thinking. Von Strife's evilness was always about doing whatever it took to save his daughter's life. But if she's alive in this world, then maybe he's not so evil anymore."

"She's alive?" asked Ernie.

"According to the school computers, she's a student at Iron Bridge."

Max turned at the sound of a thud and a flutter of wings. "What was that?"

"Just a crow," Harley replied, picking up a stone and taking aim. "He keeps coming back, though. Or maybe there's more than one."

Max hated crows, ever since a flock of them attacked the school last year and nearly tore everything and everyone apart. Freakish things with beady eyes. "Let's be more careful about what we say and where we say it— you never know who's listening."

"Yeah," replied Ernie. "Like Harley's lurking girlfriend."

"Keep it up, Agent Thunderbutt," warned Harley hotly. "I'm going to say this once. Loud and clear. Raven is a weirdo. She's a freak. I wouldn't be caught dead with her."

As the Griffins went back into the house and turned off the lights outside, the figure of a girl emerged from the bushes. Her dark hair shone silver in the moonlight, and black mascara ran down her face. She sniffed, wiped away a tear, and glared so violently at the Sumner mansion that it might have burst into flames. She stalked away, her black nails pressing sharply into her closed fists.

BACK TO SCHOOL

On Monday morning, ready for school, the Griffins boarded the *Zephyr*, an enchanted underwater subway. Like the bridge Max had seen earlier, the *Zephyr* connected Avalon with New Victoria island. But no kid in his right mind would take the bridge. Hungry dragons above and slithering tentacles from the deep weren't ideal conditions for walking to school.

Besides, unlike the dilapidated train they'd known in their world, this *Zephyr* was a work of art. Leaded glass windows were etched with flowers. Brass poles gleamed. The leather seats smelled terrific. There were even bookshelves lined with volumes of poetry, Templar history, and MERLIN Tech. All that was missing from the *Zephyr*'s Victorian finery was a marble fireplace.

Natalia fit right in with the dated style in her tan cargo pants, high buckle boots, canvas corset, and red leather trench coat. "The other Natalia happens to be just my size," she said with a smile. "I'd say that's just a little bit of fabulous."

Natalia regarded the *Zephyr*'s posh interior with a hopeful smile. So far, the moody machine hadn't paid her any attention, and that suited her just fine. Back in their world, Natalia and the *Zephyr* were mortal enemies. Their animosity had been Natalia's fault, and she'd tried to make up with it. But the *Zephyr* wasn't interested in apologies. Instead, it toyed with her. Doing nothing for weeks at a time, then suddenly dumping a bucket of rotten fish heads onto her lap.

Max glanced out the window as the *Zephyr* passed beneath the shimmering green waters of Lake Avalon. The Templar's use of MERLIN Tech—a way of hot-wiring machinery with faerie magic—made the impossible possible: hidden cities, flying cars, talking clockworks, and even this train. At the moment, the *Zephyr* was whizzing along a completely transparent underwater tunnel, which kept the ride dry and sea-monster-free. As for the lake itself, it wasn't exactly a swimmer's paradise. In those fathomless depths lurked creatures of such terrifying vastness that any ship less than a hundred feet long was considered bait.

Safe and dry inside, the Griffins were planning out their day when the Toad brothers burst into their car.

"Wow, your folks sure know how to throw a party, Max!" Todd said as he patted his belly, his two rabbit teeth gleaming as he stared at them with an expectant smile. His polarized goggles still hadn't shifted from dark to light yet, and he was wearing a Round Table jersey. Max spotted his own name on it.

SUMNER CHEATS DEATH

"Nice shirt," Natalia said.

"Good eye, good eye. The detective hath returned! Everyone's gonna be wearing them today. Not a detective. A shirt. These shirts. Well, not everyone. All the Round Table players. Ross designed them. You like it? Out of respect to the Maxter. The man is back. The fox is in the henhouse. The shark is in the water. A giant is in the…oh, you know what I mean. Right? Of course you do, Maxie. Not like the other card jocks. There's no duelist like you. Man, we missed you. Round Table hasn't been the same. Am I right or am I right?" He punched his brother in the arm enthusiastically. "Man, coming back from the dead? How many people have done that? You guys are legend, and you're not even in high school yet."

"Totally legend!" echoed Ross Toad. His bushy hair was extra fluffy today. As he launched into a dizzying gush of admiration, he and his brother abruptly disappeared in a swirl of mist. A moment later, they were replaced by Aidan Thorne, aka Smoke, a teleporter and a primo jerk back in the Griffins' world.

Smoke folded his arms, his eyes scanning the Griffins from under a set of amber-lensed goggles. "Welcome back." His voice dripped with sarcasm as he swept his trench coat out of the way and plopped down beside them. "Sorry I couldn't make it to your big party. You guys really pulled it off. Hey, did I tell you that you look pretty good for being corpses?"

"You're such a ray of sunshine," said Natalia with a frown. "I don't suppose you'd mind telling us what you did with Todd and Ross."

"They're at school. In a Dumpster with the other garbage."

Agent Thunderbolt quietly watched the changeling. Ernie had had more than his fair share of bullying before he discovered his superpowers. But here was a bully who could teleport his victim over the side of a cliff. Ernie wondered about his newly enhanced super speed. Would he finally be a match for Smoke?

"What do you want?" Max growled.

"Stop playing stupid. I want to know what your game is." The blond thirteen-year-old took off his goggles and began to clean an oil smear on a lens. "So what's your angle? Playing it low-key? Expect me to just play along? You can forget it."

"We have no idea what you are talking about," Natalia responded. "Please leave."

Smoke's glaring eyes fell on Max. His devilish smile gleamed. "So, I bet you're glad to be back. Thinking about looking up anyone in particular? Maybe Brooke? Then again, maybe not. She'd see through this lie of yours in a second. Face it, Sumner, she's too good for you."

Max's mouth slammed shut. Harley moved toward Smoke. "Natalia asked you to bug out. You gonna vamoose or is this gonna get ugly?"

Smoke smirked, thumbing toward Natalia. "Your new girlfriend, Eisenstein? When Raven finds out, you're dead." As Harley lunged for the boy, Smoke disappeared with a laugh.

"Geez, I hate that kid," Natalia said, seething.

"Do you think he knows something?" asked Ernie. "Man, why does this place have to have a Smoke? Wasn't one enough?"

"Relax," said Harley, sitting down next to Max, who was distracted. "Smoke might be playing us. He's a liar. It's what he does best."

"That doesn't make him any less dangerous," said Natalia. "The last thing we needed on our first day of school is an enemy." She paused thoughtfully. "Then again, this might just be the lead we've been looking for. There's no one I can think of who would want to see the Griffins disappear more than Smoke. Griffins, we may have our first suspect!"

As they ascended the wood and leather escalator from the subway platform, the high gates of Iron Bridge loomed before them. The school was identical to the Griffins' Iron Bridge. However, this one hadn't been blown up by Von Strife a century ago. The arched windows, flying buttresses, marble halls, pedestals with illustrious busts — those were all the same, except they were the originals, rather than restorations. To Max, it was like looking back in time — to a time he never knew. In this world, Iron Bridge, not Stirling Academy, was the big cheese among the Templar schools. And it liked to show off with hallways packed with trophy cases, ribbons, championship rings, and pictures of past stars.

The paranoia brought on by Smoke's strange visit evaporated the instant the Griffins walked into a hall of cheering faces and clouds of confetti. Banners fluttered, flags waved, and there wasn't a kid in school who hadn't signed the lockers of the world-famous, death-cheating Grey Griffins. No matter what any of the four said or did, there was an explosion of applause. A pen was forced into Max's hands, and he quickly found himself autographing casts, notebooks, and even the faces of giggling girls. By the first bell, Max hadn't even made it past the lockers, and his hand was cramping up.

Ms. Merical soon intercepted them, pulling the Griffins into homeroom and closing the door on a dozen disappointed faces. "Well," she said, smiling and looking them over, "how does it feel to be famous?" The Griffins smiled right back. It felt good. "Why don't you four relax for a bit, and I'll let you go out and get your books after the bell rings. We don't want another mob scene, do we? Though, lord knows, you four certainly deserve it."

The Griffins thanked her and moved to their seats.

"Max?" said Ms. Merical, pointing to the other side of the room. "You sit over there. Did you forget?"

Max gulped and gathered his things. That was stupid of him. And he had five other classes with different seating assignments. Plenty of opportunities to blow their cover. Other kids soon piled into the classroom.

Natalia leaned over to Max and whispered, "Hey, notice anything different?"

"Besides my seat?"

"No, silly. I mean, at least half the class are changelings. There must not be any restrictions. No rules keeping them locked away in Sendak Hall like in our world." She paused, looking around. "And I think more kids have Bounder Faeries, too, though I haven't actually counted." She bit her lip in thought. "I wonder if the other Natalia has a Bounder Faerie. If I had a faerie that did whatever I wanted, I think I'd choose a shape-shifter. Or maybe a unicorn. Of course, a shape-shifting unicorn would be better, you know, so they don't take up so much room on the subway."

"Bounders don't do whatever you want," said Max. "If they did, Sprig would be here, instead of off on her own adventures."

"Well, there have to be more reliable faerie protectors than Sprig. What about Honeysuckle? Brooke's Bounder pixie? By the way, have you seen Brooke yet? No? Well, I'll keep my eyes peeled and let you know." She patted her *Book of Clues*. "This is going to be a very interesting day. Yes, very interesting, indeed."

"Hey, Natalia," said Ernie, raising his thick brows expectantly. "You've sure got a lot of new friends. Girlfriends, I mean...what's the name of the changeling girl? The one with the glasses?"

"No, I am not introducing you," said Natalia.

"What? I didn't mean—"

"Oh, yes, you did. Besides, I thought you had a thing for Raven."

Ernie glowered. "But now I'm not the only one," he muttered quietly.

Max looked over at Harley, who nervously chewed on his pencil. Max knew his friend was thinking about Raven. Harley would have to face her in the hallway at some point. The boy watched the clock intently, as if willing time to freeze. Anything to stop that bell from ringing.

And it rang. Impossibly fast. Harley stuck to his seat as long as he could, waiting for everyone else to clear out, then quietly snuck into the hall. He looked left, then right. No Raven. He quickly moved toward his locker. Most of the other kids had already disappeared. If he was just fast enough...

"Harley?" He nearly jumped out of his shoes. It was only the school nurse, though — or rather, a lipsticked clockwork with a red cross painted on its forehead. It had no legs; instead it glided on a single pedestal and wheel. The gyrostabilizers whirred constantly to keep the top-heavy machine from tipping over. "Please reroute yourself to Dr. Trimble's office. Just a quick diagnostic to make sure your system integrity checks out." Harley looked at the clockwork strangely. "I mean, that you're all healthy." The English was perfect, but the voice sounded like it was rattling around in a tin can.

Harley smiled. Excellent. Doc Trimble was downstairs. No chance of seeing Raven. Max, Ernie, and Natalia were probably already down there waiting for him.

Harley crossed the stained-glass skywalk to the next building and then went down two sets of marble stairs, reaching the dark patch of hallway leading to Doc Trimble's office. As he stepped off the final stair, a chill swept over him. Someone was in the darkness, watching him. Harley spun around.

"Is someone there?"

"Not very bright, are you?" said a voice with a familiar French-Canadian accent. Raven stepped out from behind the stairs and walked up to him, her eyes glittering like the edge of a knife.

"Uh, R-Raven," Harley stuttered. "How have you been?" This Raven was prettier than the one Harley knew. Something about the makeup and the way she dressed. Still Goth and a little vampirish, but with a touch of sophistication.

"How have I been? You come back from the dead and don't call, don't text? *J'ai vu neiger.* How do you think I am?" She was practically standing on his toes and looking defiant.

Harley backed up. "Well, it's been kinda weird. And I didn't want to freak you out or anything."

"Freak? Oh, is that what you think I am? Is that what your little buddies call me?"

Harley paused. "Um, no. It's an expression. Geez, why are you so mad? What did I do?"

"You are such a coward. Don't bother breaking up with me. We're through."

"Wait, I'm not breaking...look, I don't understand."

Raven pushed her magenta-streaked hair behind her ear. "If you aren't smart enough to figure it out, then you aren't worth the explanation." She moved toward the stairs, then looked back. "We're over. O-V-E-R. *Oui?*" She stormed up the staircase.

Harley stood there wondering why he felt so terrible. After all, didn't this solve his problem?

BACK FROM THE GRAVE

"Well, I don't know, but apparently portal travel agrees with you," said Doc Trimble. His office was a rather scary-looking laboratory of damp concrete, moldy brick, and steel shelves crowded with bubbling beakers. He raised a steam-powered arm and clicked off a few toggle switches on the control panel. A stovetop hat, dingy and blown-out, hung from a rack. "Chronologically, you haven't aged in three months. But other than that, you're all perfectly healthy." He turned to Ernie. "Except you, Mr. Tweeny."

"What do you mean?" Ernie suddenly felt naked. Doctors always made him feel that way. "What's wrong with me?"

"You're undergoing the changing process. Aren't you taking your medicine?"

Ernie sighed in relief. "Oh, that's all. Well, I ran out of dragon dung tea a couple of days ago."

Doc Trimble set aside his chart and looked at Ernie quizzically. "Dragon what?"

"Oh, he's just messing with you," Natalia said quickly. "Something he read in a comic book. Do you have any more medicine? He lost his in the portal."

Doc pulled a small bottle of pills from a cabinet marked Changelings Only and handed it to Ernie. "Take one a day. No more. No less. You remember what happened last time."

"Oh, yes, don't worry about a thing," promised Ernie awkwardly.

As the Griffins made their way down the dark hallway, Max suddenly pulled them into a corner. "He took our blood. You can bet he'll do a DNA scan."

"So?" said Ernie. "The other Griffins are exact copies of us, right?"

"Yes and no," said Natalia. "We were the same when we were born. But our lives were different. And little changes add up. Like mutations or cell damage. Max is right; if they spot a difference, we could be in hot water."

"Well," said Max, "at least we haven't run into Von Strife yet. That's good news. Maybe he doesn't know about us?"

"So where's Brooke at?" asked Ernie as they passed a

66

long wall of lockers. Brooke's looked like it hadn't been opened in months. "Do you think she was abducted?"

"She was pulled out by her dad," explained Natalia. "I heard it from a girl in the bathroom. No one knows why. Or where she went." She turned to Max. "I'll try to find out more. I know how you..." She paused, noticing Max's discomfort. They all knew how Max felt about Brooke Lundgren. Natalia smiled and dropped the topic respectfully.

"It's all right," said Max after a moment. "Whatever you can find out. Maybe it's better she's not around. I mean, Brooke's always been able to see right through me. She'll know I'm a fraud."

"Speaking of which, we should be more careful what we talk about," Harley said. "Raven can make these walls tell her everything we've said. And she's got every reason to do it."

"And whose fault is that?" Ernie said. "You had your chance to be nice to her."

"What are you talking about? She's the one who jumped me."

"Ha! You wish."

"Ernie, I am so going to belt you."

"Why hasn't Logan's name been cleared yet?" asked Ernie later that day as the four Griffins made their way across the grassy quad leading to the dining hall. Recess was in session for the younger students, and with all the shouting, it was hard to hear one another talk. "We've been back for days. I mean, isn't it obvious he didn't kill us?"

"Obvious to who?" asked Natalia. "It's not obvious to me."

"You know what I mean. Everyone thinks we're the other Griffins, so if we're alive, they couldn't have been killed. Wait. I think I just confused myself. Umm..."

As Ernie tried to untangle his thoughts, a crowd of students rushed past. Their Bounders chased after them: Turtle Dragons, Dandelion Duffles, and even a nasty little Spider Pixie. Max wondered about Sprig. He hadn't seen her since she flew out his bedroom window, and he was starting to worry that Ernie might be right about Yellow Eyes's being an assassin. Any creature powerful enough to take out his Bounder was capable of anything.

Farther up in the air, two fourth-grade teams of flying changelings were playing a game of dodgeball. Every now and then, a player would tumble down, skid across the lawn, then leap back into the game with a growl.

Down at ground level, Harley picked up a loose stone and flung it at a crow. Then another. "Man, what is it with these birds? I haven't seen so many since—"

"Since Blackstone was after us last year," Max finished. The last thing Max wanted was to run into a copy of the shape-shifting werewolf who had masqueraded as their teacher.

"Let's not get paranoid," said Natalia. "Things seem pretty good so far, apart from Smoke. Look, we've got new lives. New families." She touched Harley's arm. "So, Harley, how's that house of yours on the hill? I can see it from my backyard. So amazing! Are you, like, pinching yourself every time you wake up?"

"I try not to think about it." And he tried hard. He was rarely home. And when he was, he locked himself in his room. Said he didn't feel good. Which was true. The problem wasn't in his stomach, though. It was in his head. This place was messing with him.

"You're not fooling anyone," said Natalia. "We all know what a big deal this is for you."

"I'm dealing with it on my terms, okay? You got a problem with that, Miss Nosey?"

"You aren't dealing with it. You're hiding from it. And don't put on that tough-guy face. We all know what a softy you are on the inside. I'm just saying we're here. If you want to talk."

"Whatever," he replied as they moved toward the crowded dining hall.

On their first day, they'd already met almost every changeling student who had been kidnapped by Von Strife back in their world. It was a little spooky, seeing them walking around, laughing like nothing was wrong: Becca, the girl who could walk through walls; Stephen, the frost elemental; and, of course, the shape-shifting, Round Table–sweeping Hale with her shimmering skin and perky antennae. They were all here. And all very much alive.

As the Griffins entered the dining hall, they found it exactly the same as their own, complete with the same clockwork cooks and lunch-bots. The marble floors, the chinks in the towering pillars, the sheen of the lunch trays. Even the silverware. It was all so familiar that the Griffins soon forgot they didn't belong here—until Ernie let out a squeak and dropped his tray, spilling a mountain of mashed potatoes. The clatter rang out across the expansive room, with its fifty-foot-high windows and cavelike acoustics.

"Look who's back from the dead," Ernie said breathlessly to Natalia. In front of them stood Robert Hernandez, Ernie's best changeling pal, who'd been kidnapped and killed, thanks to Von Strife and his soul-ripping technology. It had been Robert's abduction that had driven Ernie to form the Agents of Justice. Stupid idea. And Hale had been kidnapped as a result. Like for Robert's abduction, Ernie blamed himself when Hale disappeared.

Ernie gaped stupidly at his old friend. He gathered his wits when Natalia pinched him. "It's a copy of Robert," she reminded him. "Not the real one."

"Should I go talk to him?" Robert's death had been the single most devastating event in Ernie's life. Depressed, alone, and angry, he had sulked his way through the last school year. He needed to talk to Robert. He just had to.

Natalia understood this even better than Ernie. "Yes, silly. You can go talk to him. Just do it fast. People are staring at you."

Taking in a deep breath of courage, Ernie cautiously approached Robert near the condiments station. Ernie cleared his throat. "Hey, uh, Robert."

Robert took off his shabby derby hat and ran it around in his hands nervously. "Um...did I do something wrong?" A splat of ketchup landed on his scuffed toes.

"What?" Ernie scratched his head and decided to start over. "Hey, why didn't you come to the party at Max's house?"

"Look, is this a game or something?" asked Robert, backing away like a kid about to get a wedgie.

Ernie frowned. "Hey, I thought we were friends."

Robert studied Ernie. "Sure, yeah. Whatever you say..."

Natalia caught Ernie's arm and whispered, "Everyone is staring at you. You need to stop talking to him right now."

"But this is crazy...."

"We'll sort it out later," she replied. "Something is wrong here."

"Boy," Harley began as the four Griffins sat down together, "first Smoke, then Raven. Now this. We're blowing ourselves up, and it's not even fourth period!"

Several students piled in next to Ernie, grinning like hyenas. "Hey, Thunderbolt, why were you talking to Hernandez?" asked one of the students as others leaned close. Most of them were changelings. "Is he the new mark? You just let us know. Man, you've never gone after him before."

"And disobeying a direct order from Von Strife," said a green-skinned boy. "We knew you were tough, but now you're just crazy. Crazy awesome. Dude, what's he like? I hear he's a transmuter. They're, like, only the most dangerous — can suck your powers right out and use them on you. Freaky."

"Oh, he's a total freak," agreed a boy with ram horns. "I wouldn't touch him with a ten-foot pole."

"You've got that right," said Denton, as the lion boy joined the fray, putting his arm around Ernie's shoulder. "But Thunderbolt here is the man. He does what he wants and when he wants."

Ernie gulped down his regret as he watched Robert slink out the side door. "Oh, you know me," he stuttered. "I guess I like living on the edge." The next thing Natalia knew, a sizable crowd of changelings had gathered around him, egging him on. Caught up in his new celebrity, Ernie was soon standing on the table, recounting some of his best adventures. Some of the tales were even true. But all of them were loud. Too loud, considering the low profile the Griffins had hoped for.

Natalia looked over at Max, who silently agreed:

Ernie had to be shut up. Max and Harley said their good-byes, then extracted Ernie from his fans.

"Hey, where are we going?"

"Your appointment with Doc Trimble. Don't you remember?" Max shook his head. "I was afraid of this...."

"Doc Trimble?" Ernie mumbled, scratching his head. "Wait, what were you afraid of?"

Max turned to Ernie's fans. "A side effect of being trapped in the portal for so long," he explained casually. "He forgets things sometimes. Just a glitch. I'm sure we'll get it fixed."

"Amnesia?" Ernie exclaimed nervously as Max and Harley escorted him out. "Oh my gosh. Is it true? You've got to help me, Max." He paused in his panic. "You're Max, right?" Max smiled. Good old Ernie.

VON STRIFE

Max and the Griffins nearly finished out their day without further incident. Until the last bell. As they exited the classroom, they found a clockwork attendant waiting for them. The human-shaped robot was brass-plated, with flickering blue eyes and a quirky ticking sound. It bowed with a squeak as it presented a card to Max.

OTTO VON STRIFE REQUESTS THE HONOR OF TALKING WITH THE GREY GRIFFINS AT THREE THIRTY SHARP. LOOKING FORWARD TO OUR REACQUAINTANCE.

Max looked at the clock on the wall. Three thirty. Of course this was going to happen. They'd all known it. They just hadn't wanted to think about it.

The Griffins reluctantly followed the clockwork through the halls, over the bridge, up several flights of stairs, and finally to the director's door. In their world, this was the Baron's office. Here, however, one of the Baron's deadliest enemies would be sitting in his place.

The attendant opened the door, and the Griffins filed in. The dark-paneled office was a mirror image of its counterpart, with a few notable changes, such as photographs of Von Strife's daughter, smiling and as healthy as could be. Von Strife stood behind his desk as they entered. He greeted them with a nod as the attendant closed the door behind them. Next to him stood a young woman, perhaps sixteen years of age, with fiery hair. Literally on fire. Max had met her before. She was Naomi, Von Strife's second-in-command and one of the most powerful changelings in the world. She said nothing, but her eyes smoked as she watched the Griffins intently.

"Please sit down," Von Strife said, motioning toward the red velvet couch. Von Strife wore a black suit with a high collar and a jeweled cravat. His silver beard was trimmed neatly and his eyes were a frigid blue. His hair, as silver as his beard, was cropped close in military fashion. He moved like an aristocrat, with a polished cane at his side. While they'd never met the villain in person, there was something in his face that seemed hauntingly familiar to Max.

"I am very pleased to see you have returned," he said with a smile, revealing a set of flawless teeth. "Few of us who had hope remained. But, as always, the Griffins have emerged victorious."

Natalia nudged Max. She'd noticed the familiarities as well. They'd met this man before.

"And how are you enjoying your first day back? I hear the good doctor has given you the green light?" Ernie was gravely quiet. Robert's reaction to him at lunch had unnerved him. Now here was the man responsible for Robert's death back in the Griffins' world, making nice. Ernie's face flushed.

Max's eyes caught movement outside the window. A crow was peering in at them.

"We're fine," answered Natalia blandly.

"I understand that you met with Smoke this morning."

Max remained silent. Smoke tattled on them already? Great.

Von Strife studied them for a moment, reading their faces. "Yes, well, I apologize if he offended you. My son has anger issues. I work too much, he tells me. Yet when I ask for his help, he turns everything into a competition. I must not be much of a father." Max looked over at Natalia. Smoke was Von Strife's son? This was news! "Then, of course, he's never fully taken to being adopted.

76

Feels he has something to prove. Nonsense, of course. But I thought you should know...."

"So how is your daughter?" Natalia asked, keeping a cautious eye on Naomi. The fire elemental returned Natalia's gaze with a condescending smirk.

Von Strife moved back to his desk and sat down. He ran his fingers through his hair, as if something was gnawing at his mind. "Unfortunately, she has taken ill. It's been several months since she'd first been confined to bed. Frankly, I'm very worried. I'm a doctor, after all. And somehow I can't even make my own daughter well."

"Oh, I'm sorry." Natalia had a soft heart, even for villains. "Is it...the changing process?" After all, she thought, that was what had nearly killed Sophia in their world.

Von Strife shook his head. "That was my first thought, Ms. Romanov. But thanks to my medicine, her changeling blood is stable. No, this is something else. Something new...something..." His eyes drifted out the window for a moment, then returned quickly. "I will be taking a few days off to personally attend to the lab work, hence my desire to see you before I go." He was familiar. Dangerously familiar. And yet, Max knew quite well that they'd never met Otto Von Strife.

"We're sorry," Max offered. "We know how much Sophia means to you."

"Do you?" Von Strife's eyes scanned Max, as if searching for something. Then he sighed. "I have to admit, I don't find many people in this world who do.

Nor do they understand what I have sacrificed to ensure her safety. What I've gone through." The Griffins did. Von Strife had killed countless people on his monstrous quest to save his daughter from changing. Yet there was something odd going on with this man. He wasn't acting like a monster. He acted like...an old friend!

Natalia shot to her feet, pulling Max up with her. The others stood as well, pulled by her force of will. "Oh my gosh. I totally forgot my grandparents were coming over tonight! They're going to kill me."

"Of course, Natalia. The boys can catch up with you later and fill you in."

"No," she replied quickly. "What I mean is...the other Griffins are supposed to come, too. It's a party. We all have to go. Right now." Ernie tried to argue but quickly remembered his "amnesia" problem.

"Well," Von Strife said, "as you wish. I do need to attend to my daughter. But let's continue this chat when I return. In a few days, perhaps?"

A few moments later, Natalia pushed open the double doors and stamped across the lawn, her fists clenching and unclenching.

"Okay, what was all that about?" asked Max.

"Are you serious?" she replied, walking down the hedge-lined Green Corridor that led to the subway platform. "Didn't you see it? Didn't he seem just a little familiar to you?" She pulled on her jacket as she cut through the damp flower bed.

"Well, I guess he did seem kind of familiar. But we've been after him for so long...."

"Take away his beard. His hair. And put round glasses on him. Ring any bells?"

Ernie stopped short. "Holy smokes! You mean you think he's Obadiah Strange? You can't be serious."

"No one has fingernails exactly like someone else. And Von Strife's were the same as Strange's. They also sit the same way, cross their legs the same way, and even breathe the same. They are the same. I'd stake my reputation on it!"

"But Obadiah Strange had wooden teeth," argued Max. "Von Strife's were perfect."

"False teeth, Max. He also shaved his head and wore glasses. Easiest game in the book. Man, was I stupid." Natalia kept up her pace as she trotted down the escalator. "We have to get out of here now."

"Wait a second," Ernie said. "What if the Obadiah in our world is the Von Strife in this one, and vice versa? It could happen. Wouldn't that explain how nice he was?"

Natalia shook her head. "I could see it in his eyes. He's the same guy we've been trying to stop. He's also the same guy who pretended to be our friend all this time. I know it. And he knows I know it. That's why we have to get out of here."

"Leave?" asked Harley. "Like, where are we going to go? The only way back to our world is through the

Paragon Engine, and last I checked, Von Strife is the only one with the keys to that ride."

Natalia came to a halt on the subway platform and glanced up at the elaborate exposed gears of a ticking clock on the wall. The *Zephyr* wouldn't be coming for a few minutes. She then looked over at a security camera. It was aimed right at them. She growled.

"I can't believe I was so blind. I'm better than this. I'm a detective, for heaven's sake. And here he was, under my nose the whole time. Someone take my license away!"

"Well, I guess it makes sense," Max said. "I mean, how else did Von Strife always manage to stay one step ahead of us? He was in the room when we were making our plans. He even helped with the plans himself."

"It also explains all the times he went missing just when we needed him most." Natalia rolled her eyes and tapped her foot irritably. "Then there's the whole Smoke angle. The nastiest kid in school just happens to have Von Strife — I mean Obadiah Strange — for a daddy. Isn't that convenient? No wonder the creep is on to us already. This just smells like a plot."

Ernie sighed and kicked a pebble over the side of the subway platform. "You know, I just started liking this place. I'm popular. Finally."

"Looked like you were more of a bully to me," said Harley as the *Zephyr* arrived. "And did you see those friends of yours? They were cheering you on." Ernie shook his head. "Come on. Only bullies have little packs of friends like that. I'm starting to think the other Ernie wasn't so nice."

"Oh, like I'm supposed to take advice from a guy who steals his best friend's girlfriend."

Harley's mouth dropped as he slid into his seat. The train doors closed. "Look, I didn't steal.... Wait a second. Raven wasn't your girlfriend."

"Oh, thanks. That makes it all better." He glowered out the window as they shot along the underwater subway corridor. The transparent walls of the tunnel allowed Ernie to peer into the inky depths of Lake Avalon. Somewhere down there lurked a monster just waiting for a train-sized snack. "Well, at least Robert is alive. They all are. All the changelings who went missing, like Hale and Becca. And they're happy. With the new medicine, none of us have to worry anymore. We're finally safe. I guess."

"Are you saying you want to stay?" asked Harley incredulously.

"Don't you? Now that you have Raven, what else could you want? Oh, and then there's your new daddy!"

Harley clenched his teeth. "You just remember that isn't your family you're going home to see tonight. It's just a bunch of lonely people you've tricked into thinking all their prayers have been answered. Well, they haven't. It's just a game we're playing. You know it, and I know it."

SCARECROW

Harley parked his bike and made his way to the front door of his house, which was an unquestionable marvel of engineering. With its glass and curving horizons, the house just seemed to flow. Harley had no idea how Henry Eisenstein had designed this illusion. He wanted to find out, but he still couldn't bring himself to ask the man who was supposedly his father.

Henry was nice enough, of course. He and this world's Harley had been pretty close. But that Harley didn't seem very interested in what his father did. He was all about sports. Harley thought it was strange that he was more like Henry because he never had his dad around.

"Hi, Harley," said Candi as she glanced up from the kitchen counter. "How was your day?"

"Same," said Harley as he hung up his sweatshirt on a coat hook.

"Okay. Well, would you like to join us for dinner? I'm making catfish, just the way you like it."

"Can I eat in my room?"

"Again?" she asked, disappointed. She walked over to him. "You can't live your life in your room."

"I think it's for the best," said Harley. His voice was bland and cold.

"It's not."

"Trust me, it is."

"You act like you hate us, Harley," she said. "You know, I've talked to your friends' parents. Everyone seems just fine. But you...what happened to you, Harley?"

"I just need more time, that's all," said Harley. "Look, it's nothing personal. It's just something I have to deal with."

"Let us help you. Let us at least—"

"I'll let you know." Harley cut her off. He made for an escape up the stairs, then paused guiltily at the railing. He turned to find Candi Eisenstein shaking. She wasn't crying. Even in this world, she wasn't the type. She was too tough. Apparently it wasn't their poverty that had made her a survivor after all. It was inside her all along. When he considered that, Harley's heart softened.

"Look," he said, "you guys are great. I know that. Probably the best parents in the world. What's going on... well, it's not your fault. I just need some time. I'll work it out. Can you do that?"

She quietly returned to the kitchen. Harley slunk up the stairs feeling awful. He'd been honest. But somehow that didn't make him feel any better.

Sitting down at his desk, Harley glanced at the pictures on the wall. Pictures of a family he'd never known. In his room back home, there were only three pictures: one of his mom and him; one of his dog, Roscoe; and another of Monti McGuiness on the bridge of the *Graf Zeppelin* handing Harley the keys to his laboratory — the official symbol of Harley becoming Monti's apprentice. That had been a great day, and as Harley sat there, he found himself wondering what had happened to Monti in his world. The inventor had been so sick, confined to a wheelchair, and getting worse. Harley missed the quirky engineer. Without a father of his own, Harley had looked up to Monti an awful lot. More than even Harley had realized. Then Harley's eyes fell on the telephone near his DE Tablet.

"I wonder if he has the same number...." Harley picked up the phone and began dialing. He smiled. He didn't know why he hadn't thought of calling until now. If there was one person he could talk to, it would be Monti. The line rang. It rang again. The voice mail picked up.

"Hi, uh, this is Harley Davidson Eisenstein. I guess, well, I don't know if you'll get this. But when you do, it would be great to talk to you. Yeah, I mean, if you want. I could drop by, or whatever. If you have time. Anyway, this is kind of a stupid message. You know me. It's just all weird, you know? I mean, of course you don't. But you do. Anyway, call me back. Or whatever."

Harley hung up. Then he waited for the phone to ring. It never did.

The Griffins survived the rest of the week without blowing their cover. At least, as far as they knew. Of course, Von Strife might be on to them, but he had been absent for several days, attending to his daughter's sickness. Smoke, too, had gone missing. Apart from the occasional glimpse of Naomi, Von Strife's rather-frightening fire elemental, the Griffins could finally relax.

Max couldn't have had a better week. Movies and popcorn with the family. Long drives in his dad's sports cars. Hours of throwing the football. He couldn't remember the last time he looked forward to going home after school. Of course, he was living someone else's life, as Harley liked to point out. Still, sometimes Max would close his eyes and find himself imagining that he belonged here. It felt great.

Despite the setback with Robert Hernandez, Ernie

was just thankful his friend was still alive. He made sure to give him space, though. Harley had been dead-on about the bully thing. This world's Ernie had built quite a reputation using his super speed to make other kids look like idiots. It was time to change all that. Ernie was a hero, and heroes weren't bullies. Unfortunately, change wasn't easy. Most of his fans wanted him to be exactly the way he used to be. He tried to blame his amnesia whenever possible.

"So how are things with you?" asked Natalia as she sat down across from Harley in the school library. Harley scanned her wardrobe with little interest, despite Natalia's obvious pride: the gold corset was floral velvet, the airship aviator jacket matched the brown leather of her cavalry boots, and her faded jeans had two lines of properly distressed rivets running down the side of each leg. Her new girlfriends had gone on and on about her sense of style. But to Harley, Natalia might as well have been wearing a pumpkin on her head. "You seem a little distracted."

Harley shrugged as he flicked a paper football over her head. "It's Monti. We were pretty close, right? Well, this Monti doesn't even return my calls. It's not like he doesn't know me. I mean, I know he knows who I am. He's a Templar, after all. No, it's more like he doesn't like me." Harley kicked his feet up on the table. "I keep wondering what this other Harley did to make Monti dislike him so much."

"He can't be that bad. His parents sure love him, if you couldn't tell." Natalia smiled warmly, but Harley shrugged it off. She pushed her schoolbooks aside. "Well, my mom and dad are exactly the same as they are back home. I can't decide about my sister. Either she's more annoying than my sister, or it's because she's had time to get worse. I have to lock my room when I go to school in the morning just to keep her out of my stuff." She quickly looked around for eavesdroppers. They were still alone. "Anyway, I know these aren't our families and all. I know that, Harley. But we need them, just as much as they need us. And we love them just as much as they love us."

"Speak for yourself." Harley drummed his pencil on the table, then got up and began pacing. "Our Monti was in rough shape when we left. I wish we could find out what's going on with him. I mean, maybe he's even worse. What if he's dead? I feel so useless, you know?"

Natalia sighed miserably. "Oh, Harley... I don't know. I don't know what to do. How to act. What to say. Even my family... sometimes it's so easy to just forget I don't belong here. And then I feel all guilty about it. Can you believe that? I feel guilty for kissing my mom good night. Like I'm somehow cheating on my parents. This is so weird I don't even know where to begin."

Harley grinned. "Trust me, I get it. So, how are things in the world of glamour and gossip magazines?"

"If you are referring to my friends, you can knock it

off. They aren't like that. Well, not all of them. Well, Brittany is. And Katie. Big-time. Okay, I get your point. Anyway, I'm just playing along for now. It's not like we'll be here for very long. I've got a lead."

"Serious?"

"Well, you remember that my dad in this world is an acquisitions agent for Von Strife? I've been working in questions in our conversations. Not too often, though. I don't want to make him suspicious."

"He's a Relic Hunter?"

"Ha! He works for the museum. Can't you just see my dad swinging across underground rivers and fighting off zombies with his umbrella?" Natalia snickered. "You know, until this happened to us, my dad and I never had much to talk about. Now we talk all the time. I never knew how interesting he was."

"So what is he working on right now?"

"He won't tell me. He doesn't bring his work home. And he won't take me to his office." Natalia sighed. "It's like he's hiding something. Someone in my family finally does something interesting, and he won't tell me a thing. Agh! How frustrating."

"I imagine your sister feels the same way about you."

Natalia's eyes narrowed. "It's not the same. Anyway, how are things with Raven?"

"Having a changeling like her hate your guts is a little freaky. Still...she's different, in a way that...well, you know."

"Different how?"

"Um, she's not as insane as the one from our world. This Raven, well, she has class." He smiled to himself, his eyes falling to the table in thought.

Natalia watched as he spoke but said nothing.

Saturday morning rolled lazily toward afternoon as the Griffins strolled through New Avalon. So much was the same. But the changes were impossible to miss: colossal airships sailed over their heads, horses clattered down the cobblestones, and adults they had known forever were now doffing their top hats and curtsying as they passed on the street. The stores catered to more than just humans these days. There were video games next to anti-troll pepper spray. Wireless phones with brassy rotary dials. The past and the present—with just a dash of the future—seemed to be painted together on a canvas larger than life. Only the Griffins seemed to notice how strange it all seemed.

As they walked along the cobblestones, they found themselves pausing to look in the window of the Shoppe of Antiquities. Iver's place. The lights were out.

"I still can't believe he's dead," Natalia sighed. "It's been a year, you know?"

"He'll never be really dead," said Ernie. "Not to me."

"It'll be weird to meet the one from this world. Lying

to everyone else is one thing. But lying to Iver? When he comes back from his Templar mission, he won't even know who we are. I mean, who we really are." She paused, thinking back to Iver's death. It had been so sudden. So horrible. "I wonder if anything happens to you when your other self is killed."

"Apparently not much," Max replied. "I mean, the other Griffins are dead, and we're just fine."

"True."

"I wonder if Iver still leaves the key to the back door in the same place," said Harley.

"You want to break in?" asked Natalia. "We're in enough trouble, don't you think?"

"Come on, Iver wouldn't mind."

As they moved down the side alley and rounded the corner, they found a very large, very black crow perched on the window ledge. One of its eyes had been removed and replaced with a telescoping lens of brass that zoomed in and out with a whir of invisible gears. Its head cocked to one side as it examined the Griffins with its mechanical vision.

"Okay, this is officially the creepy zone," said Ernie. "Maybe we shouldn't be back here." But as they turned around, they found their way back thick with crows. Dozens were clinging to the brick wall and fluttering down from the rooftops, creating a canvas of beady eyes.

Natalia scanned the area with her Phantasmoscope. She frowned. "Guys, we're officially in monster territory.

These crows aren't the only nasties nearby. I'm picking up some pretty-big-time monster signatures coming our way. If we're going to get out of here…"

Harley grabbed a broomstick and handed Max a garbage-can lid. "This could get ugly." More crows flapped down, surrounding the Griffins in a field of gleaming metal eyes.

Max looked down at his hand. If he'd had the *Codex Spiritus*, he could have made short work of these little monsters. However, Logan still had the ring. "Maybe my Skyfire…"

"No, Max," said Natalia. "Without your ring, you can't control the fire. You could kill one of us."

A flicker of blue suddenly appeared on his fingertips. "Uh, guys, I think we have a problem. It's coming whether we want it or not." The fire leaped up his arms. Max swallowed hard, trying to concentrate. He had to extinguish it before it got out of control. It was the crows. They were somehow triggering his Skyfire. Max had forgotten how little he understood about his powers. The ring had made it all so easy. His vision blurred. His stomach turned.

Natalia turned. "Max, your eyes!"

Max's Skyfire raged within him, trying to get out, and as a result, his grey eyes blazed an electric blue. It was building up inside him. Fast. "You guys need to get out of here!" Like Ernie's, Max's powers seemed to be supercharged in this world. Without the ring to control it, though, Max was a walking time bomb.

"We're not going anywhere!" Harley yelled back as the crows doubled and tripled in number. They were only a few yards away and closing. All of them croaking and whirring with their clockwork hearts. Harley desperately stabbed at a bird that had hopped uncomfortably close to Natalia. It angrily snapped at the broom, then jumped away. "We need a wall. Just long enough for Max to get himself together." He turned to Ernie. "How fast are you? Can you run around us and create a speed shield, like they do in comic books?"

Ernie scratched his head. "Hitting a crow at three hundred miles an hour isn't going to feel so good."

"You're a changeling; you'll heal. We won't." Harley handed him the garbage-can lid. "Just hold this in front of you. Go!" Sensing the Griffins were going on the defensive, the crows launched their attack. "Now!"

As the tidal wave of crows swept toward them, Ernie bolted into action, sizzling through the wall of crows. Around and around he sped, faster and faster, until he was nothing more than a ring of silver light.

"He's doing it!" Natalia exclaimed in amazement. Black feathers drizzled down like rain. She'd never been more proud of Ernie.

Unfortunately, there were so many birds that Ernie couldn't see where he was going. Finally, he dared to lower the garbage-can lid to get his bearings. *Smash!* Feathers struck his face. Blinded, Agent Thunderbolt catapulted into the air. He landed hard, a tangle of limbs.

His changeling blood would heal him, but he was out of the fight.

Harley tried to shield Natalia from the shower of beaks and feathers, but there were far, far too many. No matter how fast he swung that broomstick, or how mercilessly she tore the claws and legs from her hair, the Griffins' bones would soon be picked clean.

Suddenly the birds were yanked away. When Natalia opened her eyes, she found Max standing in the midst of a cyclone of black crows. The helpless birds were locked in orbit, like unwilling satellites around a fiery star that was about to explode.

Skyfire leaped from Max's eyes, fingertips, and mouth. The sky grew dark. Thunder crashed.

"Get down!" Harley yelled, tackling Natalia just as a jagged bolt of lightning hammered down. Everything exploded.

Ernie, who was just able to turn his head, could see the whole thing from where he was. If he hadn't been a changeling, he would have been blinded in an instant. As it was, the brightness still felt like daggers in his eyes. But that didn't stop him from watching every one of the thousands of helpless crows suddenly burst into flames, then to dust, and finally, as the fire ebbed, to wisps of smoke.

Max fell over face-first. The sky cleared. Sirens could be heard from the fire station on the other side of town.

"He's all right," said Natalia, checking Max's breathing. "I think he just blew a fuse. Wow, did you see that?"

"I sure did," replied Ernie, clearing his goggles of bird feathers. He looked up and down the alley of shattered windows. "I think the whole world did. What were those crows after?"

"Your livers," said a very distinctive baritone voice. Turning, they found a menacing figure in a broad-brimmed hat that hung over a set of shining, malicious eyes. The man's body, thin but rigid as a flagpole, was draped in a black leather trench coat. This was a man they'd known well. A man they'd hoped to never see again. A man whose ambition and taste for assassination had earned him a top spot in the leadership of the Black Wolf Society.

"Blackstone," Harley growled. He stepped protectively in front of Max's body.

"Father Blackstone, if you please," the man replied as he moved into view. In a tight fist, he held the leashes of two horribly grotesque creatures. Black skin lay slick over their backbones of jagged vertebrae, and their mouths sprang with rows of bloodstained teeth. These were the jaws of Slayer Goblins, monsters that had nearly finished off the Griffins more than once. Yet these monsters had been changed: like the crows, parts had been removed and replaced with clockwork machinery. Their empty eye sockets had brass machinery housing camera lenses stapled to the monsters' faces. Their teeth were serrated knives, and blue-zapping coils shot out of the backs of their heads to connect to various pistons just above the shoulders.

"They make for charming pets. Don't you agree?" Blackstone stroked the head of one of his Slayers. Its jaws hungrily snapped at the air.

The Blackstone from their world was as mean as villains came, a shape-shifting assassin with a kill list a mile long. Most of his murders had been of the easy sort, though. He preferred targets who didn't put up too much of a fight. That, and he wasn't particularly brave. This Blackstone, however, didn't seem to have a problem with attacking kids in broad daylight.

"What do you want?" asked Natalia, her fists clenched. She wouldn't go down without a fight. Even if Blackstone had a dozen Slayers.

"Would you believe me if I said 'world peace'?" Blackstone said with a sneer.

"Not a chance."

"Good. I'd hate to find anyone thinking I was getting soft. And now"—he glanced at his pocket watch—"I believe it's lunchtime." He knelt down beside his Slayers and patted their nasty heads. Then he dropped the leashes. "*Bon appétit*, my pets."

The Slayers leaped at the Griffins.

OUT OF THE BLUE

Instead of feeling slashing teeth, Natalia felt herself falling through a hole in space. An instant later, she was facedown on a freshly polished oak floor. Her friends were next to her. A big hand reached down as Natalia looked up. It was Olaf Iverson! His white beard, his plaid shirt, and his wire-rimmed glasses were unmistakable, as were his mountainous shoulders and round belly.

"Iver!" Natalia exclaimed, leaping up into the man's arms. "Oh, we've missed you so much!" Harley and Ernie joined the crushing hug. They couldn't help themselves.

"It's wonderful to see you four, as well," he replied,

running his hand through Natalia's tangled red hair. He scooped up Max from the floor and laid him on the couch. "Let's get our Master Sumner back to health, shall we? I'll be right back."

Iver quickly disappeared into the kitchen. He returned and passed a small white object beneath Max's nose. The Griffins watched in amazement as Max's eyes suddenly shot open and he sat bolt upright.

"Magic..." said Ernie.

"Smelling salts, actually." Iver winked.

"Iver?" Max breathed weakly as his vision cleared.

"Yes, Master Sumner, I'm here."

"Where are we?"

"My apartment. Just above the Shoppe of Antiquities, of course. How are you feeling?"

Max looked around. It certainly was Iver's old place. But it was very empty, as if Iver wasn't planning to stay long.

"Oh, Iver!" exclaimed Ernie. "Thanks for saving our lives from Blackstone. Did you see those Slayers? All Frankensteined up and on leashes?"

"Father Blackstone," Iver corrected. "Though he's no priest. He's a killer for hire." He chewed on the stem of his pipe thoughtfully. "So I see Logan has not yet returned your ring, Master Sumner?" He studied them for several long moments, waiting for a reply, then broke into a chuckle. "You Griffins. So secretive. So mysterious. And indeed, so lost in this strange, new world, unsure of whom to trust. Don't you recognize me after all this time?"

The mouths of the Griffins sagged. Had he just said what they thought he said? Could it be true? Could he be...?

"Yes, it's me—your old Iver," he said softly. Natalia's lip began to quiver. Iver leaned in closer. "I am very sorry, my dear friends, for putting you through such a difficult ordeal. I had to make my death believable, you see." He held out his big arms and scooped them all into them. Max found himself smiling: not only had their friend returned from the dead, but now the Griffins were no longer alone in this strange world.

"But how did you come here?" Max asked after clearing his throat. The boys reluctantly sat down. Natalia, however, wouldn't part from Iver. "And why?"

Even in their world, Iver was a mystery. As were his miraculous powers. Was he a changeling? Perhaps a wizard? Was he from another world entirely? What was, however, a decided fact was that Iver could do the impossible when it mattered most. This time, instead of fighting off monsters or knowing the future, he had shown himself quite capable of escaping death itself.

"Because I serve a higher order, Max. One that spans infinite worlds. I go where I am needed most. And I am needed here, on Earth Beta." He regarded their blank expressions. "Apparently I didn't spend enough time with you on the topic of parallel universes. As it happens, the world you and I come from is known as Earth Alpha, while this world, where we sit, is Earth Beta. They were once the same universe, but they split from each other, as near as I can tell, about a century ago. So, as you'd imagine, while most things are the same, there are still startling differences."

"Then you must know how to get back, right?" asked Max.

"Of course. But I am afraid you Griffins cannot travel the same roads I do. No, Von Strife's Paragon Engine is your one and only hope."

"Then you know where it is?" asked Natalia.

"I have my suspicions. But I think you, Ms. Romanov, are just the detective we need to bring the engine to light." Natalia beamed. "There are a number of leads. But I suggest you begin with Von Strife himself. With his daughter so ill, I do not know when he'll be back, but I know he trusts you, and that can work to your advantage. In the meantime, you four will need to continue your covers. Be the Griffins of this world—and that means you, Harley. I have heard reports that you are sticking out. Don't. You will only hurt those whom you are trying to protect." Harley sat back on the couch and sighed. "Yes, be the Griffins. Be friends with their friends. Do what they did. It is imperative that no one doubts you."

"What about Brooke?" asked Max. "I mean, we've met Logan and Raven. Is it safe to talk to her? Should I be talking to her, you know, just to keep up the cover?"

"Brooke and her father are busy, Master Sumner," said Iver in a cautious, firm tone. "I suggest you put her out of your mind. She has her task. You have yours. Perhaps, before this is all said and done, you two will be able to compare notes."

"You mean she knows about me?" asked Max.

"I said nothing of the kind. Please focus on the task at hand."

"Then what about Blackstone?" pressed Natalia, ignoring Max's exasperation. Iver had a spectacular way of telling them only what they absolutely had to know and not one crumb more. "You have to know something about him."

"Well, this version of Blackstone is particularly dangerous but luckily rather dim. I don't believe he knows who you truly are. That is to our advantage. As long as he is in the dark, his master will be as well."

"Von Strife? He's still the bad guy, right? I just want to be sure."

"That depends. This Von Strife is a model citizen who wouldn't so much as break the speed limit. His only care is for his daughter. However, I advise you to be on your guard. Your Von Strife is somewhere. As is his Paragon Engine."

"How can you be sure?" asked Max.

"How else did you come here if it wasn't for his Paragon Engine? And if it is here, so is Von Strife." Iver stood up suddenly and clapped his hands together. "I know

100

you must have many questions. But the main thing you need to know is that you are no longer alone."

"Are you going someplace?" asked Natalia.

"You are going somewhere," Iver said. "You just disappeared into thin air in front of Father Blackstone. He'll be quite put out about his crow collection. If he didn't want you dead before, he most certainly will now. He'll be looking for you. In all your usual haunts. Be careful. And never go out alone." Iver walked over to a dressing mirror and ran his hand over it. The surface rippled like a pool of water. A portal! He motioned for them to step through it. "Yes, I'll be in touch. And in the meantime, do as I instructed. Fit in. Do nothing to draw suspicion. Your lives depend upon it."

EAVESDROPPING

The Griffins of Earth Beta apparently often traveled by portal, because when Max and his friends popped back into their homes after leaving Iver's, their families didn't think anything of it. After dinner, Max and Natalia were back online, reviewing what they'd learned.

> **Natalia:** Blackstone is going to be a problem.
> **Max:** Iver said he'd take care of it.
> **Natalia:** That's not exactly what he said.
> **—Ernest Tweeny joined the discussion—**
> **Ernest:** Hey, what's up? Did u see what Iv

—Ernest Tweeny has been disconnected from the discussion—

—Ernest Tweeny has been blocked—

Natalia: someone needs to teach him how to use encrypted chat.

Max: ;-)

Natalia: Just so you know, I won't be waiting for Von Strife before starting my detective work. I have other options.

Max: Like what?

Natalia: Smoke. He knows something. And if he's Von Strife's kid, then he probably has an inside track. I'm going to tail him a bit. See what he's up to.

Max: Be careful. Smoke could teleport u off a skyscraper.

Natalia: Leave everything to me.

Max: I have a bad feeling about this....

The police investigation had stalled. Sheriff Oxley tried to reschedule the interviews with the Griffins three times, but each time, they were canceled at the last moment. Perhaps Iver had stepped in. Max was fine with that.

The next week at school was easier than the first. They were settled into classes, wore the right clothes, and hung out with all the right people. Ernie avoided Robert and instead spent his time relishing his new popularity. Harley avoided Raven—or perhaps it was the other way around. And Max spent some time getting to know the other Round Table duelists. After all, there was a big tournament coming up fast. The biggest of the year. And Iron Bridge simply had to win.

"We don't have much time to get you ready," said Hale. Coach Wolfhelm had assigned the changeling girl with the perky antennae to get Max back in shape. On Max's world, Hale had been a top duelist. One of the best. "You're a little out of practice," she continued with a smile. "So just follow my lead."

Round Table was played the same here as it was in Max's world. Both worlds used custom-built decks of trading cards filled with amazing creatures and perilous traps. And both used elaborate dice known as knucklebones. The combination of card draws, placements on the field, dice rolls for chance, and a solid strategy made for some intense duels. And that was before Max put on his 3-D Kinematic goggles. With a flip of a switch, the whole game moved into a virtual-reality video game. Dice and cards might be played, but what the duelists saw was something out of a movie. Fire-breathing dragons, hordes of goblins, missile-launching elves...they were all there, as real as magic could make them. And twice as dangerous.

Over the next fifty minutes, Hale tore Max apart. At first there were hushed giggles from the other top duelists as they gathered around the table to watch. Then embarrassment. Then came the stunned silence. Max shouldn't be losing. Not like this.

Meanwhile, Natalia was in detective mode, artfully interviewing people who knew Smoke, gathering information without their realizing it. She found herself really liking this world. Sure, it was different. But in a good way. Her dad enjoyed working for Von Strife. He had money now. And time. So he tended to fix things around the house and take Natalia's mom on surprise lunches. Then there was Natalia's sister, who, despite her blatant thievery, was somehow sweeter. And who knew? Her ransacking skills might come in handy one day if Natalia ever needed someone to join her detective agency.

She discovered that Smoke was definitely a loner. When he was on the scene, people scattered like fish from a shark. He seemed to like it that way, sometimes sitting down at a crowded table to see how quickly it would empty. This tendency made it easy to track where he'd been. But predicting where he'd pop up next was the real trick. He attended class from time to time but rarely handed in homework. He wasn't into sports or Round Table. He didn't eat in the dining hall. He had no friends. After a few days, it because quite clear that Smoke was rarely at the school at all. And when he would appear, he looked as filthy as a grease monkey. It was up to Natalia to figure out where he was spending his time.

The big break came when Natalia walked by the girls' bathroom. There was a sudden scream followed by a flood of girls pouring out the door, blushing and furious. "What's going on in there?" Natalia asked Katie.

Katie grumbled as she buckled her jeweled belt. "Smoke. That creep! He just teleported right into the middle of the bathroom. Can you believe that? I don't care how powerful he is. He's going to get it! He has to sleep sometime."

Natalia smirked. "Is he still in there?"

"No. Anyway, I have to go. I'll call you tonight, okay?" Natalia could definitely see why the other Natalia and Katie had been friends. Katie was cute, fiery, and a verbal sharpshooter. She said what she thought, no matter who was listening. Natalia respected that. And Katie and Brittany weren't her only friends. Christina and Gwen called her practically every night, mostly to talk about clothes. Natalia had been suspicious at first. After a while, though, she found herself enjoying the calls, even looking forward to them. Of course, she hadn't confessed this to the Griffins. She hadn't even admitted it to herself.

Inside the bathroom, Natalia found dirty footprints in a splash of water. Boot prints, to be exact. Smoke's. Natalia smiled as she knelt close to the floor with her Phantas-

106

moscope. She immediately recoiled from the smell. Something between rotten tomato and wet dog. She swapped out the lenses on her Phantasmoscope, pinched her nose, and moved closer.

"Hmm...oil. But why does it smell so terrible?" she muttered. She rubbed the grit from the footprint between her fingers. "Okay, it's not motor oil. Something else. Like lubricant for a big machine. A big clockwork, maybe? Where have you been going, Smoke?" Smoke could conceivably teleport anywhere in the world. She needed something more. Something specific.

When Smoke reappeared at school a few days later, Natalia was back on the hunt. Having learned his habits, she picked up his trail quickly and was soon tailing him through the dark, lonesome hallways of one of Iron Bridge's neglected wings. She stayed in the shadows, keeping her distance, when suddenly he disappeared.

Natalia sighed. He did that a lot. Just teleport away for no good reason. She decided to walk a bit farther down the hallway where he'd disappeared, and that was when she nearly tumbled down a hidden staircase. She caught herself, twisting her ankle and stifling a cry. She sat down and nursed her foot, cursing her nearsightedness.

Natalia was about to limp back when she heard voices floating up from the darkness of the stairwell.

"Are you sure that's what they said?"

"I'm not an idiot, Smoke," replied a female voice. "I know what I heard."

"So if they aren't the real Griffins, who are they?"

"I don't care," said the girl. Natalia thought it might have been Raven.

"Then why are you telling me? You've never been nice to me before."

"*Sacre bleu de*... If you so much as touch me again, I'm gonna put your head through that wall." Definitely Raven.

"You didn't answer the question. Why are you telling me all this?"

"Let's just say they need to be taught a lesson."

"You mean Harley...?" Natalia could almost see Smoke's leering smirk. "I know it had to be hard to find out the way you did, Raven. If you ever need—ow!" Natalia heard a thump and a body slumping to the floor. "What did you do that for?"

"I don't like to be touched."

Natalia quickly hobbled behind an old door as Raven stormed up the stairs and down the hall. As for Smoke, either he was still down in that stairwell or he'd teleported out. Either way, it was time for Natalia to inform the Griffins that their story was about to go public.

THE REPLACEMENT

Max: Raven just sold us out 2 Smoke?

Harley: I knew I shouldn't have made her so mad. Agh!

Max: U think she eavesdropped on us?

Natalia: Of course she did. That's her changeling power. She can eavesdrop on conversations that happened a hundred years ago if she wants. We should have been more careful.

—Ernest Tweeny attempted to join the discussion—

—Ernest Tweeny was dropped from the discussion—

Natalia: At this point, I don't know what Smoke will do with the information. He doesn't have friends. But the big risk is him telling his dad. And if Von Strife knows who we are, we can kiss finding the Paragon Engine good-bye.

Max: Wait a sec. Iver's sending me a text.

—**Max has suspended the discussion**—

—**Max has rejoined the discussion**—

Max: Okay, he's going to arrange for us to talk to Monti.

Harley: Seriously??? The guy's been dodging me for weeks.

Natalia: Excellent. You cover the Monti thing, Max. I'll stay on Smoke. But Raven is still out there. We need someone to talk to her. Get her to shut up somehow. She's going to get us killed.

Max: Harley?

Harley: ???

Max: I'm sorry to ask you to do this.

Harley: Then don't.

Max: Just be nice to her. Say you want to be friends or something.

Harley: Oh sure. That ought to fly like a brick.

Max: Come on, Harley. You are the only person who has a chance with her.

Natalia: Please, Harley?

Natalia: Harley?

Natalia: Harley!!!

Harley: Fine. But u owe me.

Max walked into the Grand Auditorium of Iron Bridge holding a new deck of Round Table cards. As he stepped onto the stage, he scanned his teammates. There were so many changelings. Easily half. And in this world, they could use their powers to their advantage. As Coach Wolfhelm had told him, Round Table was a warm-up for the real thing. If you couldn't deal with a changeling in a Round Table duel, you wouldn't stand a chance on the field of battle.

Max looked over to see Tejan Chandra shuffling his cards. The genius kid from Bengal had the changeling power to erase a single thought or wipe your memory clean. His only downfall might be that he was too nice of a kid to use that to his advantage—Max hoped. Max said hello. Or did he? He couldn't remember. Tejan winked knowingly.

Todd and Ross Toad soon arrived like a couple of vultures, with notepads at the ready. They were there to watch the duelists, study their moves, and get the inside story. The brothers' side business was publishing the *Toad Report*, a must-have guide to every top player in the league, their strategies, and their weaknesses. If you were playing someone, and you needed the skinny on how to win, the *Toad Report* was the final answer. Of course, the other duelists could easily get the same information about you if they chose to buy a copy—which meant that the *Toad Reports* didn't come cheap.

As the Toad brothers swept by, they hastily saluted Max. "You're the man, Sumner," Todd called. "Don't forget it. The man!"

"Hey, there you are," called Coach Wolfhelm. The man was dressed in brown-buttoned spats, pin-striped pants, and a matching vest. His sleeves were pushed up high, and a derby was perched atop his grizzled head. He put a hairy arm over Max's shoulder. "Well, Max, you didn't lose any of the old magic, didja? It would do my heart a turn to think you had."

Max shrugged self-consciously. "If I did, you've always got Hale. She's a great player."

"Aye, but we need more than a great duelist to send old Stirling to the deep. We need Max Sumner. The old Max Sumner!" Max caught the look of embarrassment in Hale's eyes as she overheard. Wolfhelm smiled broadly, exposing a set of rather pointy teeth. "You just worry about yourself. There're a lot of folks depending on us. I won't let you down; you don't let me down likewise?" His furry knuckles gave Max's shoulder an uncomfortable squeeze. "See?"

Max saw, all right. If he lost the tournament, his cover would be blown.

After days of Natalia's nagging, Harley finally agreed to talk to Raven. He had a feeling the conversation would be ugly. He was never that comfortable around girls, anyway. He'd say something wrong, or wouldn't say something he should. Still, he'd try. Raven was currently in the library for sixth period. It was the best shot Harley would have at catching her alone.

As he made his way toward the library, he reflected on the last two weeks and what it was like to finally have a father. Not that he was an expert on the subject or anything. He avoided the man at every turn. Pretending to be someone else's kid wasn't right. Whenever he slipped and used the terms *dad* and *mom*, he wanted to hit himself. His parents here were pretty cool, though, and they gave him all the space he wanted. But it hurt them. He could see it in their eyes. Then he thought about the Paragon Engine, and what it would be like for them to lose their son all over again. They'd be devastated. And this time, Harley would be to blame. He already hated himself for it.

Harley looked up at the sign above the double doors: Rosenkreuz Library. Est. ad 1616. He spotted Raven near the back, dressed in her familiar black leather pants and jackboots, both with rows and rows of buckles. Over her rock-concert T-shirt was a dark hooded cloak that completely hid the chair beneath her, giving her the illusion that she was floating over her boots. She was alone and pretending to be asleep. Taking a deep breath, he moved ahead.

"Don't even think about sitting down," Raven warned, not bothering to open her eyes. Harley sat down anyway. Raven turned her head the other direction and sighed. "Please, go away."

"We should talk."

"That would not be a good idea."

Natalia had invented a good story. He'd run the details over and over in his head to make sure he'd remember. He hoped he'd get it right. "You don't have to say anything. I can do the talking. And if you don't like it, you can leave."

"I can leave now," said Raven, standing up quickly and gathering her books. *"Au revoir."* Harley pulled her back down. She ripped her arm away and stared menacingly at him.

"Please. Give me a chance." Harley took a deep breath. "So, anyway, the whole dying thing. I'm sorry I didn't talk to you sooner. Things have been weird. Maybe it was the portal, but sometimes I'm not myself. It's getting better, but you can even ask my mom. I'm not the same. I just need a little time, that's all."

Raven's glare softened for a moment, then returned with intensity.

Harley kept going. "I'm not asking for things to go

114

back the way they were. I know you're angry, and I know why. I'm just asking you to take it easy on me. And maybe, you know, we can"—he swallowed a lump in his throat—"hang out. You know, if you want."

Raven studied him intently, then shook her head. "Nice story. Give my compliments to Natalia."

Harley sighed, then slumped in his chair.

She continued after a pause. "It was good, though. The story. If I were a cheerleader or a yearbook chick, I might have bought it."

Harley looked over at her. She was smiling. "I don't understand."

"You never were that bright when it came to girls," Raven replied. "But I know you well enough—whoever you are—to know you can't lie to save your life."

Harley whistled softly, running his hands through his hair. "I'm pretty terrible at it, huh?" He found himself smirking. "You do a pretty good job, though."

"I have more practice. So who are you, anyway?" She watched him intently.

"I'm Harley. I've been Harley all my life. It's the truth. Am I really that different?"

"You guys are sloppy, you know. Talking everywhere. The walls can hear you. And if they do, I do. And I may not be the only one." They should have stuck to secure chat, Harley thought. "But we're safe here. No one is listening except me."

"How do you know?"

"I can talk to walls, chairs, toothbrushes, toilet brushes, if I really wanted...even the air. And the air is telling me no one is listening right now, okay?" Harley was astonished. This Raven was more powerful than the one in his world. "So, who are you, really?"

"I'm Harley," he repeated, realizing he was about to do exactly what Iver had told them not to do. "And the others are the Griffins. But we're not your Griffins. We're from a different Earth. Believe me, we don't want to hurt anyone. All we really want is to get back home."

"What about my Harley?" Raven pressed. "Is he in your world?"

"I know as much as you do. When we arrived, your Griffins had already been missing for three months."

A lonely sadness filled Raven's eyes. She bit her lip, and her silence only made Harley more anxious.

He paused. "You won't tell anybody, will you?"

Raven raised an eyebrow. "Oh, you mean Smoke?" Harley blanched. "Don't worry. I knew Natalia was eavesdropping the whole time."

"But why talk to him at all?"

"So you'd finally talk to me, idiot." She grinned as one of her dark-nailed fingers played with a silver earring. "All he knows is that the portal changed you. And that could mean anything."

She stood up as the bell rang. Harley took hold of her wrist. "Wait. I'm sorry. Sorry for everything."

"Can I have my hand back?"

116

"We need your help." If there was one person who could find out what Smoke was up to, it was Raven. Harley had to at least try.

She looked at him in genuine surprise. "You have a lot of nerve."

"I know. But we're desperate to get back to our world. There's a Raven there, too. She and two of our best friends are in a lot of trouble right now. You might be able to help."

"You come in here, pretending to be my Harley, then give me this whole crazy story about being from another world? You have got to be nuts. You guys are pathetic. The other Griffins were so much better."

Harley nodded. "I guess I'm not much compared to your Harley."

"No, you're not," said Raven. Her smoky eyes softened as she regarded Harley's desperation. She reached out to him instinctively, then withdrew with an icy scowl. "But you're the only Harley we've got left."

As she moved toward the door, she turned with a sly smile. "Fine. I'll hear you out. But if you guys are messing with me, I'm out." She disappeared around the corner, her buckled boots leading the way.

Harley didn't move from his seat for a long time. His eyes were locked on the doorway through which Raven had left. And then he realized he was smiling. A real, honest-to-goodness smile.

KILLER FOG

The crows were back. One here, another there. Looking in windows, peering down from trees. Max didn't wander alone, and the crows didn't attack. There was an understanding. They would watch. Observe. And there was nothing Max could do about it.

A deep fog had set in over New Avalon. Weather advisories had been posted, people had been warned to stay inside, and Iron Bridge had canceled school. This wasn't an ordinary fog. This was a killer fog, thick with poisonous mists.

"People can die in this soup," Natalia had told Max over the online chat session that morning. "I looked it up. These killer fogs just pop up out of nowhere, kill a bunch of people, then disappear. No one knows why, but it's been like this for years." She sighed. "Well, we take the good with the bad. And so far, this world has been pretty good. And as for Smoke, you'll be happy to know, I've had the gunk from his shoes analyzed. Whale oil!"

"Isn't killing whales illegal?" asked Max with a shudder.

"In our world, yes. But here? Who knows? And would a bad guy care? Anyway, it's a very specific type of whale. And only one company has a license to sell the oil. Now all I need is a customer list."

As for Sprig, she had popped into Max's pocket a few times but hadn't said much. She'd just slept nervously and twitched her tail. When Max tried to find out if she'd discovered who was following him, she only shook her head and changed the topic. Then she disappeared again. She'd been gone for several days now.

Max sat in his living room, playing a video game, while his little sister played close enough to keep a wary eye on him. His parents had called earlier, letting him know they were stuck at his grandmother's house until the fog lifted. Max had to admit that he was enjoying these parents more than his real ones. Everything here was so impossibly perfect: the perfect sandwich, the perfect cookie, the perfect throw of the football. And, strangely, even his underwear was being ironed.

As Max blew up an alien spaceship, a blue spark

suddenly leaped from his fingertip to the game controller. Max jerked his hand away and shook it. He looked at it closely, then continued playing. Another spark. This time, when he pulled his hand back, a band of electrical current appeared between his fingers. And it didn't stop.

Max felt a chill, and he looked out the window. Through the thick fog, he could see two shadows approaching.

He knew instantly. Father Blackstone's Slayers. They were coming for him!

Max quickly picked up his sister and ran into the kitchen. She protested, demanding to be put down. Max opened the cabinet beneath the sink and shoved his sister inside.

"Stay in there."

"Let me out!"

"Stay in there, or Mom and Dad are going to be very mad at you."

"You're not my brother!"

Max peeked around the corner. The shadows were gone. But the Skyfire raced over his skin in bands of blue energy. "Fine. I'm not your brother. But if you stay under there, and promise not to say a word, I'll let you play with my video games for the rest of the day."

She shut the door herself.

"And stay there. Remember," Max warned as he checked the security-system console. Not that it mattered. If someone wanted in badly enough, an expensive noisemaker wasn't going to stop him.

Max heard something on the roof. There was a sound of scrambling and falling tiles, followed by a rumble and smash in the great room. Stepping quietly through the hallway, he peered around the corner. Everything looked normal enough. *No! Wait.* The fire irons were scattered on the floor.

A black blur shot from the shadows and plowed into Max. He flew through the air and landed hard on the tiles. The room went silent again, except for a familiar ticking of a clockwork eyeball. The Slayer watched him, waiting. Then it leaped again, pinning Max to the ground with its razor claws. Max flailed his hands, pushing the gnashing teeth away. He beat at the monster, smashing his soft fists into its clockwork eye implants.

Somewhere nearby, Max heard the other Slayer roar. In the kitchen! It was looking for Hannah. Max struggled under the monster's weight but couldn't budge it. His sister screamed, but he couldn't move. He couldn't save her! Max's control snapped for the second time since arriving in this world. His vision flattened into a field of blue, and like the rushing of a great flood, the Skyfire burst free. There was a torrential wind, a blast of thunder, and an explosion so violent that the Slayer was ripped away from him with a helpless yelp.

Max's eyes stung. His mouth tasted like bleach, and

his nose burned. He rolled over onto his chest, breathing hard. Then he noticed how very quiet the house had become. Max got up on his unsteady feet. He looked around, unsure of what had just happened, and then rubbed his eyes in amazement. A hole the size of a locomotive had been blown through the back of the house, and the poisonous mist was beginning to seep in.

The Slayer that had attacked him was gone, and the other, Max could see, was sneakily picking its way through the destruction out of fear of being spotted. It looked up at Max and howled, leaping out into the night.

Max jumped to his feet and raced into the kitchen, flung open the cabinet doors, and knelt down—his heart in his mouth. There, looking back at him, sat Hannah. A smile lit her face.

"That was fun," she said. "Let's do it again!"

With his sister in the safe room, Max donned his breathing mask and headed up to his room. He fired up the DE Tablet and sent a message to Iver. Max needed his help to get the *Codex* back. The Skyfire was too much to control. It was blind luck that his blast hadn't blown through the kitchen, taking out Hannah instead of the monster.

When the police arrived, Max was happy to name Blackstone as the chief suspect.

"I'll personally set a Templar THOR unit on the case," Lord Sumner stated icily as his eyes smoldered. In his hand, he held a dented, tarnished clockwork eye that had been blow off one of the monsters. "No one attacks my family. No one."

PART TWO

THE PLAN

THE MACHINE

Max: U guys better be careful. Those Slayers could still be out there.

Natalia: Blackstone could have a whole petting zoo full of them. Wouldn't that be cute. Ugh. At least the fog has lifted.

Harley: Heard u had a slumber party, Natalia. U dumping us for your new friends?

Natalia: A slumber party? What am I, nine? And no, I am a Griffin first. I'm just pumping them for information. You'd be surprised how much they know.

Harley: Yes. Yes, I would. LOL

Natalia: ANYWAY…How's it going with Raven? Any progress?

Harley: Sort of. But now Ernie won't talk to me. I can't win.

Ernest: Harley's using her.

Harley: It was Natalia's idea. Hey, if u like her so much, she's all yours.

Ernest: I'm sorry. Was somebody just talking?

Max: Let's stay focused here. Okay? Raven could be the answer to finding the Paragon Engine.

Natalia: When can she meet with us?

Harley: She has a fencing tournament this weekend. Maybe next Monday, after school?

Ernest: Oh, he knows her schedule. How sweet.

Natalia: Ernie, I am giving you one warning.

Ernest: I'm giving you one, so there.

—Ernest Tweeney was disconnected from the discussion—

Max: Let him rejoin. He'll get over it.

Natalia: FINE

—Ernest Tweeny has joined the discussion—

Natalia: U going to behave or what?

Ernest: Or what.

Natalia: AGHGHGHGHGGH

Max: Hang on. I'm getting a chat request. Secure line.

—Max has suspended the discussion—

—Max has rejoined the discussion—

Max: It's Monti!

Harley: What does he want????

Max: He wants us to meet him. Saturday morning. Told us to head to subway platform 13.

Natalia: That's near the Masonic Hall, right?

Max: 10:13 AM, he says.

Natalia: What an odd time.

Harley: He's an odd guy.

Max: Okay. My mom said I could go. Everyone who can make it, let's meet up at Ernie's house at 10. We'll walk over to the platform from there. The Slayers won't attack if we're all together.

Natalia: Let's hope.

Harley powered off his DE Tablet and walked over to the window. Of course, his whole wall was a window. The house was glass from bottom to top. Since Iver's warning to fit in, Harley had started having dinner with Candi and Henry. He tried to fake his way through conversations, but he was terrible at lying. And so they looked like a normal family only from a distance.

Harley tried not to think too much about it. After all, if the Griffins ever got out of this world, Candi and Henry would only be more devastated if they thought he was their Harley. He planned to tell them. At some point. But first things first: Monti.

He tried not to get his hopes too high. This wasn't his Monti. But he couldn't help it. Tomorrow was a big day. He wondered what Monti looked like. What would he say? Would it be like having an older brother again? Or a father? All Harley knew was that Monti was the closest thing he had to family outside the Griffins and his mother. And Monti seemed to understand Harley better than any of them.

At precisely 10:13 the next morning, the Griffins boarded the *Zephyr* and quickly sat down. If this was anything like their world, the *Zephyr* would take them to a well-trafficked station in New Victoria, and from there, they'd have to hoof it across the cobblestoned city streets until they reached Monti's lab. They knew the way very well and had dressed to blend in with the strange city folk, who, like New Avalon, still seemed stuck in the nineteenth century. The *Zephyr* was rolling along the familiar path as the Griffins chatted when suddenly their car broke away from the rest of the train and pulled off onto a side rail. It stopped. The lights flickered, then shut off.

"Oh, this is just perfect," Natalia complained in the darkness. "I suppose the train is going to eat us now." She immediately wished she hadn't said that. So far, the train had treated her pretty well. The last thing she needed was to make an enemy of the *Zephyr* in both worlds.

"Hopefully, just you," said Harley. He'd never admit it to his friends, but he wasn't feeling so hot about meeting Monti anymore. Being ignored by the guy you once counted among your best friends hurt. Even when it wasn't on purpose. Harley was glad they were in the dark. Natalia would have seen through him in a second.

There was a boom, then a lurch. Max felt the train car descending. How fast or how far, he couldn't tell. Another boom and a jolt of clamping iron. The lights flickered to life, and the car began moving again down what appeared to be an old, rocky passage that might once have been a coal mine. For several long minutes, they bounced along. Then the car came to a sudden stop at what appeared to be an abandoned platform. Cobwebbed chandeliers wobbled over a weather-stained Persian carpet. The place hadn't been a regular stop in decades.

Monti stood near the stairs, reading a holographic paper that disappeared when he looked up. He pushed his glasses up on his nose and approached the Griffins. It was the same old Monti, with his floppy hair and boyish face. Though instead of jeans and a blazer, he wore a rubber lab apron, and a pair of welding goggles sat atop his head.

"Follow me," he whispered, keeping his eyes averted. He led them along several cramped brick passageways, up and down countless flights of iron stairs, and finally to an elaborate doorway covered in Masonic carvings and symbols. He pulled out a pocket watch, turned the hands to different positions, then wound the stem. A moment later, the back of the watch broke free and a clockwork beetle emerged. It ran along Monti's hand, leaped onto the door lock, and inserted itself. A moment later, the door swung open. They entered.

"Excuse the mess," said Monti as he moved ahead into the darkness and began flipping on the lights. In a few moments, the Griffins found themselves standing in Monti's laboratory. The brick monstrosity, large enough to hold an aircraft carrier, was mostly empty. And the few clockworks that served Monti squeaked and whirred beneath the stained-glass and wrought-iron ceiling. This was a laboratory of possibility. But for now, it sat quietly.

They picked their way across the oil-stained floor, past a row of pinball machines, and just to the right of the automated disassembly chamber. Monti led them up a short flight of iron stairs to his office, closed the door, and then sat down. They sat across from him, waiting for him to say what he had to say. Instead, he took a dirty cup, rubbed the inside with his shirt cuff, and poured himself some coffee. He didn't say a word or raise his eyes as he sipped it quietly.

After several uncomfortable minutes of silence, Harley rose from his seat and moved around the office, absently picking up different bits of machinery. The office doubled as Monti's toy box. Clockworks of every size and shape sat quietly on shelves and leaned in corners. Half-finished weapons hung from the walls. In the center of it all was a large recliner, more duct tape than leather, and a waist-high stack of comic books. Ernie moved through the collection in a second, pulled out his favorites, and plopped into a chair, completely checking out.

Harley moved to the workbench, then quickly reached into a bin and pulled out a small device. "Wow, how'd you get a phase inducer that works at room temperature? I've only seen this talked about in books. This is incredible!"

Monti brightened, looking up for the first time. "Thank you. You know, phase inducers are all about…wait a second. How could you know? I just invented that."

Harley quickly put down the gadget and sat down. "Oh, just a lucky guess." Harley picked up a stack of Hulk comics and handed a few to Ernie, who refused to accept them. The two hadn't yet spoken that morning.

"Lucky guess…right…" Monti murmured as he sipped his coffee. He seemed to withdraw into himself for a few moments. Then he raised his eyes again. Spotting a dirty sock on the floor, he discreetly kicked it under a chair. "So, let's talk about Paragon Engines," said Monti. "And let me get right to the point. I don't know where it is. And no, I can't help you find it. But I don't think it matters anymore. It's been shut down. Hopefully for good."

"You brought us all the way here just to tell us that?" said Natalia incredulously.

"Well, I can see how it might look that way." Monti paused uncomfortably and cleared his throat. He sighed and let his shoulders sag. "Let me start over. I'm not very good with people. I spend all my time here in the lab. So I'm sorry if I am coming across all wrong. The real reason for bringing you here was because once Iver told me who you were and that you came from Earth Alpha...well, there's so much we don't know about interdimensional travel. I was hoping I could...interview you?" He looked at them with pleading eyes.

"Interview us?" Natalia exclaimed. "Are you crazy? We aren't a science project." She growled. "I bet you weren't even friends with the other Griffins. If you were, you wouldn't do this to us."

Monti paused, glancing timidly at Harley. "I...to be honest, the Griffins here really weren't that interested in me or what I did. Iver said something about Harley being my apprentice in your world. But the Harley here was a tough guy. An athlete. He didn't know anything about machines." He cleared his throat. "Sorry if it seemed like I was avoiding you, Harley. Until Iver told me what was going on, I thought your calls were just a prank." Harley said nothing.

Natalia, however, was on her feet. "A joke? I'll have you know that Monti is one of our best friends. And he's dying. Yes, that's right. He's dying of some strange sick-

134

ness while you're sitting here trying to interview us for your science magazine. I can't believe this...."

Monti swallowed a lump in his throat. "Dying?"

"As if you care," she replied testily. Then she softened as she caught sight of Monti's trembling hands. "And...don't worry. It wasn't genetic or anything, I'm sure. You...you'll be all right."

"So what do we do now?" asked Max. "The Paragon Engine is our only ticket back."

"Von Strife is the only one who knows where it is," answered Monti quietly. "And he's also the only one who knows how to use it. Unless you persuade him to help, you aren't going anywhere."

Natalia pushed herself out of her chair. "If you'll excuse me, I am going to go sulk in my frustration. You don't mind, do you, Monti? I'll be back." With a sympathetic glance at a very disappointed Harley, she headed out into Monti's lab. She felt terrible for her friend. The worst part was the irony. In their world, Monti was the closest Harley had had to a father. But now that Harley finally had a dad, Monti wasn't interested in him.

Max looked around at the lab. While it was not as impressive as their own Monti's, it was far more secure. The whole thing seemed to have been built with a sense of paranoia. There were bioscanners at every door, small camera drones zipping around the rafters, and storage areas secured with zapping plasma fields.

"Every gadget I make," explained Monti, "everything

you see in this place, is funded by Von Strife. And as you can see, he likes to keep things locked up tight. But it's a small price to pay. If the linear guns or the singularity bomb ever fell into the wrong hands, I couldn't imagine…" He shuddered.

As Natalia walked through the lab, her thoughts returned to the Paragon Engine. The Griffins had to find it if they wanted to get back to their world. And if Von Strife was the only one who knew where it was, then they'd just have to find some way to get close to him without his knowing about it. Natalia suddenly paused in front of a room full of portal mirrors. All of them were marked with the initials v.s. And then she had a luminous idea. She rushed back to her friends.

"Does Von Strife come here very often?" she asked.

Monti glanced up and scratched his head. "Sure. He always likes to check on my progress."

"Does he take the *Zephyr*, like us?"

Monti laughed for the first time. "With Naomi with him all the time? You've met her? All right, then you know what she's like. The *Zephyr* is terrified of her. So Von Strife only comes here via portal mirror. That one over there, in the Archives room. The Zeta Class. Some of my best work. At least, I like to think so. It connects this lab directly to his private office in Iron Bridge."

"What about the other mirrors?" asked Harley.

"They're deactivated. And dangerous. Von Strife won't use them."

"You don't say." Natalia smiled to herself as she scribbled something down in her *Book of Clues*. That portal mirror could be just the thing. It was too perfect. All they needed was a plan. And plans were something Natalia was particularly good at. First, they'd need to talk to Raven.

RAVEN

"You want me to break into someone's house?" Raven folded her arms. She and the Griffins were up in her dorm room, safe from spies and eavesdroppers. Rock posters covered her walls, and a music system, taking up most of a wall, pumped out angry music. It played endlessly to drown out the disembodied voices that were constantly talking to Raven: the walls, the pipes, the floorboards, and even her toilet. They all had a story, and Raven was the only one they could talk to.

"Not his house," Natalia corrected. She moved her goggles up and over the brim of her hat and stuffed her gloves into her jacket pocket. "His lab. And we're not going to steal anything." Raven had listened to the whole story of their world, and their plan to return, without interruption. Until now.

"Hey, we're the good guys," said Ernie with his most charming smile. His lightning-bolt shirt was pressed and his Agent Thunderbolt helmet was polished to a shine. He'd been looking forward to talking to Raven all weekend. This was his big chance to win her away from Harley. "You ever worked with real, live superheroes before?" He moved beside her, arching his eyebrow. "You know, we're not that different from you. We just live large. You want to hang out sometime?"

Raven looked at Ernie and snorted. "Did they grow you out of some test tube or something?" Ernie wilted.

"The Raven we knew was the best there was at this business," said Natalia.

"The girl you knew wasn't as smart as you think," countered Raven. "I mean, just look at her choice in friends." Deflated, Ernie moved away, sulking. "Okay, so you break in. Then what?"

Max stepped forward. "We avoid Monti's security system—that's where you come in. Then we make our way to the Archives, and we fire it up—Von Strife's personal portal mirror."

"Fire it up?"

Harley raised his hand. "It takes some MERLIN Tech know-how, but I can do it."

"I thought you only threw footballs," she replied with a smirk.

"Guess I'm just full of surprises." Harley grinned.

Ernie rolled his eyes and sat down in the corner. "Does anyone else here feel like throwing up?"

"So you'll just waltz into his office?" Raven continued. "Just like that?"

"Just like that," said Max.

"And what about me?"

Max shrugged coolly. "You stay in the lab until we get back."

"Why? You hiding something?"

"Just didn't want to put you in any more danger. If we get caught in his office..."

"You say Von Strife is out?"

"His daughter is sick," Natalia explained.

"Fine. Then what?"

"Then we search Von Strife's office for clues about the Paragon Engine," said Max.

"What if Von Strife is there, waiting for you?"

"He won't be."

"Okay," continued Raven. "So basically you are asking me to break into a high-security laboratory, possibly get myself killed, and I could get expelled while I am at it. What's in it for me?" It was rhetorical. She knew exactly what she wanted.

Max clenched his jaw. Raven was the only one who could get the Griffins in and out of Monti's lab without being spotted. No camera, no microphone, no clockwork could ever sneak up on her. Max sighed. "What do you want?"

Raven's eyes gleamed. "Nothing big. But you either do it or the deal's off."

"Anything. What?"

"Before you leave this world, before you step through your little Paragon thingy and leave us behind, you have to find out who killed my Harley." Her voice broke, and her shoulders sagged for a moment, but the second she felt Natalia's hand on her arm, Raven shrugged it off and grew rigid. "That's the deal. Got it?"

"But that could take us years," Max argued.

"And it could get us all killed," Natalia added. "It's better if we just disappear."

"Better for whom?" Raven replied in an icy tone. "You owe the other Griffins. You waltzed in here, stole their lives, their families—everything. And now you just want to leave without making it right? You're not heroes. You're just a bunch of cowards."

The Griffins fell silent. Uncomfortable glances passed among them. Any quick escape would be out of the question if they did what Raven asked. Then again, she had a point. A very painful point. The Griffins shared a silent conversation of glances and nods. Then Max turned back to Raven.

"All right. We'll do it."

THE PLAN

Natalia: So once Harley locates the Zephyr's control computer, I help him hack into it. Is that right?

Max: Unless u have a better plan to get to Monti's.

Natalia: Not at the moment. Between Harley and me, I think we can do it. The only thing that worries me is Raven.

Max: That she'll rat us out?

Natalia: No. I mean, finding out what happened to the other Griffins. It isn't going to be easy considering everything else on our plate. We're

kind of swamped, with all the hacking of security systems, reprogramming of the subway,
and laying out an invasion plan into a top-secret
laboratory.

Max: U have a solution?

Natalia: I have an idea. But it's up to you to
make it a success. Logan. Supposedly he was
there when the other Griffins were killed, right?
He has to know something. And he's more reliable than Smoke, you know. If you can chance
it...

Max: But I don't know where he is.

Natalia: But he knows where you are. You can
count on it.

As Max turned off his DE Tablet, he sat back in
thought. *Logan.* He was still out there somewhere. And
he still had Max's ring. It wasn't clear which side he
worked for, but Max knew one thing for certain: if he
wanted to kill the Griffins, they'd have been dead long
ago. That was all Max needed to be convinced that it
was worth a try to talk to him.

Max noticed a small ladybug nestled among his
books. As he reached out to pet it, it took flight, landing
in the ferns. Curious, Max followed it, then felt the skin
on his neck tingle. Turning, he spotted a flash and a swirl
of mist in the corner of his bedroom. Smoke grinned
back at him. The blond creep was dressed in a beat-up

143

leather trench coat, and his golden-tinted goggles were slid up on his forehead. From the grime on his face, Smoke looked as if he'd spent the better part of his day rolling around inside a car engine.

"Heya, Maxine. Talking to your girlfriend on the DE again?"

"Lurk much?" Max shot back.

"Just dropping by to remind you that we have some unfinished business. Number one, you need to fill me in on your little game. I'm tired of waiting. Just tell me what you want. Number two, you better get Natalia off my back or she's gonna have an accident, if you catch my drift."

"I think you might be trespassing."

"I usually am."

"Did the league of evil kick you out already?"

Smoke snorted. "Good one." He looked around the room, his eyes drifting from one object to the next. "Say, where's that little Bounder of yours? The shape-shifter? Shouldn't she be sitting on your head or whatever?"

"Maybe you need to be shown out." Max stood up. His vision flickered into the blue spectrum as his Skyfire danced on his fingertips.

Smoke took a cautious step backward. But he didn't leave. "Maybe you should know when to stay dead."

"You mean when Logan supposedly killed us off?"

Smoke laughed proudly. "Nice, huh? I can't believe the police bought that line."

Max's eyes narrowed. So Smoke was the one behind that crazy lie after all. Of course he was. Who else? Max's fists burst into ghostly flames. "You know, I'm beginning to think you might not be a very nice person," Max said.

"Coming from you, I'll take that as a compliment. You could have cleared Logan's name a dozen times by now. I mean, just being alive pretty much proves he didn't do it. But not you. You just let him twist in the wind. That's cold, Sumner. Even for me." Smoke vanished in a swirl of mist.

The following day brought rain and a steely determination in Max. He would find Logan. One way or another.

Max stepped out into the rainy mist wearing his kung fu uniform, padded down the stairs of his back deck, and followed a white rock path through a hedge-trimmed cornucopia of flowering trees, statues, and rose trellises. He passed like a ghost through the labyrinth and unlocked a door obscured by a thick wall of wet leaves. It squeaked open. Max shut the door behind him and looked around.

Before him lay the red pagoda where Logan had spent tireless hours training Max to become a Templar warrior. For days on end, they'd talk about Max's future, his hopes, his dreams, and his fears. This place was special to Max. Perhaps it was special to the other Max as well. He walked over to the rock garden and took up the rake. He wondered what he should draw. Some sort of sign or symbol. Something clever that only Logan would understand. After a half hour in the wet, Max was still staring at the rocks.

"This is stupid," Max said out loud. He sighed. "He'll never come...."

"You'd probably be right."

Logan was perched atop the roof of the pagoda, his figure blending with the dim shadows of the ornamental dragons beside him. The Scotsman silently dropped to the ground. "You got something to say?"

Say? Max's mind had been completely wiped by Logan's sudden appearance. He stumbled over his words. "I want to clear your name."

Logan silently watched Max. Among all the people in the two worlds, Logan was the most like his counterpart. The same leather jacket. The same five o'clock shadow. The same way of talking. The only difference was that Max's Logan wore sunglasses while this Logan wore an eye patch.

"Smoke framed you," Max blurted out. The Scotsman didn't move. Didn't twitch. "But you knew that, didn't you? I don't know...I don't know what to say to you. Just let me help. Like you always helped me."

Logan bristled. "You and I have never met."

Max straightened, recalling the interrogation he'd undergone. "If you know that, then you also know that I am Max. Maybe not yours. But just as real."

146

"Don't worry about me, kid. I don't need your help."

Max brushed the rain from his face. "In my world, Logan would never have run away from his problems."

"Running away? You seem a little smug on the topic seeing as how you plan on hijacking the nearest Paragon Engine and hightailing it back to your world."

"I don't see how I…" Max's voice trailed off as his mind caught up with Logan's words. How could Logan have known about their plans for the Paragon Engine? Unless…no. The computer chats had been encrypted.

"You don't need to break any encryption," said Logan, reading Max's mind, "when you have a camera." He raised his gloved hand to show a small ladybug perched atop his knuckle. It raised its wings, exposing tiny clockwork gears of etched silver. "She's a pretty thing, isn't she?"

Max slapped his forehead. He'd been such an idiot! "If you're reading our chats, then you know we're not running away. We're going to help Raven find the missing Griffins." Max's teeth chattered as his damp uniform snapped in the wind.

Logan placed his leather jacket over Max's shoulders. "Which is why I'm gonna help you. First things first, though. No clearing my name. I work better from the shadows. There's more at stake here than you know."

"But…"

"Now, about the Griffins. They were on the trail of something big. Never mind what it was. The important thing here is that Smoke was in on it. I told the Griffins to tail him. They did. But that's where they got into trouble. They sent me a message. Said they'd found a giant machine blazing with blue fire. The Paragon Engine. Smoke had gone through. They asked if they could follow him. I told them to hold off, since there might not be a return ticket. But…I never heard back."

"So Smoke killed them. I knew it wasn't you!"

"They're not dead—not yet."

"How could you know that?"

"One night, about a month after they disappeared, I was shaving in the mirror, and I see Max looking back at me. Then he started talking. He sounded like he was a million miles away. Said there'd been an accident. They'd never found Smoke. They'd never even made it to the other side. They were stuck in some sort of in-between world. They were in bad shape, and getting worse. I don't know how long they'll be able to last. But one thing is clear. You find the Paragon Engine, you'll find the other Griffins. You tell Natalia to kick her snooping into high gear."

Logan walked over to a hatbox sitting on the bench. He lifted it gently and handed it to Max. "Now, about the real reason I came here." He frowned. "Open it up—carefully."

Max peeked inside, not knowing what to expect, and found two amber eyes blinking up at him. There was Sprig, purring weakly in the form of a kitten. She was shivering. She tried to get up but fell back on her side with a pitiful squeak.

"Your Bounder was found lying in a ditch just outside town," Logan explained. "No footprints. No car tracks. Nothing." He watched Max stroke the spriggan's ear tenderly. "Stayed up with her half the night to make sure she pulled through. She's a strong one, though. Already on the mend. If you ask me, she's been poisoned. But I'm no expert on faeries. You might want to ask Doc Trimble."

"But how? Who...?"

"No answers. When she's up to it, she'll tell you. Meantime, keep her warm."

As Max looked her over, he noticed a small metal gleam underneath her makeshift blanket. Reaching down, his fingers closed around a ring. A slender ring. Max's breath caught in his throat. It was his *Codex* ring. When Max looked up again, the Scotsman had vanished.

Max stood silently as water from his hair dripped onto the ground. He shivered as he began the cold trek back to the house, Sprig's box clutched tightly in one hand, the *Codex* ring gleaming cold and blue on the other.

THE BREAK-IN

Max sat down at his desk shortly after dinner. Next to him curled his spriggan, still snuggled in her box. She hadn't spoken a word, but she seemed peaceful. He'd take her to see Doc Trimble in the morning. As for Logan, Max had shared their conversation with the Griffins. It had been exactly the breakthrough they needed. The other Griffins were alive! And if they could find the Paragon Engine, they'd be halfway to saving them. Harley suggested just putting the squeeze on Smoke, since the creep could lead them right to the Griffins. But Smoke had gone missing yet again. Their best bet was to stay on track with the big plan. And, as it happened, tonight was the night.

Ernest: Are you sure about this? What if Von Strife is there?

Natalia: Max's plan is good. What about Raven?

Harley: Don't worry. She'll be there.

Ernest: Oh, so now you are speaking for her? Maybe one of us should ask her.

Harley: Be my guest, Thunderbutt. You seemed to be doing so well back in her room.

Ernest: …

Harley: What about Smoke? We know about him, but does he know who we are yet?

Natalia: I don't think so. He keeps asking Max what game we're up to. That sounds like he's pretty much in the dark. And if I were to guess, I'd say he's afraid of something. Maybe the other Max knew something juicy about him.

Max: He knows you are on to him, Natalia.

Natalia: Like I'm scared.

Harley: No, I think Max is right.

Natalia: So I'll be careful. Okay? There, satisfied?

Ernest: Sorry about Sprig, Max. Food poisoning is rough. There was this one time I ate a tuna sandwich that had been lying out for a couple of days. Man, I heaved out my guts all day. And at super speed, my throat was like a power hose of death. Talk about splash factor. Dude, total MELTDOWN of the bathroom.

Natalia: Um…anyway…

Max: Have we considered Naomi? What if she's waiting for us in Von Strife's office?

Natalia: If Von Strife is gone, she will be, too. But just in case, if we see her, let's not give her a reason to turn us into charcoal.

Harley: I just reconfirmed. Raven will meet us at seven.

Max: Good. Monti won't be back until after ten. Plenty of time. Is the Zephyr ready?

Harley: Natalia and I tested it yesterday.

Ernest: I sure hope you know what you are doing.

Max: Relax. We're the Grey Griffins. What could go wrong?

At precisely 7:12 PM, the subway security cameras clicked off. Ten seconds later, the *Zephyr* rolled up to the platform, and the Griffins, along with Raven, emerged from the shadows and quietly boarded the train.

"This had better work," Ernie whispered.

"Did the Ernie of your world complain this much?" Harley asked Raven.

"Only when you didn't change his diaper," Raven replied.

"Hardy har har!" Ernie said grumpily.

Ten minutes later, the Griffins were standing outside Monti's lab. "Follow me," said Harley, leading them into a dark alley flanking the building. "Monti has a service door for his recycler clockworks. It will be a tight fit, but we can make it."

"And the security system?" Max asked.

"I guess we'll see."

The service entrance was a hydraulic door about knee high. It was monitored by cameras, which Harley disabled with a signal jammer. He then pulled out a small device from his pocket and spun a crank on its side several times. It began to blink.

"This should interrupt the security-field sensors." Harley reached into his mouth and pulled out a thick wad of bubble gum. "Thimble Wicket Gum. Stickiest gum known to man." He smiled at Raven but returned to work when he spotted Ernie glaring at him. Applying the gum to the bottom of the device, he stuck it to the metal door. *Click!* The door swung open.

Max looked over at Raven. "Okay, your turn."

The changeling girl placed her hand on the wall and concentrated for several seconds. "The nearest clock is on the other side of the main room. Once you clear the door, you're going to…oh, forget it." She dropped her hand and ducked under the door. "Just follow me."

Between Harley's knowledge of the lab and Raven's ability to keep them hidden from the roving security patrols, the Griffins made excellent time. They moved like shadows from one crate to the next, up a ladder, over a catwalk, and back down into a subterranean corridor lined with throbbing steam engines and sliding pistons. It smelled of grease and salt water. Max stopped and wiped a smear from his goggles, only to have Raven suddenly pull him by his collar into an alcove. A flybot swept by, scanning the area for intruders. That was a close call. But they were quickly back in action.

"This is it," Harley said as they neared a set of steps leading up. "The Archives are up there. Follow me, and don't touch anything, Ernie!"

Ernie smirked. "I've been all over this place a dozen times—including upstairs. And I licked everything! Twice!"

"Great…" Natalia rolled her eyes. "How'd it taste?"

"Like chicken."

As they emerged into the shadowy room, Max rolled up his sleeve. "Mind if I light up?"

Raven nodded. The *Codex* ring quickly melted and spread up Max's arm like a twisting snake. It twined around his forearm in thicker and thicker cords until the outline of a gauntlet appeared. Then the magical liquid

154

solidified, revealing the *Codex* gauntlet wreathed in blue flame. Max smiled. Having the *Codex* back felt good. Really good.

"*Sacrement!* What happened to this place?" Raven said as Max's Skyfire illuminated their surroundings. "It looks like a bomb went off." The walls and floor were charred black. Apart from three shining portal mirrors, everything else in the room had been completely obliterated.

Harley whistled. "It wasn't like this a few days ago. Maybe an accident with one of his machines?"

"Let's find out." Raven placed her hand on the wall, frowned, then stepped away. She pointed to a floor-length portal mirror lying against the wall. "That's VS's personal mirror over there."

"But what happened to the room?"

Raven returned to the wall. "Okay, I'm picking up something. Hang on. It's getting clearer. A few days ago a changeling chick came through another mirror—that one next to VS's mirror—a pyrokinetic. Hold on...I can see her face. *Sacre*...it's Naomi. The fire witch. She's looking for someone....No, she's following someone.... She's saying something. I can't hear over the fire—it's like a furnace in the room. She's mad, though. Wait, here she goes." Raven let out a cry and pushed away from the wall, shielding her eyes. After a moment, she straightened and rubbed her head. "She blew the place up. Man, that chick has got some serious juice."

"She's bad news...." said Natalia.

"You think she's bad news? Who do you think she was following?" The Griffins looked at Raven blankly. She sighed and rolled her eyes. "Smoke! She was tailing Smoke."

"What was he doing here?" asked Natalia.

Raven shrugged. "According to the mirror, he's here all the time. Using the mirrors. He uses this place like a train station, always leaving, then coming back a few minutes later."

Natalia pulled out her *Book of Clues* and flipped through several pages. "Okay, let me get this straight in my head. Smoke is using the Paragon Engine. But he's also using portal mirrors. That's a whole lot of portal travel for a kid who can teleport himself around the globe under his own power."

Max agreed. "But why would Naomi be following him? And why blow the place up?"

Raven shrugged. "My guess is that Smoke wasn't supposed to be here, and this was her little way of sending him a message. One thing's for certain: he hasn't been here since."

Harley moved to Von Strife's mirror and examined the clockwork dials and gears, the wires, the coils, and the fluid tubes. All seemed in order.

Raven pointed toward the door. "Better move fast. Monti's environmental systems have picked up elevated levels of carbon dioxide in this room."

156

"Carbon dioxide?" asked Ernie.

Natalia sighed. "Oxygen in, carbon dioxide out. That's how your lungs work, Ernie. Don't you ever pay attention in class?"

"And changelings breathe faster than humans," said Harley. "We should have put a respirator on Thunderbolt's mouth."

"Great. Maybe I should stop breathing," Ernie retorted. "Would that help you out, Harley?"

"It might." Harley glared at him.

Harley fired up the engine. His hands flew over the machine, flipping toggle switches, and synchronizing the field stabilizer. Within ten seconds, the mirror blazed to life. He looked back at his friends. "I'll go first. If I'm not back in five seconds, something went wrong. Get out of here fast." Harley stepped through before the others could argue.

Five seconds. Four. Three. Two. One. Max's heart sank. And then a familiar hand appeared through the portal, waving for them to go through. Max let out his breath and smiled. He turned to Raven. "Okay, you still cool staying behind?"

"If you're not back in thirty minutes, I'll clear out," she replied, pulling down her brass goggles. "Meantime, it'll give me a chance to check out this geek-crazy place of Monti's."

The Griffins stepped into the swirling mirror and disappeared.

BUSTED

The Griffins stepped out onto the polished wood floor of Von Strife's office. It was quiet. Scarily quiet.

"Okay," said Max. "Stick to the plan."

"We have twenty minutes, tops," Natalia warned, drawing out her Phantasmoscope.

They moved fast. Natalia covered the shelves, Max checked the desk, and Harley searched for hidden panels or walls. Running lookout, Agent Thunderbolt was a perpetual blur. The plan was bulletproof, and the Griffins had the experience to make it look easy. Unfortunately, it wasn't enough. They came up empty-handed.

Suspiciously empty-handed. Almost as if someone knew they were coming.

"This doesn't make any sense," Natalia said, flipping through lens after lens of her Phantasmoscope: amber, emerald, ruby—none of them helped. "There has to be something!"

"If we don't get back soon," cautioned Harley, moving toward the portal mirror, "Raven will leave without us."

"Please don't leave on my account," came a voice from behind the desk. Suddenly, the chair that had been empty only a moment before was now occupied by Von Strife himself! Behind him stood the smoldering figure of Naomi, her red hair flickering blue at the ends. Von Strife fingered a familiar brass device that Max instantly recognized. "Yes, an IPA," the man confirmed. "Similar to the one I gave you back in our world."

The Griffins froze. Had he just said *our world*?

The man rose with a friendly smile in his eyes. But those eyes were like exhausted batteries, on the verge of going out. His daughter's sickness was eating him away. "Your secret is safe with me. After all, we are both strangers in a strange land, as they say. We must stick together. Although I am curious: how did you manage it? Your journey here. You used my Paragon Engine, no doubt. Yet you arrived in the Old Woods, I've heard, rather than on my doorstep. Why?"

"We didn't exactly have an instruction manual," said Harley.

"True," said Von Strife, his voice tired. "And yet here you are. Curious. Very curious, my young friends."

"So, what are you going to do with us?" asked Max, keeping a wary eye on Naomi. The fire elemental wasn't quite as charming as her master. "Kill us?"

"Kill you?" Von Strife said, following Max's gaze to Naomi. He nodded in understanding and turned toward the changeling with a kind smile. "Would you excuse us for a moment, my dear? I'd like to have a quiet word with my friends." Naomi cast a venomous eye toward the Griffins, nodded, then walked out of the office, each fiery footstep a full five inches above the ground. The door closed behind her. Von Strife turned back to the Griffins.

"I would sooner cut off my own arm than cause you harm," he explained. "You four mean the world to me. You always have—and you know it."

"So you admit that you're Obadiah Strange!" Natalia said.

"Guilty," Von Strife replied. "Please forgive my necessary alias. There is simply no better way to learn the plans of my enemy than to be among them. But that does not change the fact that I have always been your friend. If you will allow me to explain?"

Ernie trembled. Obadiah Strange had been his friend. The only one who'd understood his pain about Robert's murder. And here he was, confessing to be the murderer himself. Natalia's hunch about Strange and Von Strife being the same man had bothered Ernie, but he hadn't really believed it until now. Ernie found himself scheming to re-form the Agents of Justice and put an end to this creep once and for all. Then again, the changelings here would never believe the story. Von Strife was a friend to the changelings. After all, he was one of them. And so was his daughter. Ernie would be laughed out of the dining hall. Ernie's scheme fizzled in seconds. But he had three more ready to go.

"We're listening," Max replied as the Griffins sat down.

Von Strife settled into his chair. "First, you will not be returning to your world anytime soon, and I recommend you give up this quest of yours to find the Paragon Engine. The machine has proved unstable lately and has been taken offline. In the meantime, before you judge your predicament too harshly, I will say this: consider remaining here. After all, you may find that this world is a much nicer place than the one you left behind. Your families, for instance. That alone would be sufficient for almost anyone." His eyes strayed to Harley, then Max. "And trust me. I know. With Sophia alive...why would I ever want to return?"

He picked up a picture frame and smiled at his daughter's portrait. "As for my personal journey here, it all began when I first discovered the existence of parallel worlds. A limitless canvas of possibilities. Endless choices. A wrong in one world might be righted in another. A lost loved one, for example, might yet be living. My inability to save my own daughter suddenly had an alternative possibility. Somewhere out there, there might be a happy ending after all. And so I constructed the Paragon Engine to find that world."

Natalia looked up from her *Book of Clues*. "What I don't get is that the Templar were convinced that Sophia was in the Shadowlands, and that's where you were heading all this time."

"A simple case of misdirection," Von Strife replied offhandedly. "You'll recall my changeling power is immortality: the ability to live and relive my life, making different choices each time. Indeed, nearly a hundred lifetimes passed before I finally found this world. Not only had Sophia survived here, but she'd never been sick at all. The Von Strife here had discovered a cure—the very medicine that you, Ernest, are now taking. I sent my daughter over as soon as I was sure. Nearly a hundred years ago, by your reckoning. But when you travel through the Paragon Engine, time is no more a barrier than space. To her, she's been here but a short while. I followed as soon as I could."

"What about the other Von Strife?" asked Natalia, her eyes narrowing in suspicion.

"Ah, perhaps Detective Romanov thinks I killed him and assumed his identity?" He sighed. "I am afraid it is nothing so dramatic. I came here as Obadiah Strange, to work alongside this world's Von Strife. But a curious side effect, one neither of us had expected, began to manifest. The longer the two of us were in proximity, the more alike we became, until ultimately we merged. I am not the Von Strife you knew before. I am the Von Strife of two worlds."

"And your daughter?" asked Max incredulously.

"The two Sophias became one. And you should be aware that if the other Griffins were here, you four would similarly cease to exist as yourselves and become the Griffins of two worlds. Luckily, my changeling power had properly conditioned me to this duality. My daughter, however, doesn't remember our old world at all. Assimilation. It's the universe's way of tidying up anomalies."

Natalia shivered. The thought of losing her memories and becoming someone else, even if it was another Natalia, horrified her.

"The other Griffins," said Max. "They are trapped in your Paragon Engine. We have to get them out."

"So I have heard," said Von Strife. "But it's quite impossible. I am the only one capable of operating the engine. Yet I wasn't even in this world when they disappeared. I was with you."

"What about Smoke?"

"Smoke?" He paused thoughtfully. "You can't be serious. No, I am afraid you are on the wrong trail. If the

Griffins are alive, they are not in the Paragon Engine. Trust me."

Natalia frowned. "Trust you? After what you did to Robert?"

"As for Robert, what you saw that day in the snow was a machine remotely powered by Robert's mind, not Robert himself. When it was destroyed, Robert's mind returned to this world." Ernie's mouth fell open. He'd been grieving all this time for nothing? Well, almost nothing. "As for the other changelings, the explanation is quite simple. There was no cure for the changing process in our old world, despite my best efforts over countless lifetimes. All too often, they died in my arms as I attempted to stall their horrific metamorphosis. When I found this world, I knew I had to bring them across. What you call kidnapping, I call rescuing, Natalia. All those changelings who went missing are here, in this world, safe and with no memory whatsoever of the horror they'd once faced."

"Don't try to play the hero card," warned Ernie. "We know what you really are."

"I make no claims to being a hero. I am simply a father who did the best he could with what he had. It was a long journey, but it was ultimately a success. And along the way, I managed to save the lives of countless change- lings by bringing them here. Far more than anyone can even guess."

"Then why keep the Templar in the dark?" asked Max. "Maybe they would have helped you."

"And have them take control of the Paragon Engine? Whereas I would use it to save lives, they would use it to extend their quest for power. They could not be trusted."

"So you're saying we can never go home?" asked Ernie.

"Ernest, you are home. All of you are. A better home than any of you could have in a thousand possible worlds. Trust me. I know."

EPIPHANY JONES

Von Strife's revelation stunned the Griffins. For many days, they walked through the hallways of Iron Bridge in a fog. They barely noticed the passing classes, the homework assignments, the changelings flying overhead, or the Round Table practice sessions. They'd been taught to hate Von Strife, but they'd loved Obadiah Strange. If indeed the two were the same man, and if what Von Strife said was true, the Griffins had better come to terms with this new world, because there didn't seem to be a ticket home.

Then there was Ernie. After learning that Robert hadn't died at all, he didn't know how to feel. His stomach was in knots. But those knots were loosening. If Robert was alive, even if he didn't remember where he'd come from, things didn't seem quite so bad after all. He tried to keep that in mind whenever he saw Robert in the hallway. He'd attempted to talk to Robert again but made a fool of himself even worse than before. Natalia told him to let it go. "You have to give it time," she'd said. So that was what Ernie did.

However, the piece of news that struck all the Griffins the hardest was Von Strife's refusal to help them get home. They were stuck here.

"Like I'd buy his story," said Natalia to her friends. "I mean, he lied to us the whole time by pretending to be Obadiah Strange. He's probably lying now. As far as I am concerned, the Paragon Engine is still open for business and the Griffins are still alive. The only difference now is that we can't count on Von Strife to help us. That leaves Smoke. By the way, remember the oil on his shoes? Well, Brittany told me that her dad is a commodities buyer in New Victoria. Apparently Von Strife is the biggest purchaser of whale oil on the island. He buys it by the truckload to use as a lubricant for a big machine. And is there a bigger machine than the Paragon Engine? See? Now you can lay off my friends. I told you they knew things."

Harley rolled his eyes. "So why is it on Smoke's shoes?"

"Aren't you paying attention?" Natalia sighed. "If Smoke doesn't know how to run that machine, you explain to me what he's doing with whale oil on his boots and grime all over his face. I hate to say this, but I don't think Smoke is as stupid as he looks."

Max agreed. Over his chair hung Logan's black leather jacket. He'd kept it with him. It was warm and comfortable, if a little big. But it made Max feel safer somehow. "I wonder if that's what Smoke's so worried about. That we know he was using the Paragon Engine."

"And that we'll tell his daddy? You might be right. But before we tattle, let's make sure we have our ducks in a row."

"Oh, come on," said Harley restlessly. His life at home was getting more difficult. Candi and Henry were pressing him for answers, even threatening to bring in a telepathic counselor if he didn't start talking. If the Griffins didn't find the Paragon Engine soon, their cover would be blown wide open. "We already know Smoke is our biggest threat. Let's deal with him now before he pops into our rooms and stuffs a pillow over our faces."

"And what about Blackstone?" said Ernie. "He's still out there. And twice as scary as Smoke. You think they are working together?"

Natalia bit her lip. "Blackstone hates kids. There'd have to be something in it for him. But I can't think what Smoke would have to offer."

"Raven could figure it out. Send her to Smoke's room. Five minutes in there and she'd have the whole story."

Harley bristled. "Are you crazy? If he spotted her, he'd drop her off a building."

Ernie put his hands to his heart and batted his eyelashes. "So protective. So romantic. You're my hero." Harley rolled his eyes.

On Saturday morning, when Max arrived at Iron Bridge for Round Table practice, he was greeted by the cheers of his teammates. The Round Table championship was fast approaching, and despite Max's fear of not measuring up, he had recently pulled off some spectacular wins. He wasn't quite to Hale's level. Not yet. Though the more he played, the more things started to fall into place. The biggest challenge was playing against changelings. In his own world, using changeling powers in a game was considered cheating. But here, Max had to deal with it whether he liked it or not. When he stopped fighting his fear about facing down a mind reader or dream weaver, his luck began to change.

"Man, your scores are skyrocketing," said Todd Toad, his leather boots worn thin and tattered at the toes. His jacket was in a similar state of neglect. If it wasn't Round Table, it didn't matter. "Xander Swift's your only real competition, and not even he has your adaptive skills," Todd continued as he walked with Max toward the practice room.

"Xander's with Stirling Academy?" asked Max. This must be the same Xander who had transferred to Iron Bridge back in his world.

Todd looked at him in puzzlement. "Are you joking? Of course he's with Stirling. He's Stirling's version of you." Todd sighed, then smiled. "Sorry. I guess I keep forgetting your brain got a little fried in the portal. Anyway, remember that you're my favorite and richest customer. I don't want to lose you. You need something else? Some other information on the game? The teachers? The judges? You just let me know. We're at a whole new level with you. You got it? We're with you all the way, Maxie. You need something done, we'll do it. No questions asked, you know what I mean?"

Max smiled. "Uh, I'll let you know."

Max felt a hand slap his shoulder. It was Tejan Chandra. His smile was kind, and his eyes shone with excitement. "The scores are really quite impressive, Max. I think we may very well be able to defeat Stirling. What a coup!"

At the moment, Max was practicing against Epiphany Jones, an eleven-year-old girl with the changeling ability to plant ideas in your head. After three rounds of fending off her mental attacks, he was exhausted and asked for a break. He took off his Kinematic goggles, detaching the MERLIN-phased electrodes from his temples. The scientists of this world had managed to bring all the virtual reality of the SIM chamber into the Kinematic goggles, allowing for not just the five senses, but even the sensation of pain—horrible, crawl-into-a-ball-and-cry sort of pain. Duelists were known to get hurt. Round Table was a deadly serious business.

"So who do you hang out with at school?" asked Max as they set up for the next round. "I don't see you around much outside of practice."

"Nobody." Epi reached into her bag and pulled out a new set of knucklebones. Each side of her dice shimmered like stained glass. Her posture was prim in her canvas jacket and riding boots. But her eyes had a cloudy, forlorn look, the kind that Max imagined belonged to a fun-loving girl who had been stuffed into a dark closet.

"Why not?"

"With Brooke gone, who else do I have to hang out with?"

Max laid down his cards. "You're friends with Brooke? Brooke Lundgren?" This might be Max's chance to find out what Iver wouldn't explain: what Brooke was up to and what she knew.

Epi looked at him with suspicion, and then Max remembered that his other self would have known they were friends. "I mean, uh, do you ever see her, you know, outside of school?"

"Her dad's got her locked up like Rapunzel in a tower. She doesn't e-mail or text or anything. I thought she was just messed up about you—the whole dying thing, you know? But now that you're back...I guess I thought she'd come back, too." She bit her lip.

"Maybe she's sick?" Max reached into his pocket and stroked his Bounder, who was curled up in the shape of a grey squirrel. She still wasn't back to her old self.

"What? Nothing can hurt her. She's a healer, remember? Man, did something fall on your head while you were gone?" Max laughed it off as best he could. He'd have to leave the subject of Brooke alone when it came to Epiphany Jones. He couldn't lie nearly as well as Natalia, and he wasn't as quick on his feet as Ernie. Max's honesty could cost him.

When Max got off the *Zephyr* at Lake Station, the first of three stops in New Avalon, he tried to put his mistake out of his mind. After all, what did Epiphany Jones know? Nothing. He'd just need to do a little more research before jumping into conversations like that.

As he walked across the tiled floor toward the escalator, he felt a clammy chill sweep over him. He looked around, his eyes slowly adjusting to the dim. Sure enough, lurking in the shadows was a set of gleaming teeth. A single flashing clockwork eye peered back at him. There was a familiar snarl.

"The Slayer," Max breathed. He willed his *Codex* ring to turn into the gauntlet. Skyfire immediately arced across his metal fingertips. "Okay, let's see what you've got!" Max called angrily. The monster stayed where it was. "What are you waiting for? I'm right here." The two adversaries stared back at each other, neither attacking nor retreating.

Then Max heard another growl. He spun to find the other Slayer crouched just behind him. It let out a roar. Max stumbled backward into the leaping claws of the first Slayer. It had been a trap all along. Then Max heard an explosion, and the claws fell away. Two more explosions. The Slayers disappeared from view.

Max felt a strong hand pull him up. "Time to move," he heard Logan warn as the Scotsman turned Max on his heels and pushed him toward the stairs. In Logan's other hand was a plasma gun, its barrel still smoking from its attack on the Slayers. Logan and Max, with Sprig curled up in his backpack, raced up the stairs. Glancing back, Max saw a thick cloud of crows pour like a black flood out of the subway tunnels and sweep toward the stairs.

"There're too many!" Max exclaimed as Logan pulled him up the last of the steps.

"We'll see," said the Scotsman, taking a silver canister from his belt. He pulled the pin and lobbed it down the stairs. "Now, quick, behind this wall!" Max just made it when he heard a muffled boom below. There was a flash of fire. The smell of propane. Then it was over. Logan put on a respirator and headed back down the stairs. He returned a few moments later, brushing ash from his black T-shirt.

"Well, the night shift won't appreciate the mess, and

neither will Blackstone. But I can't imagine that creep's got many crows left now."

"What was that you threw in there?"

"Captain Tristan's Fontabulus Thermobaric Goodness. Also known as a TRM-66A. Great for cleaning bats out of the chimney, as it were." He opened a gloved hand to reveal a fistful of cogs, small clockwork bits. "Blackstone is modifying the crows just like he's done with the Slayers." He pushed the pieces around in his hand thoughtfully. "Well, at any rate, we know what he's up to now. And I think we just bought ourselves some time. As for the Slayers, I wasn't expecting to see them tonight, so I didn't bring the right equipment. Those two snappers will be back in action in no time. Let's get you home. You need a lift?"

Max saw his mom's car pull into the lot. "I better go with her. She doesn't know that you've come back."

"Good. Keep it that way. I'll tail you, just to be sure."

Max leafed through his homework later that evening when Sprig took the form of a tabby cat. She leaped up onto his desk. Max set down his pencil. "Feeling better, huh? I saw you teleport earlier today.... Where did you go?"

Her voice was quiet. "Max must listen. When Sprig followed Yellow Eyes before, it was very dangerous.

Mountains. Cities. Islands. Yellow Eyes is fast. And clever. But not clever enough. It dropped something. A paper. Sprig found it and hid it. Then Yellow Eyes found Sprig...." She coughed and wrung her paws. "Sprig was too weak to return for the paper. Until today. Sprig has brought it to you...." She produced a small scrap of note-book material. It was crumpled and filthy, and smelled of oil. As Max tried to decipher the writing on it, Sprig sprouted wings. "Sprig will try again. Sprig will find Yel-low Eyes. Max is not safe until the creature is gone." With that, she flew out the window.

Max turned on the Tiffany lamp and looked closer at the scrap of paper. Then he looked again. He rubbed his eyes. He'd need some help with this.

Max: Hey, I know you're online.
Natalia: Just doing some digging. What's up?
Max: Sprig just gave me a piece of paper that Yellow Eyes accidentally left behind. Could be important. I need u to look at it. I'm taking a pic-ture now. Sending it over...hang on.
—Max requests to transfer a file to Natalia—
—Natalia accepts Max's file transfer—
Natalia: Got it. Okay, let's see.... It's really torn up, Max. Couldn't you get a better picture?
Max: It's pretty nasty. Oil stains or something.
Natalia: Does it smell like a wet dog?

175

Max: How did you know?

Natalia: It's rancid whale oil. Isn't that an interesting coincidence....Anyway, this paper doesn't say anything except the word Wormwood-6. What's Wormwood-6?

Max: I was hoping you could tell me.

Natalia: I'm on it.

THE BIG DAY

The weeks leading up to the big tournament were a parade of parties, banners stretched across the halls, late-night Round Table cramming sessions, and about a million and one e-mails telling Max how much everyone depended on him to beat Xander Swift and keep Iron Bridge on top.

Max's focus on the game was so intense that he had pushed everything else to the side: Von Strife, his promise to Raven, and even his own friends. He missed meals. He missed sleep. He even missed tests and countless homework assignments. But the school gave him a pass. Nothing was more important than the star player and his preparations. The same went for his mom and dad. They held all his calls, kept his stomach full, and tiptoed around the house.

It was nearly two in the morning when Max noticed a flashing light on his DE Tablet. He laid aside the latest copy of the *Toad Report* and stumbled over to the desk. He flipped up the lid of his computer, and a message popped up: an encrypted chat request from I Want My Jacket Back. Max smiled and glanced at Logan's leather jacket, still hanging from a peg on his bedroom wall. Max pulled up a chair, pushed the books from his desk, and swung the screen around to face him.

"Don't bother," said a voice, and the Scotsman stepped through the window and into Max's room. "We can do this live." Outside, an airship passed lazily in front of the moon. Logan spied his jacket and pulled it from the peg, surveying its contours. "Looks like you took good care of it. Much obliged."

Max closed the DE Tablet and grinned. "So what's up?"

"I see you've been studying up pretty hard for the big tournament." Logan picked up a few of Max's books from the floor and glanced through them.

"I just don't want to let anyone down."

"You won't." He set the books aside. "Just heard. Von Strife's daughter. She's taken a turn for the worse. He left Iron Bridge a few hours ago."

"What's wrong with her?"

"Million-dollar question, Grasshopper." Logan pulled

on his jacket. "Changelings don't get sick. Not in the way that she is, anyway." He paused thoughtfully, then turned a grave eye to Max. "If she dies, Von Strife won't take it well. Which means you need to work fast to locate that Paragon Engine, while he's away."

As Logan made to leave, Max caught him by the sleeve. "Sprig said something about a creature with yellow eyes following me. Have you seen anything like that?"

Logan shook his head. "I haven't seen anything, but then again I've been busy. Could she describe it or what it wanted?"

"Just that it was after me."

Logan rubbed his stubbled jaw thoughtfully. "I'll check into it. In the meantime, you focus on winning the tournament and finding the Paragon Engine. Tall order, both. But you can do it, if anyone can."

The day of the big tournament had come at last. The sun was shining. The stone and glass buildings of Iron Bridge were draped with banners. Everywhere Max looked, flags were snapping in the breeze. There was the white-and-red of the Templar. The Golden Griffin of Iron Bridge. The Stars and Stripes of the United States. The familiar blue of the Minnesota state flag. And, of course, all the flags of the visiting schools, including Antioch, Rome, Carthage, and Stirling.

As Max walked down the white rock path, his yellow-shirted fans swarming around him like bees, he smiled upward to find Sprig flying overhead as an eagle. She smiled back down. The spriggan was back to her old self, and Max couldn't be happier.

Everyone in the crowd was talking all at once, and Todd and Ross Toad were pouring advice into his ears. Everyone wanted his attention, ignoring Hale completely. Not that she seemed to mind. Her antennae had never looked perkier. She was ready to fight.

The crowd pulled Max along like a leaf in a river's current. They shouted and cheered for the Iron Bridge team and booed whenever another school was spotted. By the time Max reached the auditorium, he was dizzy from the canvas of euphoria that spun around him.

The auditorium was immense and opulent. Red velvet and soft oxblood leather were everywhere, accented by silver fittings, shimmering chandeliers, and snow-white statues. The balcony swept overhead in a great golden arch, and the box seats, appointed for Templar royalty, looked out over a stage, which was, at the moment, hidden behind the quiet curtains of expectation.

Max found the other Griffins waiting for him near the stage, all smiles for their friend. They'd been through a lot together. Max didn't know what he'd do without them. Even Harley and Ernie seemed to have patched things up on Max's account.

"Have you seen Xander yet?" asked Ernie. "People

are talking. They say you've got him spooked. How's that for a better world than the one we left behind?"

Harley handed Max his pair of Kinematic goggles. "I had them overhauled and added a few modifications myself."

"What sort of modifications?" asked Max as he flipped the clockwork goggles over in his hands. They were heavier than standard goggles and outfitted with toggle switches, multiple lenses, leather padding, and a maze of complex channels and shielded skin-interfacing nodes. The goggles connected wirelessly to a massive virtual grid, translating sight, sound, touch, taste, and smell to the wearer in a way that was indistinguishable from reality.

"A target tracking system. It's like any video game where you track enemy targets. A green reticle will appear on them. Makes tracking multiple targets, like missile barrages and Fireball Pixie swarms, a lot easier."

"Is it legal?"

"Ha! You should see what the other kids have. I just hope I leveled the field a bit for you."

Max looked at the crowd as the velvet seats of the Grand Auditorium began to fill up. His parents and grandma would be here soon. But no Iver, no Logan. Both of them were continuing to live in the shadows, and they were up to something that Max hadn't yet pieced together.

He turned at the sound of a familiar voice calling.

Waving at him from the luxurious red and gold box seats was his family. Grandma was there, with his grandfather's championship medal glittering on her dress. Her arm was proudly around Annika. Behind them stood Lord Sumner. Hannah was perched on his shoulders. It was a picture-perfect moment.

"Xander's over there talking to his parents," Ernie said.

"Max has better things to worry about," replied Natalia.

"Oh no, he doesn't." Ernie grinned. "I just went through Xander's cards. Wanna know what I saw? He's got at least four dr —"

"Ernest!" Natalia interrupted. "That's against the rules."

"Fine. Be that way. But it's not cheating to tell him that Xander's goggles have a bunch of custom dials on them. Never seen them before."

"Were they silver with red dots?" asked Harley.

Ernie nodded.

"He's got Obscura filters, Max. That'll make it hard to hide or fake him out. He'll be able to see you as you really are, no matter what you throw at him."

"I'll deal with it," replied Max as he tried on his own goggles. "How about you guys? All set?"

"Don't worry about a thing," said Natalia, waving at Katie and Brittany as they bounced by. "With everyone busy watching you, they won't notice me and Harley slipping out the back."

"And I'll keep an eye out for Smoke," Ernie promised as he patted his helmet, dropping the brim to a rakish angle. "Agent Thunderbolt's on the job, folks."

The trumpets rang out, announcing that the tournament was about to start. Max took in a deep breath. "Okay, this is it! Wish me luck!"

The Griffins laid their hands together in a pile. "One, two, three! Griffins can't be beat!" Max hugged Natalia, high-fived Harley and Ernie, and ran through a side door.

THE GAME'S AFOOT

A crash of applause, the ring of a bell, and a whiff of black powder. Max powered on his Kinematic goggles, drew his cards, and waited for the game to come online. A moment later, the opaque goggles flatlined, then exploded into color. A world grew beneath his feet, or perhaps he was falling feetfirst. He could never tell which.

He stood atop an oil-rig tower suspended above a roaring ocean. The wind howled. Rain pelted. The only way to see anything was to wait for a good flash of lightning. These goggles were definitely light-years ahead of those on Earth Alpha. Here he could feel the rain stinging his face and smell the oil leaking from the nearby crane. He also felt the grid work under his feet. Max rapped the metal railing with his knuckles. *Yep. It'd hurt. This will be interesting.* He'd practiced for this moment for weeks.

Across from Max stood a matching tower. His opponent, a duelist named Nikon, was there, laying out his cards. Those cards, like Max's own, hovered in midair, within easy reach, and ensured that the game could continue even if the player jumped or scaled a ladder. Max had read Nikon's stats in Todd and Ross's latest *Toad Report*. The duelist was from Novgorod Academy. His ability to unnerve better players, then take them apart, was legendary. Nikon rarely waited past the first round to launch an attack. Sure enough, Max spied several small drones materialize in the mist. With a whir of helicopter-like gears, they shot across the windy expanse toward Max's defensive line. Max settled into the game like it was an old leather chair. This was going to be fun.

The game didn't last very long. Using a Ring of Invisibility card, Max snuck up a series of slippery catwalks and dropped a sea monster on Nikon's defensive line. Once the creature polished off the cards, it turned to Nikon, who screamed as he disappeared down its gullet. The game was over before the bell sounded. Nikon threw his knucklebones and sulked offstage.

Max won the next three duels handily. The stakes continued to rise as the brackets closed and top players clashed. Iron Bridge lost only two of their nine players. Max ruled the leaderboard, with Xander close behind.

While Max's fans were cheering, Natalia and Harley slipped out the back door, then split up. Harley began tracking down Raven. After hearing about Von Strife's revelation to the Griffins, she seemed to have given up any hope of seeing her Harley again. She'd become morose—well, more morose than usual. Getting her back on the team meant rekindling her hope of finding her Harley. He had mixed feelings about that.

As for Natalia, her detective work had a few open-ended questions that Monti might be able to help with, such as Smoke's use of portal mirrors when he clearly didn't need them with his powers. She felt sure this was extremely important.

Monti was already at the subway platform, pacing nervously. "Of course Von Strife told me all about the break-in, Natalia. He personally delivered the news. He wasn't happy, let me tell you." Monti sighed. "If you needed my help so badly, why not just ask?"

"Would you have let us use the portal mirror if we'd asked?" Natalia batted her eyelashes innocently.

Monti sighed again. "Fair enough. Follow me." The *Zephyr* quickly appeared. The elegant doors swung open, and Monti entered. As Natalia stepped inside, the train rumbled angrily and nearly snatched her velvet handbag in its closing doors. She'd seen this sort of behavior before. And she didn't like it.

"The *Zephyr* didn't appreciate you hacking into her systems," explained Monti. "And neither did I."

"I couldn't hack my way into a Jell-O salad," Natalia replied demurely.

"That's what the *Zephyr* said." Monti snorted. Natalia scowled.

The train jerked to a sudden start, sending Natalia to the floor. Exasperated, she tried to pull herself into a seat, but the train kept toying with her, stopping and starting just as she got her balance. After a few moments, Natalia finally managed to wedge herself onto a bench. "You know, this train and I have a long history back in my world."

"I can imagine," said Monti, giving no sympathy to Natalia's white-knuckled determination to stay in her seat. "At any rate, as long as we're on the move, no one can monitor what we're saying. So, why don't you start at the beginning?"

Natalia quickly detailed how the Griffins broke into his lab and how they avoided his security cameras, roving clockwork patrols, and even his environmental sensors. Monti seemed visibly impressed, if a bit disappointed that his efforts hadn't proved more challenging.

Then, when she explained Smoke's hijacking of the portal mirrors, and Naomi's burst of fiery anger, Monti

187

began pacing nervously. "Naomi. Of course. Of course. I had a hunch. But a little hard to complain. She doesn't appreciate anyone asking her questions."

"But why would she be following Smoke?"

"Well, Smoke has always been a problem. That's what Von Strife gets for adopting a pickpocket from Cutthroat Bay."

"What's his angle?"

"Oh, he's not so hard to figure out, I guess. Smoke is the neglected son of a very busy man. What does he want? What would any kid want in that situation? Attention. Validation. The usual suspects. An average kid in that situation might play hooky or steal a candy bar. Smoke, well, he has taken it to a whole new level." Monti shivered. "No, that kid is trouble."

"So why would a teleporting changeling need to use one of your portal mirrors?"

"Well, for one, his natural teleporting leaves a smoky residue in the air, while portal mirrors don't leave a trace. Perhaps he's trying to stay below radar."

Natalia wrote everything down carefully in her *Book of Clues*, pausing to check her notes from time to time. "Whose radar? Von Strife's? Naomi's?" Monti shrugged. Natalia glanced at her watch. She needed to get back soon. "So, one more question?"

"Fire away."

"The Paragon Engine. Is it possible the other Grey

Griffins could still be alive in there? Logan is convinced they are."

Monti paused. "Well, I mean, anything is possible. It's just not likely."

"Why?"

"Well"—Monti scratched his chin—"for one, clockwork portals use technology rather than magic to get you from one place to another. They deconstruct you into tiny little particles. Then a matching machine on the other side reconstructs you bit by bit. Of course, for a very short time, your particles are stored in what we call a pattern buffer. But it's not a place to hang out. The particles pass through at light speed; then the buffer is wiped clean. So getting stuck in the engine is nearly impossible to conceive... unless..."

"Unless what?"

"Well, it's highly technical. And theoretical, for that matter. Let me think about it and do some research. I'll let you know." The *Zephyr* quickly returned to the Iron Bridge subway platform. "Your stop."

Natalia studied Monti as the door opened. "You know, the other Monti was one of our best friends. Inside, you're the same guy he is. I can see it. And I think you see it in us, too. We need your help, Monti. The other Griffins, they need your help. You're the only one who can...."

Monti cleared his throat. "I'll do my best, Natalia."

THE FISH

With the single-elimination rounds over, only sixteen players remained, and three schools had been knocked out entirely. At the moment, Max was standing in another rainy world. This time, however, his feet were set firmly on the muddy ground. The battlefield was a slimy grave-yard of broken tombstones, rotting grass, and deep pits blooming with the hungry arms of zombies.

The opponent standing across from him, according to the *Toad Report*, was Jay Fish: a smarmy, conniving kid from Rome who seemed to have stopped growing in the fourth grade. He had a Brillo pad of hair, colorless eyes, and a sneering sort of smile — or was it a smiling sort of sneer? Even his own team detested him.

Fish won the roll of the knucklebones and drew his first card. He laid it down on defense. Then he looked up at Max, offering a friendly smile. But there was no smile in his eyes as he said, "Good luck! And if you need a breather, just let me know. It can get pretty tough out here."

Max rolled his eyes.

Fish continued as they both laid down their defensive lines. "So how was it being stuck in a portal for so long? I heard it can mess you up pretty bad. Your brain, you know?"

"I think you talk too much." Max drew another card and kept it in his hand.

"Still," the duelist continued, "you did change, right? Being dead has to change a person."

"You should really pay attention to the game," Max warned.

"Oh, don't worry about me. I'll be all right. Hey, you should know that some of the kids are whispering that you've gone a little crazy since you've come back. They say you are wandering around school mumbling to yourself."

"What?" Max couldn't help himself.

"Your turn to draw. So, anyway, yeah, they say you're not exactly in the pink, missing the final screw, out to sea...you know how kids are."

Max's vision turned blue. He squeezed his eyelids shut to extinguish the Skyfire. If he flared up in here, he would fry the game and probably everything connected to it. He'd be disqualified. That was most likely Fish's plan all along.

"Not feeling well? You just take your time."

"I'm feeling just fine." As Max's vision cleared, he saw that Fish had launched an attack. Four burned and charred forms were crawling out of the pits toward him. One had a lightning-bolt T-shirt, and another had long, braided hair. It was the Griffins. Zombified!

As they dragged their rotting limbs toward him, Max raised his eyes at Fish. "You know, kid? You're kind of a creep." Max unleashed a three-card chain attack.

Fish's smug little grin evaporated as a colossal dragon, armored and spiked, dragged its great belly over the graveyard, leveling tombstones and rotten trees. With a bulldozer-sized foot, it trod the zombie Griffins into the gurgling mud. When it reached Fish's ogre and rock masher defense, the dragon let loose with a fury of flames. The dragon pressed on until it leered hungrily down at Fish, its black reptilian eyes expressionless. Unable to help himself, Fish shrieked like a little girl. The fiery jaws snatched the boy up, playfully flipping him into the air. With a quick snap, it swallowed him whole.

The dragon burped.

As the duel ended and the goggles were lifted, Max

looked down at those three cards: a fire iguana, magic growing beans, and a three-round chain attack. Not a bad combination.

Fish stood up after making sure he was all in one piece. He held out a shaky hand to Max. "Good duel!"

"Not for you, it wasn't." Max ignored the hand and walked away.

"Boy oh boy, you really handed Jay Fish his lunch!" exclaimed Ernie as Max walked backstage. "He didn't score a single point on you."

"Because he's a terrible player. How'd he get this far?"

"He's the nephew of one of the judges," answered Todd Toad as he pushed by to lay the *Toad Report* into the hand of another paying customer.

"Are you sure Smoke's not here, Ernie?" whispered Max.

"I've been all over this place a hundred times, I bet."

Max sighed. Smoke had to be here. Somewhere. "Any word from Natalia or Harley?"

"Natalia will be back in a few minutes. She sounded a little freaked out, but wouldn't say why."

"What about Harley?"

Ernie was trying hard to stay mad at Harley, but it wasn't easy. "He said Raven will help. But she thinks we're crazy."

"She thinks everyone is crazy."

"Maybe she's right." Ernie sighed, then grinned. "I love this world. I wish my powers were like this back home. Being here, well, it's the closest I've ever come to actually being as fast as the Flash."

Max smiled. "And you're only in sixth grade. Wait until you get older."

"But if we go back to our world, I won't be as fast. Plus, back there I have to go back to drinking that dragon dung tea just to stay alive. I hate that stuff. It tastes like poop."

"That's because it is poop."

STIRLING RISING

Max slogged his way through the next duel, losing several points while knocking Antioch out of the running. It was Hale who was shining now. She'd sent Rome packing without losing a single point. The changeling girl was on fire, striking down attack after attack. Bets were being made, mostly by the Toad Brothers, that she'd win the tournament all by herself.

The next duel pitted Max against Carthage hero Titus Marcus. This was the first match where Max had to really work. Titus launched an avalanche of attacks that kept Max breathless. But his luck didn't hold. Eventually, Titus simply played the wrong card, stumbled, and fell into a gravity well. That was the end of that. Carthage was out.

Four players remained: two from Iron Bridge, two from Stirling. Stirling remained ahead overall. Each duel would have to be carefully thought through.

Next up: Hale versus Xander. It would be a good fight, but Coach Wolfhelm wasn't about to take any chances. He called Max over. According to tournament rules, every team had one chance to change out players.

"I'll be swapping you and Hale on this one," said the coach.

"What?" Hale exclaimed, her antennae drooping. "But I've got just as many points as Xander. I can do it. I know I can."

Coach Wolfhelm shook his head. "Xander's a bit too strong, I'm thinking."

"But you see the way I've been playing. I can beat him. I know I can." Hale turned to Max. "Max is the team captain. He makes the call. What do you say, Max? Let me fight Xander. You know I can take him."

The coach grunted. "If Hale goes down, Max, you'll have a hard time of it in the final duel. No margin for error."

"Max," said Hale with fiery eyes, "I won't let you down. I promise."

Max looked at Hale. This match meant everything to her. More than it would ever mean to Max. After all, this wasn't even his world. He averted his eyes from the coach and smiled at Hale. "Xander's all yours." Hale let out a squeal of delight and sprouted a pair of wings. She took a victory lap around the backstage area. The coach slapped his forehead and walked away.

A single table was set up on the stage. Hale walked out, greeted by cheers from the Iron Bridge fans. Then Xander appeared, his black dreadlocks and smoky good looks capturing the attention of the cameras. The crowd roared as the king of style took off his tinted brass goggles, flashed a smile, and bowed. Here was a kid who aced tests without attending class. He led in scoring without showing up for practice. If he ignored people, they only loved him more. Everything he did was right, even if it was wrong. If he lost tonight, he'd still be a winner. Everyone knew it. And he knew it best. He had nothing to lose, and Hale had everything.

The duelists sat down, their Kinematic goggles were activated, and the hourglass was turned. The duel began.

Max stood next to Ernie under the big screen, watching the virtual field of battle. Hale wasted no time. Her offensive line of trolls rushed toward Xander like a wall of rock, blowing through his defenses and punching a hole through to Xander himself. As the trolls leaped toward him, Xander fired up his jet cycle and raced into the sky, spinning and looping to avoid the chunks of earth the trolls were lobbing up at him. It was a crushing first attack. Xander had been taken by surprise. But he was far from finished. He flicked the red triggers on his flight stick and a barrage of dragon-fire missiles raced toward the changeling girl's defenses. Hale quickly activated her Falling Sky card, and the rockets were hammered to the ground in a fiery explosion.

As the smoke cleared, the crowd cheered. This would be a great game.

Over the next seven rounds, Xander and Hale fought toe to toe. But Hale had her rock-star moves tonight, and Xander couldn't seem to touch her. She had him on the ropes, with his forces all in the sky, fighting off Hale's Flight of Giant Eagles. Below, he was open. Hale activated a Cloak of Invisibility and rushed toward him, sword drawn. Xander didn't seem to suspect a thing.

And then Max recalled the Obscura filters Ernie had seen on Xander's goggles. No matter what he was pretending to be doing, Xander could see Hale perfectly well. The crowd roared as Hale's invisible avatar shot toward the seemingly distracted Xander. Twenty feet. Ten. The crowd held their breath.

There was a blinding flash as Hale ran face-first into Xander's Field of Disintegration. A cry. A messy explosion of red. And the duel was over.

There was a stunned silence. No one had seen it coming—except Max and Ernie. Someone cried, "Cheat!" Another person cried, "Prove it!" It looked like there would be a fight among the parents. But when the replay was shown, exhibiting the special filters on

Xander's goggles, the Iron Bridge fans sunk morosely into their seats.

Hale slowly set her goggles on the table. She was as stunned as everyone else. She'd played perfectly. She could have won. She should have won. As she passed Max, she patted his shoulder. "I guess the coach was right about me."

The bell rang, and Max was rushed out to play Stirling's second-best player. Max won the duel in three rounds. But all he could think about was that he'd let Hale down. He'd let his whole team down. He felt horrible. And now everything was riding on the upcoming fight between the two best players in the league. A fight Max wasn't sure he was good enough to win. The announcer called out, "Next duel: Max Sumner of Iron Bridge versus Xander Swift of Stirling. Winner takes all in the closest game in Academy history!"

THEFT

"Max, you're doing great!" Lord Sumner said as he led Max backstage. "All those late nights paid off." Max's dad was, as always, the best-looking man in the room. It was his mom, though, turning heads in her velvet gown and diamond necklace. Another place, another time, and she'd have been a queen. But a queen who baked brownies and wore sweatshirts on the weekends.

"We're so proud of you," Annika Sumner added, hugging him close. "Max, you just amaze me. You've always been good, but this is, well, I said it already. It's amazing!" She wiped her lipstick from Max's forehead with a lace kerchief, then gave his hair a playful tousle. "I have

a surprise. I was going to wait, but I just can't anymore."
She winked over at Grandma Caliburn, who nodded
with an approving smile. Then she handed Max a small
box. "Open it."

Max did. Inside lay shiny silver dog tags with the
name of Max's grandfather stamped on them. "Do you
like it?" Annika asked with searching eyes. "The Templar High Command made these exact copies for us. We
had to pull a few strings, of course. But aren't they just
beautiful?" Max's eyes flickered in excitement. His grandfather in his own world had been buried with his dog
tags, and Max never knew how much it would have
meant to have them around his own neck. He missed his
grandfather. A lot. "They are to replace the ones you lost
when you...disappeared. And, well..." she continued as
she wiped away a happy tear, "you were still young when
he died. But now look at you." She regarded him quietly.
"I missed you so much....And now I'm starting to feel
you're back again. You're really back. Aren't you?"

Max hugged Annika quickly, hiding his guilty eyes.
"For luck," he said as he was swept away by his friends.
Annika waved as he receded into the crowd.

Max's teammates crowded around, each with their
own bit of advice. The Toad brothers squirmed their
way to the center. "Real quick," said Todd. "We've got
Xander figured out. He's not watching his left side. And
his deck is totally aerial. Get him on the ground, and
you've got him. If there is no ground, you better make

sure you've got something that can go toe-to-toe with him in the sky. Oh, and don't forget that his reaction speed is still better than yours. Your best bet is to do the unexpected. Did you eat anything? A banana would be good. Potassium is brain food. Would somebody get Max a banana? Hello? Anybody? Yo! Get this man a banana!"

"And almonds," added Ross Toad.

"Totally. Almost as good as bananas. You, over there, change that order. I want..."

The bell sounded. The Griffins gave their cheer and pushed Max out onstage, where he found his chair waiting for him. He sat down and reached for his Round Table deck, realizing only then that it wasn't there. "What the heck?" he cried. He'd had it only moments before. He was sure of it.

"You have five minutes to find your cards," the official warned. "Otherwise, you'll have to forfeit." Max raced backstage, his heart pounding like a jackhammer.

"Are you kidding me?" he exclaimed, turning his backpack inside out. "This is crazy. They have to be here."

"What about the cleaning crew?" asked Natalia. "Did you leave them on the table when you finished?"

"I don't remember." He'd been thinking about Hale's loss, not the game. Now he'd blown everything.

"Two minutes left," warned the official.

Ernie suddenly appeared. "Bad news. Smoke was here."

202

"This is not the time," Natalia responded. She pulled Max's coat off a hanger and burrowed into it with searching hands. "Can you help us look for Max's cards?"

"But it was Smoke who took them."

Max jumped up. "Are you sure?"

Ernie held up a single familiar card. One of Max's. "I found it in his jacket pocket when he wasn't looking."

"Where are the rest of my cards?"

Ernie shook his head. "I searched everywhere."

"One minute!" warned the official. Max's mom and grandma looked horrified. His father had cornered the official.

"Stolen or not, the rules are clear," the official deflected.

"We have to get you a new deck," said Natalia.

"A new deck?" Max exclaimed in panic. An unfamiliar, untested deck would be dangerous. Too many things could go wrong.

"Don't even think about it," said Hale. The changeling girl approached the Griffins, her antennae drooping like withering flowers. Hale pulled out her own deck and handed it to Max. "You've played me enough times. You know my deck."

Max nodded, putting his hand on Hale's shoulder. "I owe you."

"Just beat that kid...."

While Lord Sumner had the deck approved by the official, Max raced to the stage bathroom to splash water on his face. Glancing up at the mirror, he gasped. His reflection looked terrible. He hadn't realized the game had taken so much out of him. Then his blood froze. That wasn't him in the mirror. His reflection was wearing different clothes. And a sickly Sprig—with white fur— was wrapped around his neck.

Max nearly shouted when he realized what he was looking at—or rather, whom he was looking at. Then the bell sounded, and he ran back to the stage.

The sky was a pale blue, whipped with marshmallow clouds. Max's steam-powered jet pack roared and strained against his shoulder straps. He checked the iron gauges, then checked his watch. Should be enough fuel.

Across from him hovered Xander, wearing jet boots. Sunshine glinted off his smile, and his aviator scarf streamed behind his leather jacket like a movie star.

Behind each boy flew a large airship flanked by a swarm of brightly colored biplanes. The sky would be their battleground this duel. Winner takes all. No mercy. No regrets. Max braced himself for what would be the toughest duel of his life.

Ernie turned to see Denton, the lion boy, sitting next to him. Like any cat worth its salt, Denton could sneak up on anyone, anywhere. Even Ernie. "So, I hear you're looking for Smoke."

"I've been all over this school a hundred times," said Ernie. "I can't find him anywhere."

"He's nearby," said Denton quietly as his eyes scanned the crowd. Then he touched his nose. "I can smell him. I can even hear his heartbeat if I listen close enough."

"Where is he, Denton? You've got to tell me."

Denton smiled, exposing his fangs. "I've got a feeling you Griffins are going to punch his ticket pretty soon. I'm cool with that. All of us are. He's not one of us. He doesn't deserve to be called a changeling."

Ernie eyed him warily. "Are you sure you want to help? I mean, what if Von Strife finds out?"

"Everyone knows Von Strife only cares about Sophia. Especially Smoke. Probably why he's such a jerk." Denton licked his furry paw and smoothed back his fashionable mane. "Anyway, he's up in the balcony. Seat 82A. You can see him from here. I'd go now if I were you. He'll be too busy watching the duel to notice you until it's too late."

Ernie patted Denton on the shoulder. "Thanks, dude."

"Anytime, Thunderbolt. You're the man, right?"

"Going somewhere?" Harley said, catching Smoke by the arm as the changeling was about to leave.

205

Smoke shook himself free and glared at the Griffins through his amber-lensed goggles. His fists clenched. He clearly didn't like to be touched. "Who do you think you're talking to? You're not a changeling. You're just a stupid human. You're a nothing. I could drop you off a bridge in a second, and there's nothing you could do about it."

"You even think about teleporting," warned Ernie, tapping the lightning-bolt emblem on his T-shirt, "and I'll pull your tongue out of your face before you get a chance. So you just stick around, okay?" He looked over at Harley and gave him a wink. Nothing mended a friendship faster than a common enemy.

Smoke seemed to consider putting Ernie to the test, but instead just spat on Natalia's shoe. "So what do you want? I haven't got all day."

"First, where are Max's cards?" Natalia asked.

"Have you checked the boiler room?"

"You burned them?"

"Prove it."

"You're in way over your head, Aidan," Harley growled. At the mention of his name, Smoke's eyes became saucers.

"What did you say?" he asked.

"Aidan Thorne," Natalia replied with a smirk. "What, forget your name?"

Smoke's puzzlement turned to sudden realization. "Oh, man! I can't believe I didn't see it before. That explains everything!" An evil grin spread across his face. "You're the jerks from Earth Alpha."

"W-what do you mean?" Ernie stuttered as he and his friends exchanged nervous glances. They'd just blundered hard. "I mean, no, we're not. What's Earth Alpha?"

"You're in a lot of trouble here, Aidan," pressed Natalia, determined to stay focused.

Smoke chuckled. "Don't you lame-o's get it? My name's not Aidan Thorne. I only used that name in your world. Smoke is the only name I've ever had here." Smoke doubled over with laughter and wouldn't stop even when Harley pulled him up by the collar.

"What's so funny?" Natalia demanded, putting her finger in Smoke's face.

"Funny? It's hysterical. And what's the best part? I was right all along about the other Griffins." He wiped a tear from his eye as he continued to laugh. Suddenly, he pointed toward the stage. "Hey, what's that over there?"

The Griffins turned their heads to see the crowd cheering wildly. When they looked back, Smoke was gone. Natalia growled.

After an awkward silence, Ernie cleared his throat. "I can't believe we just fell for that." Natalia shook her head in exasperation, and the three Griffins headed back downstairs.

AN INSIDE JOB

Xander's red zeppelin was a floating fortress orbited by a swarm of buzzing biplanes. Max's smaller white airship wasn't as well protected, but it had a class-four cloaking device. Unfortunately, with Xander's Obscura filters, that was about as useful as a fork in a soup bowl.

In this final duel, a player could win in three ways: earning points, knocking out the opponent, or destroying the opponent's airship. Although multiple win scenarios were uncommon in anything other than master-level play, Xander and Max had met the requisite points. Max just hoped his training would pay off.

Using his steam-powered jet pack, Max zoomed

into position. Todd's advice to do the unexpected was a little vague. He'd have to think on that. Find an opportunity. So he laid his defense, keeping a careful eye on Xander through his goggles. Several rounds passed as the two top players got into position. Max was the first to attack.

There was a flash, and five armored Valkyries riding winged horses shot up out of his card and raced across the blue sky. They hit Xander's banshees like a train, slicing them into ribbons with a roll of the dice. Xander hit back with his vampire bats, but Max's paralyzer drones were on the job. The bats zigged and zagged, but the drones quickly gobbled them up.

Max kept the pressure on. His Valkyries wheeled right, plowing into Xander's jet-packed goblin assassins. The green-faced monsters didn't stand a chance. As they plummeted from the sky, Max spotted a wide-open gap in Xander's defense. Max could hardly believe his luck!

"Max is going to do it!" Natalia shouted, squeezing Ernie's hand as they watched the video screen.

The Valkyries charged through the hole, banners waving and spears shining. They bore down on Xander, dissecting one defender after another. However, just as they leaped over the Disintegrator Wall and landed on the other side, their horses lost traction, skidding through the air. Cinch vines shot up from the mist and ensnared the riders. The harder the Valkyries fought, the stronger the vines clenched.

"Nice moves," Xander called out in a cool voice. "Now it's my turn." He activated a card from his hand, rolled his knucklebones, and the sky turned black. Wind howled. Lightning blazed. And the rain was slashing sideways.

"Rain?" Max groaned. "Again?" As he wiped his goggles with his sleeve, Max spotted a vortex bearing down on him. His targeting system quickly engaged, identifying the attack. "A class-three cyclone?" Max shook his head. Legal. Just barely. This had to have been what Ernie wanted to tell Max.

The funnel of death sucked up the paralyzer drones first, then moved on to the Valkyries, the cinch vines, the goblin corpses, and even the Disintegrator Wall. Anything close was reeled into the vortex and spat out like the chaff from a harvesting combine.

Max backed up. Way up. He hoped the cyclone would run out of steam before it hit his airship. Max looked down at his cards. They weren't activating. Then Max realized that this was a chain attack. Xander still had another move. This could wreck Max's whole day.

Max searched his hand for a card that could jam the chain. Nearby, his Punisher Pixies, Astral Worms, and Cloud of Indecision were torn apart. The cyclone was within a hundred feet of Max when it finally spun itself out. That was when things really got bad.

As the cyclone unraveled, there was a sudden burst of fire from inside. A frantic alarm went off in Max's ears like a trumpeting elephant. A missile had locked on to him. A class-four Pile Driver. It had been lurking in the eye of the storm, waiting until it got close enough to Max to make him a sure thing.

With no other defense, Max activated his class-two Wall of Will. The missile punched right through it.

"Forget this!" Max exclaimed. He hit his jet pack and rocketed away. The Pile Driver leaped after him like a fiery hound. Somewhere back there, Max knew, Xander was already imagining a shiny new trophy.

Max dodged and looped. The missile stayed on him. The chain attack had devastated Max. He recalled Iver's advice from long ago: in the big leagues, fights didn't last long. The smallest mistake was met with merciless finality. Then there was Todd Toad's advice: do the unexpected. Max wasn't quite sure how to make that one work. After all, the only thing Xander might not expect was for Max to be the one chasing the missile rather than the other way around.

As Max circled his own airship for the third time, he suddenly had an idea. A wonderfully terrible idea. He could almost have hugged the Toad brothers. If it worked. Max reviewed the cards in his hand, nodded, then kicked the jet pack into turbo. Max shot across the sky toward Xander, weaving through his defenses like a Ferrari on a track.

"What are you doing?" Xander called as he dove out of Max's way. "You aren't allowed to attack me without defeating my defensive line first." Max buzzed him again. "You're going to get yourself disqualified, Sumner." Then Xander spotted the red glow of the Pile Driver as it blew through his defenses and headed straight for him. Xander hit his jet boots, blasting to safety like a bottle rocket.

He yelled something at Max, but Max never heard him. He was already deep inside Xander's territory, rounding the monstrous red zeppelin. He kept the speed on, giving it all the juice he had. Xander activated his squadron of biplanes. They buzzed toward Max on an intercept course, their water-cooled Vickers plasma guns at the ready.

Fighter planes rushing toward him. A Pile Driver coming from behind. This couldn't possibly look good. But Max knew what he was doing. He activated his Hall of Mirrors card. There was a disorienting flash, and the sky was suddenly filled with a hundred Max Sumners, all flying in different directions. The biplanes instantly broke off to engage the mirror images. Max sighed in relief. So far, so good.

The class-four Pile Driver wasn't in the least distracted by Max's play. It stayed right on him. Which, Max knew, was exactly what he needed. For his plan to work, he'd have to keep the missile close to him. Far too close for comfort.

With the Pile Driver hot on his trail, Max zoomed below the belly of Xander's airship, avoiding the gun

turrets and dodging radio antennas. His jet pack propelled him like a meteor. As he swept below the massive
turbines, his veins burned with adrenaline. It was the
ride of his life.

Back in the Grand Auditorium, the crowd was going
crazy. Cheering. Shouting. The Toad brothers were taking bets faster than ever.

"There it is!" Max said to himself as the airship's belly
hangar came into view. Both he and the missile would be
going inside. But—if all went well—only Max would be
coming back out. Only a few seconds more. Five. Four.
Three. Two…

Max felt a sputter behind him, and his jets let out a
gasp. "No!" he cried. He'd forgotten to check his fuel
gauges. His stomach swam as he flailed in the air. A desperate grasp landed his hand on a communications
antenna. He clutched it with all his strength even as the
Pile Driver flew by. He cringed to think when it would
be back, then realized that it had probably been targeting his jets. Xander would need to reprogram it to come
after Max again. In the meantime, though, Xander had
no idea where Max was. And that gave Max time to come
up with a plan for destroying the red zeppelin without
killing himself in the process.

He looked up into the flight hangar. With some careful

jungle-gym moves, he might be able to swing up and onto the ladder. Then he'd be inside. He took in a deep breath and set off.

Max scrambled into the belly of the zeppelin. He hid his jet pack behind a stack of yellow oil drums. Looking around the flight hangar, Max spotted a dozen more biplanes waiting to be launched. Clockwork mechanics kept the engines running, and fast-flying sensor drones zipped overhead. So far, Max hadn't been spotted. If time ran out, Max would lose based on points, but if Xander found him first, Max would be knocked out completely. Max's only option was to win.

Max looked up. Above him, suspended like great soap bubbles, were the helium cells that kept the airship flying. *That could work*, he thought. He spotted a fire ax near the door and took it. He also spotted a parachute in a nearby biplane. He deactivated his Hall of Mirrors and used his last invisibility card to nab it. "You never know when it might come in handy," he told himself. He scaled a series of ladders to emerge on a catwalk that spanned the length of the massive ship. None of the clockworks had seen him. Not yet. He moved quickly to the first of the helium cells and threw back the ax. There would be no hiding after this.

Boom! The blast of helium nearly knocked Max over the railing. He scrambled to his feet just as he saw a dozen clockworks racing toward him. He knew then that he'd never be able to destroy all the helium cells in time.

214

There'd have to be another way. As his eyes scanned for something big and explosive, his ears picked up the familiar rumble of a rocket engine. The Pile Driver. It had come back for him!

Max swallowed a lump in his throat as he watched the missile approach like a fiery locomotive. "This won't be pretty," he said as he gritted his teeth and threw himself over the railing. He fell through the hangar door just as the missile shot in, passing only a few feet away from him. The inferno of the rocket engines ignited his parachute just as he opened it, and then his hair burst into flames. Max cried out as he spiraled out of control.

As Max fell through the clouds, he ripped off the flaming parachute and smothered his hair with his shirt. As he tried to right himself, a massive explosion above painted the sky red. A shock wave slammed down on top of him. When his vision cleared, he found himself in a hailstorm of flaming debris. As he tried to cover his head, a flaming gear struck Max's leg, breaking it with a snap and setting his clothes on fire.

"Oh my goodness!" Natalia cried out. The crowd in the auditorium was on their feet, silent and horrified.

"Hold on, Max!" Harley shouted. "There're only ten seconds left in the duel."

As he fell, Max could see a biplane, torched and spinning wildly, heading straight for him. A rush of wind tore at him, and his vision blurred. His ears rang. His fingers throbbed. If he was lucky, he might just pass out before the plane smashed into him. At least then he wouldn't feel it.

Before it did, though, a second biplane plowed into the first, turning the sky into a whirlwind of twisted metal and spinning blades. The firestorm devoured everything. Including Max. He let out a weak cry, but the oxygen had been burned away. His vision blackened just as a flaming propeller chewed its way toward him. It was over.

The bell rang.

Max took in a ragged breath like a swimmer who'd been trapped underwater. He tore his goggles from his face. As his eyes adjusted to the light of the room, he found Xander standing next to him. The boy's hand was extended. Max shook it, unsure of what it meant. There was an avalanche of cheers. Max could hear his name being chanted as Iron Bridge's school song rang out clear and strong. Before Max knew what was happening, his teammates had lifted him up and carried him off into the delirious crowd.

THE PARTY

The reception hall was a crush of top hats and opera gloves as people danced and toasted their way across the floor. Balloons were as thick as clouds, and raspberry punch leaped from fountain to fountain. Hands reached out to Max everywhere. At every turn was another smiling alumnus or hopeful fifth grader. Banners with Max's name streamed from column to column, and pixies wrote his name in the air with faerie-dust sparklers. The room had just finished the second round of "For He's a Jolly Good Fellow" when Max found himself praying for an escape. He'd never been so happy and so embarrassed in his life. When he spotted Ernie at the snack table a few hours later, he made a beeline.

"Of course, I knew you had him all along," Ernie said. He ladled a scoop of peanuts into his mouth. "You were just playing with the Pile Driver, giving a show. Sweet move. Not my style, though. I'd have gone all cowboy and rode the missile into the zeppelin like a mad bull. Now that would have been wizard, huh?"

Max smiled. "Probably would have saved me from running out of gas."

"Totally. You have to think about those things. Hey, there's Xander. He's pretty happy considering you just punched his ticket."

Max regarded Xander. The boy laughed and joked as a flock of girls giggled at every word. Xander had a confidence Max only dreamed of. He was also good at everything he did, not just Round Table, which could explain why he wasn't taking his loss too seriously. "I don't think winning or losing meant that much to him."

"It's not like in our world," added Natalia as she and Harley joined Max and Ernie. "I wonder, though, if the other Max was this good." Natalia was wearing a white ball gown that glittered with pixie dust. Her hair was in tresses that spiraled down her shoulders. Long gloves, jewels in her hair, and . . . were those earrings? Max smiled to himself. Natalia was turning into a girl after all.

Then Max frowned. He'd nearly forgotten what he'd seen in the mirror earlier. Those haunted eyes, the pale

218

skin. The other Max. He shuddered as he filled in his friends.

"We need to get back to that mirror," said Natalia. She reached for her *Book of Clues*, then sighed. "Honestly, the one time I don't bring it with me."

"I agree," said Max. "The sooner we talk to the other Max, the better. Their lives depend on it."

"Oh, do they?" came the voice of Smoke. He appeared on the other side of the table, a safe distance from Harley's fists. "And here I thought their story was over."

"Nothing is over, Smoke," said Natalia. "Including your part in all of this."

"And what's my part?" Smoke grinned.

"Hitching a ride on the Paragon Engine."

Smoke didn't even bat an eyelash. "Come on. That's all you've got? The other Griffins were so much better than you."

"We're better than you think," replied Natalia.

Smoke took a bite of a cookie. "It doesn't matter. You're almost out of time anyway." He lobbed the remains of the cookie at Ernie's head. Ernie caught it in his hand without missing a beat. Smoke clearly underestimated Ernie's speed.

"Your time is coming, Smoke," Max warned.

"Oh, you know it, Maxie." Smoke grinned. "But what's coming isn't what you think." He disappeared, then immediately reappeared next to Max. "Oh, congratulations on your big win, loser. Too bad these people don't know you like I do." With a warning glance back at Agent Thunderbolt, Smoke disappeared for good.

Ernie clenched his gloved fists in excitement. "Guys?" he said excitedly. "I think I'm still getting faster. Smoke can't even teleport without it looking like slow motion to me." He grinned and looked at his fists as if they were two mighty hammers. "Now he's like any other kid. I can take him. I know I can."

Natalia tapped her chin thoughtfully. "Well, I hope you're right. Now that Smoke knows about the mirror, he could be a big problem." She turned to Max. "You just know he'll be waiting for us to try to reach the other Griffins. He's as curious about them as we are. Probably afraid they'll tell us his big secret."

Max nodded. "Let's give it a break. For a couple of days. Then we'll try again with Ernie and his new set of eagle eyes running lookout."

"The Eyes of Justice," replied Ernie as he dropped his goggles down. "Every power has to have a name, you know." The others laughed and were soon swept back into the celebration.

THE RETURN OF
YELLOW EYES

It took three days until the elation of the championship
had cooled down enough for Max to be able to walk
through school without being picked up and carried.
They all loved him. Students. His parents. His teachers.
Everyone! Max had fallen in love with this world as well.
He'd never felt like he belonged anywhere. Not like
this. Ernie and Natalia seemed to enjoy their lives just as
much as Max. Only Harley remained unaffected by the
good times. He wanted out, and he wanted out now.

But the most important thing ahead of the Griffins
was contacting the other Max. They could hardly think
of anything else since Max had told them the news. All

their answers could be on the other side of that mirror. It took some fancy talking to get Raven to lend a hand, but the moment she agreed, they were in the Grand Auditorium that very night. Max led the way into the stage bathroom and ran his hand across the mirror's face. "He was right here, looking back at me."

"Any sign of Smoke?" asked Natalia, turning to Ernie. Agent Thunderbolt gave the all-clear signal. In fact, Smoke hadn't been spotted since the night of the big party. That was both good and bad news, considering he might be up to something even more diabolical than before.

Raven walked up to the mirror and touched it. "Okay. Let's give this a shot." At first, nothing seemed to happen. Raven's brow furrowed, and she placed her other hand on the side of the mirror. She growled. "Doesn't feel like talking."

"Maybe you could hurry this up," Natalia whispered as she saw a clockwork janitor entering the auditorium.

"Shhh!" Raven hissed, moving her hands around. She dug in deep, her concentration so intense that it might have lit the mirror on fire. Then, with a satisfied breath, she released her hands and stepped back. "Okay."

The reflection had gone black, then grey. No, it was rolling mist. The Griffins stepped closer, eyes wide. A familiar face appeared. Max was there! His eyes were sunken, his face colorless. The reflection began speaking slowly, but his words were too distant. Max turned to Raven. "Can you help?"

Raven set her hands to the mirror. "I can give him a boost, I think."

"...so long here," the ghost boy finished. "I don't think we'll last much longer."

"Do you know who we are?" asked Natalia.

The reflection nodded. "You passed us in the Paragon Engine. You're from a different Earth, aren't you?"

"Yes. Are you trapped in the Paragon Engine?"

The reflection nodded again. "Not sure how long. It's bad. We're fading. We've been trying to reach you. We need your help, before it's too late."

"How did you get in there?"

"It was a trap...." The reflection's voice garbled, and Raven spent the next few moments trying to increase her power. "...doesn't matter," he said. His voice grew more rushed. Almost frantic. "...losing strength. Ernie... almost gone." Ernie shivered at the sound of his own name. The reflection's voice was getting harder to understand as bursts of static interrupted him. "...to Brooke. She'll know what to do."

"Brooke Lundgren?" Max replied.

"...her dad...with Iver. And Logan...in danger. Tell her...Omega Option. She'll know what...has to destroy the Paragon Engine at all costs."

"Omega Option?" Max repeated the ominous words. "What does that mean? And what about Logan?"

"And Harley!" Raven added in a panicked voice. "Is he all right?"

The fog around the reflection grew thicker. Raven poured her changeling power into the mirror, but all she produced was a roar of static so loud that the Griffins had to cover their ears. The mirror went dark even as the clockwork janitor squeaked onto the stage. The Griffins mumbled something about getting lost, then filed out the door, quiet as church mice.

Von Strife's absence from the school was hard to ignore. Not only had he missed the greatest Round Table win in Iron Bridge's history, but now he was missing the final exam preparations. Despite rising pleas for his return, he remained at his daughter's side, seldom answering the door.

Meanwhile, the case was firming up. Harley couldn't be more pleased. "Smoke didn't deny it when we confronted him with using the Paragon Engine. That's as good as an admission in my book. If we put the squeeze on him, he'll take us there. You'll see."

"How are you going to capture a teleporter?" asked Ernie.

"Inhibitor gun," said Harley confidently. He'd thought it all through. "One shot from that baby, and his powers go out like a light. He'll take us to the Paragon Engine, then show us how to use it. If he can figure it out, so can I. Next we free the Griffins; then we're out of here."

"If his powers are out," argued Ernie, "how do you plan on having him teleport us to the Paragon Engine?"

Natalia nodded. "Let's not forget that he has friends. Blackstone's a sure bet. Then there's that Yellow Eyes. Probably another confederate, although I have no idea why anyone would want to help that creep."

"He has something they want," said Max. "You think it's the Paragon Engine?"

"You mean he'd let them take the Paragon Engine for a spin?" asked Natalia thoughtfully. "Interesting. But why?"

"Wait," said Ernie. "You guys keep forgetting Von Strife. How could Smoke do any of this without his dad finding out?"

"I've been thinking about that," said Natalia. "Monti said if Smoke used portal mirrors, he wouldn't leave a trace. Maybe that's how he's getting there and back again."

Harley folded his arms. "Getting in and out is one thing. But how can he be sure Von Strife won't show up suddenly? It's an awful big risk."

"Unless he's helping Smoke..." said Max.

"Then why would Smoke hide his tracks? He's going through an awful lot of trouble to keep this on the down low."

Natalia chewed on her pencil. "Okay, let me think. Smoke is hiding his Paragon Engine activities from Von

Strife. We need to know why. We also need to know how he's getting away with it. Harley's point of Von Strife dropping by at any moment is a good one. Smoke would have to know where his dad is at all times."

"He's with Sophia," said Max as the bell rang. It was time to get to class. "And by the way, she's getting worse. Logan thinks Von Strife will snap if she dies. That would put a stop to Smoke's free ride real fast."

"It might put a stop to our getting home again," said Harley.

"And saving the other Griffins," said Natalia. "No, if Sophia dies, things are going to fall apart here like a house of cards. Let's hope Von Strife finds a cure, and fast."

"Hey, there's Von Strife now," whispered Harley. Just outside the window, the man emerged from a horse-drawn hover-carriage. Disheveled and exhausted, he donned his top hat and stepped out into the sun. He paused, looking up at the cheery sky, and sighed like a man with the weight of the world on his shoulders.

"I'm going to talk to him," said Natalia, pushing toward the door. The other Griffins tried to object, but instead they found themselves following her out into the courtyard on that brisk May morning. The trees were green, and the grass smelled damp and fresh.

"Ah, the noble Griffins," Von Strife said in a weary voice. "I've been meaning to talk to you. But...I am sure you've heard of my difficulties." Despite his immortality, Von Strife had aged. His eyes were sunken and his cheeks hollow, and his hands trembled on his cane.

"How is she?" asked Max.

"She's dying," Von Strife replied flatly. He paused, looking at his trembling hands. "I just don't understand it. Nothing I do works. It's as if her sickness isn't even... isn't even... I don't know." His fingers pressed his temples, rubbing them as if to reignite his brain. "The moment I cure her, the sickness returns, stronger than before. It's unlike anything I've ever seen."

"Is there anything we can do?" asked Natalia, reaching out to him. It seemed hard to believe that a man who loved his daughter this much could ever hurt another child. Natalia had spent many sleepless nights pondering whether she'd misjudged Von Strife. Was he a monster or a hero? Or was he a hero because he'd allowed himself to do monstrous things?

Von Strife's eyes glistened, and his face twitched. He soon got the better of it, however, and stoically wiped his face with a handkerchief. "I regret you had to see me like this." He smoothed Natalia's hair. "You know," he said to her, "you should really go home. I'll give your father the week off. No. The month off. Spend it with him. Spend every minute with him." He sighed, then continued up the stairs to the school. "While you still can."

"What does that mean?" asked Ernie, scratching his neck nervously. "While we still can? That sounds pretty, um, end-of-the-world-ish."

227

That night, Max was awakened by a flash of light in the hallway outside his room. He threw off his covers. He could hear a muffled cry, and a struggle just outside. "Sprig!" Max exclaimed, recognizing his Bounder's pitiful cries.

"Max!" she cried. "It's here! Yellow Eyes!"

Max raced into the hallway but was blinded by another flash. As he recovered, he found an empty hallway. He could hear his sister crying and his parents racing into her room. As for Sprig, she was nowhere to be seen. Max's stomach sank as he saw her claw marks on the carpet. She'd been dragged into a portal. Yellow Eyes had come back for her.

SIC 'EM

Something had to be done. Time was running out. For Sprig. For the Griffins trapped inside Paragon Engine. And for Sophia.

"We should go talk to Brooke," said Ernie as he sat with his friends in the school library a few days later. "Bizarro Max said she'd know what to do."

"Stop calling him that," said Natalia. "And before we go waltzing into Brooke's house, talking about some Omega Option—which sounds like a bomb, if you ask me—don't you think we should at least know what we're talking about?"

"What's there to know?" replied Ernie. "We're desperate. Sounds like a good-enough reason to me."

"You're desperate. Not me. We need to keep cool." She pulled out her *Book of Clues* and leafed through the pages. "So I have news. Wormwood-6? Monti was able to help. It's a poison extracted from a very rare mushroom. Colorless, odorless, tasteless. Once it's in your body, it goes into stealth mode. Some sort of faerie magic keeps it invisible. It could kill a human in minutes, but would take longer and a much higher dose with a changeling or faerie."

"Okay," said Max with a miserable nod. Those claw marks in the carpet had really disturbed him. "But why poison Sprig?"

"My guess is that Yellow Eyes was only interested in you," said Natalia. "Sprig got in its way, that's all. And remember that Sprig found the scrap of paper before she was poisoned. That tells me that Yellow Eyes intended to use the Wormwood-6 for something else—possibly to poison Max, or maybe even Ernie. Maybe Sprig knew something that Yellow Eyes didn't want leaking out. Maybe that's why it showed up at your house."

Max dropped his fist on the table. "You should have heard her when she was being dragged into that portal. I can't think of anything that would scare a shape-shifter like Sprig. She'd tackle a troll, a Slayer...a dozen Slayers if she had to."

"Not if she didn't have her powers," said Natalia.

"One sniff of Wormwood-6, and she's just a fluffy little animal. Even someone as annoying as Smoke would be scary."

"Wait a second." Harley stood up. "Yellow Eyes? What color are Smoke's goggles?"

Natalia's eyes became wide like saucers. "How could I have been so blind? It was Smoke all the time! Agh! When we get done with this case, please shoot me. Agh and double agh!" The Griffins sat around the table in stunned silence. It was so obvious. They'd missed it completely. How much more had they missed? One thing was clear. Smoke had to be found and dealt with. Max would reach out to Logan. There was no one better at setting traps.

After they reviewed their plans and what still lay ahead of them, Harley pushed his seat back. "Well, I gotta go. Monti is expecting me in an hour. We've got to solve the problem of getting the other Griffins out of the Paragon Engine."

"Do you think it's even possible?" asked Natalia.

Harley shrugged. "We won't really know until we're in front of the Paragon Engine and run a systems diagnostic. But that means we have to find the engine first."

"How's it feel to be working with Monti again?" asked Max.

Harley smiled. "Like I might actually miss this place when we're gone."

"So do you think Monti can save the other Griffins?" asked Raven, appearing out of the shadows as Harley passed by. She stepped onto the wood-planked escalator leading down to the subway platform.

"If anyone can, he can," said Harley. Then he paused suddenly. "Wait...how could you..." Harley gave up with a shrug. "Oh, right. You were eavesdropping on us. Man, how does a guy get some privacy around here? I don't suppose you're listening to me when I'm in the bathroom, are you?"

"Don't you wish."

As they rode down, Harley grew increasingly uncomfortable. He couldn't say why, but perhaps it was how close Raven was standing next to him. It made him angry. Not at her. But because the longer he stayed here, the more he liked her. The more he liked her, the more he wanted to stay. And the longer he stayed, the more likely it was that her Harley would be dead. That made Harley the bad guy. He didn't like it. It wasn't fair.

"So am I really that much different?" he said finally.

Raven looked at him closely. "Sometimes. But sometimes, you are him. I can't explain it. Like just now. When I was standing next to you. I felt it." She paused, blushing at her words, then pushed past him off the escalator. "Come on. Let's see what Monti has to say."

"What? You're not coming with me."

"Oh, yes, I am."

Harley folded his arms. "You can forget about it. I work alone."

"Since when?"

"Since now," he snapped.

"Who are you mad at? I didn't do anything to you."

Harley wasn't so sure. It certainly felt like she had.

"Look, my Harley would have brought me along."

"Why do you keep saying *my Harley*?"

"Why? Does it bother you?" Raven replied playfully.

Harley sighed. As the *Zephyr* slid to the platform, the doors opened and a nightmare poured out. Mechanical wings, metal beaks. Blackstone's crows had returned, and they mercilessly battered Harley and Raven to their knees.

As the last of the Frankenstein birds cleared the compartment, two larger silhouettes emerged: black-skinned monsters with their clockwork eye sockets and bloody teeth. They were leashed with studded leather and were commanded by the figure with the wide-brimmed hat behind them, the sinister Father Blackstone.

"Hi, kids," he said with a sneer. "Did you miss me? No? Well, I missed you. And so did my pets." He let the leashes fall to the ground. "Sic 'em, boys!"

An Unexpected
Invitation

"So long! See you tomorrow!" called Ernie as he sped away from the Avalon subway station an hour later, leaving Max and Natalia standing under the moonlight.

"Well, I should get going, too," said Natalia as her family's horse carriage clattered up the cobblestone. Its glass windows shone nearly as bright as the gas headlamps. When the door opened, Max saw Natalia's sister inside playing on her computer. "Depending on what Harley finds out tonight from Monti, tomorrow could be a big day."

"What was that, dear?" said her mom. Mrs. Romanov

wore a powder-blue gown, and her hair was piled on top of her head in a fluffy mound.

"Oh, nothing. Scoot over, Kat." She pushed her little sister to the other side of the leather seat. "Sure we can't give you a lift?"

"Thanks," replied Max. "Mom will be here in a couple of minutes." As the carriage pulled away, Max looked at the moon. It was late but still warm out. Locusts sang. Crickets chirped. The sleek silhouettes of airships slipped over the town. It was a good world, Max thought. At least looking in from the outside.

Max quickly shielded his eyes when a pair of unfamiliar lights shone on him. A black Bentley, equipped with MERLIN Tech engines and wings, landed in front of Max. The tinted driver-side window lowered. It was Logan.

"Get in." As he spoke, the wings retracted into the body of the vehicle and wheels emerged. It looked normal enough, apart from the gun ports that could still be seen just below the turn signals.

As Max got in, he noticed he wasn't the only passenger. A shadowy figure sat across from him, a large man in a black suit smoking a pipe.

"Iver!" Max said, moving quickly toward his old mentor. "It's been weeks. Where have you been?"

Iver looked at Max rather sadly. "I am afraid I have some bad news. Father Blackstone has returned."

"Okay," Max replied quietly. "I'm sure Logan can track him down, though." He looked toward the driver, who was taking them through the backstreets of Avalon.

"He did. The trail led to Iron Bridge."

"Iron Bridge? Why would Blackstone go there? He's bound to get caught."

Iver leaned close. "Have you talked to Harley?"

"No. He's with Monti right now."

"Monti hasn't seen him. Nobody has."

"What?" Max asked. "What are you saying? You think Blackstone went after Harley?"

Iver reached into his pocket and pulled out a small phone, shattered and broken. It was Harley's. "Logan found this on the platform. He checked the phone logs. Harley had been calling you when it was destroyed."

Max reached into his own pocket and pulled out his phone. A red light flashed. Voice mail. Max's stomach turned. He reluctantly put the phone to his ear and listened. If there were words on the other end, Max couldn't make them out. All he could hear was crashing and roaring that set his teeth on edge. There was a scream and more crashing. Then, with a bang, the call went dead.

"That roar you heard was a Slayer," Iver explained after an awkward silence. "And the scream, I am afraid, was Raven. We must assume the worst."

"No!" Max cried, shooting to his feet and nearly knocking himself senseless against the roof. "That's crazy. Harley was just with me! Are you sure? Are you sure about this?"

"The others will be sent for, of course," continued Iver. "We can't risk the Griffins splitting up again, lest you be picked off one by one."

Logan's hand reached back and squeezed Max's shoulder. "Stay sharp, Grasshopper," said the Scotsman. "This is only the beginning of a very long night."

"We're going after Harley, right?" asked Max, turning to Logan. "That's where you're taking me?"

"Max, we don't know if they are alive," said Iver grimly. "I know that's not what you want to hear. It's senseless, and it chills my heart. But I am as much to blame for this as anybody."

"You?" Max exclaimed incredulously.

"Ah, we're here," said Iver. Max looked out and saw that they were pulling into the driveway of the Lundgren mansion. "Max, put aside what you've learned of this world and the friendships you've made here. I need you to clear your mind and emotions for the next few hours. Recall that you are a stranger in a strange land—that you don't belong. Keep this close to you throughout this evening."

"Why? Why aren't you explaining anything?"

Iver opened the door and stepped out. He motioned for Max to follow. Logan was soon at their side as they marched up the stairs of the Victorian mansion. The door swung open without a sound. A gargoyle in a tuxedo stood there waiting. Its stone features were finely chiseled, its wings tucked neatly behind it. It didn't seem to breathe and was as still as a gravestone—except his eyes: yellow, cloudy orbs that swirled with energy.

"Good evening, Throckmorton," Iver said. "I've brought a visitor."

"Welcome, Olaf Iverson," the gargoyle greeted. He nodded at Logan, then at Max. "The others have already arrived. They are awaiting you in the parlor."

PART THREE

THE OMEGA
OPTION

BROOKE'S STORY

Max paused as he reached the foot of a black walnut staircase. Looking up, his eyes moved searchingly across the dark, polished paneled walls. Brooke's room was up there. He'd played on these stairs as a kid, lined up his toy cars, and read books with Brooke, mostly fairy tales. She loved fairies. He'd always wondered why until the day he found out that she practically was one.

"Hello, Max." Brooke Lundgren smiled down at him. Max blushed. She was just the way he remembered: the wavy chocolate hair, the brown eyes, the smile. She'd never looked more alive than she did at that moment. More determined, though. More...everything.

Max felt a hand on his shoulder. It was Iver. "Yes, my dear boy. She's been here, safe and sound, all along. She's been waiting for you to come. I'm only sorry I couldn't bring you sooner."

Max drew close to his old friend. "Does she know? I mean, about who I really am?"

"Of course," Iver replied. "Why don't you go on upstairs? You two have a lot to catch up on. I'll send for you later."

Max tried to push thoughts of Harley to the side. It wasn't easy. Blackstone was a killer, and there was nothing he'd enjoy more than murdering a Griffin. Clenching his teeth, Max grabbed the railing and began his ascent. Brooke waited for him, and the two walked quietly to her room.

"So you weren't sick after all?" Max began as he entered Brooke's bedroom. Despite the darkness outside her window, the room seemed effused with a soft, early morning sunshine that frosted the daffodil walls and whitewashed furniture in a warm glow.

"Dad needed my help," she replied, offering him a chair. "There's a lot going on. They'll tell you all about it tonight." Brooke studied him closely. She nodded, then closed her eyes. A moment later, she smiled. "Harley and Raven are alive. And so is Sprig. You don't need to worry."

Max sat up, astonished. "What? How could you know that?"

Brooke walked over to a small dollhouse near her

bed. She knocked on its front door. An instant later, a golden-haired pixie appeared, yawning. She had blue fluffy slippers.

"Honeysuckle, this is Max. The other Max." The faerie lifted into the air and made a few lazy circles about Max's head. "Could you give us some privacy?" The faerie looked at Brooke sharply, sniffed, then flew out through the keyhole in the door.

Brooke laughed. "She was only pretending to be asleep anyway." Brooke took down a record album from the shelf and placed it on a clockwork phonograph. A moment later, a piano waltz began as two holographic dancers took to the air and danced around the room, locked arm in arm. Brooke watched them lovingly. "It's my mom and dad," she said after a moment. "Everything was different when she lived here. Does your Brooke still have a mom?"

Max shook his head. "She disappeared when Brooke was eleven." As the figures moved around the room, Max caught a glimpse of neatly folded wings behind the figure of Brooke's mother.

"She's a faerie," Brooke explained quietly, her eyes locked on the dancers. "That's why she couldn't stay in this world. Dad doesn't think she'll ever come back." She paused, her eyes narrowing thoughtfully for a moment, then smiled to herself. "I think he's wrong. Anyway, that's where I got my healing powers, Max. It's no big mystery. My mom's a faerie."

"I never knew...." Max sat back in his chair. "Your mom always seemed distracted, but I know she loved you more than anything. I'm sure she'll come back." Their eyes met in a quiet moment of understanding. Then Max's fear for his friends returned. "You were going to tell me how you knew that Sprig and Harley are all right."

"Your Brooke is a healer, right? Well, my power goes a little further, I think. I can sense if people I care about need healing, no matter how far away they might be. Do you understand?" She curled her legs beneath her as she sat down on her chair. She hugged a lace-fringed pillow. "That's why my dad took me out of school and keeps me inside all the time. Because of my healing ability. With Sophia being so sick, Dad worried that Von Strife would try to kidnap me, like he's done with other kids."

Max hadn't thought of that. "Did he ask your dad for help?"

"It wouldn't matter. Von Strife would sacrifice me in a second if there was a chance to save Sophia. Dad knows that. And Von Strife knows he knows that. So the question never came up." She paused. "But if you're wondering, yes, I asked him. She's in a lot of pain. She needs help, Max." She let the pillow fall to the ground.

"You can sense her?"

"Of course. We were friends for a long time. She's dying, Max. And she knows it." Brooke bit her lip. For several long moments, she quietly watched the dancing holograms move around the room. She turned back to Max. "So what's it like in your world?"

"I wish I could remember. Von Strife said this would happen — that we'd start forgetting. I just didn't think it would happen so fast. Still, I remember the bad things the most. The mean kids. My parents..."

"My dad says that your parents split up. I'm sorry."

Max grinned despite himself. "Well, that's definitely one thing I'd like to forget." As Max shared his past life with Brooke, and some of the stupid mistakes he'd made, he found himself laughing and feeling better. Even hopeful. "The Griffins have been through worse," he said. "We'll get through this."

"So will our Griffins," said Brooke. "But they'll need your help. Did Iver tell you that I've seen Max, too?" She pointed to a dresser mirror in the corner of her room. "It was right after he disappeared. It was the middle of the night. My lights started flickering, and the next thing I know, I see Max looking out at me from the mirror. I tried to talk to him, but he never heard me. He kept saying my name but was obviously talking to somebody else."

"What do you think was going on?"

"My dad said that the Paragon Engine bridges two worlds, and Max is trapped between them. If you ask me — and it's only a guess — I think he was talking to your Brooke, not me."

"Then she's alive...." Max said.

"She's as alive as I am right now," said Brooke with a reassuring smile. "And so are Logan and Raven. Trust me. My father knows everything there is to know about everything. If you were so worried, you should have come here sooner... but, I guess they didn't think that was such a good idea." Max wasn't sure who "they" were, but he was sure Iver was one of them.

"So why am I here tonight?" asked Max after a quiet moment. "Iver never explained anything."

"You're here because this is big, Max. Bigger than you could ever imagine. And we need your help. Desperately."

ANSWERS

Baron Lundgren's office felt like the captain's quarters on Captain Hook's pirate ship. It was wide and planked in polished walnut. Its curving sides, dressed in bookshelves and oil paintings, rose in an arch above the mighty shoulders of six lead-glass windows that gazed across Lake Avalon. It was dark, the fire burned low, and the air rippled with a humming sort of energy that could raise every hair on a head.

Iver sat in a high-backed leather chair near the Baron's desk, puffing his pipe thoughtfully as Logan stood behind him. There were other figures in the room as well, but they seemed out of focus, like the fringes of an evaporating dream. Monti stood among them, disheveled and tired. It was nice to see a friendly face. And then he saw another.

"Hello, Max," greeted Ms. Merical. As she stepped from the shadows, her eyes flickered. Max had known there was something different about Ms. Merical ever since she took over the police station their first day here.

Iver took his pipe from his mouth. "I'd like to introduce you to some friends of ours, Max. A family, so to speak, of individuals who have been brought together for a secret purpose. But first, an explanation: we'd been tracking Von Strife's use of the Paragon Engine for quite some time. Our plan was to intercept whatever it was that he was bringing with him. We expected a shipment of clockworks. Instead, we caught you. That, perhaps, explains why you were dumped so unceremoniously in the Old Woods the night of your arrival. That should also explain Logan's disbelief when he saw you the first time. Of all of us, he was the hardest to convince. You know the rest of the story—at least from your point of view. But while I said your arrival was not planned, your timing could not have been better. Indeed, the fate of the multiverse itself may lie within the capable hands of the Grey Griffins."

"The multiverse?" Max said. That sounded kind of intense.

"Indeed," said the Baron. His thick hair neatly combed, he was dressed in a tailored suit with a silk cravat. On his pinkie was an emerald ring. His voice was tired but as commanding as a high priest's. "The multiverse is a universe of universes. It is the sum of all existence. Every parallel world—yours, ours, and countless others. And thanks to the Paragon Engine and how it connects these universes, billions of lives are now in danger."

Iver puffed on his pipe. "You see, we've known of Von Strife's interdimensional crossings for quite some time. But we didn't know how he was doing it. Nor could we explain what was going wrong: our two universes seemed to be unraveling with each trip he made between worlds. Then I discovered the Paragon Engine, and my worst fears were confirmed. I contacted the Baron immediately and arranged for my passage between worlds. The day you thought I perished on our world, Max, I was actually traveling to this one."

Max looked at Iver incredulously. "I thought you just said traveling between worlds was what was destroying the universe."

"It is the Paragon Engine that is the threat to existence. Not the travel itself."

"It's bleeding antimatter, Max," explained Monti. "Supercharged, rarified antimatter, that is. It's leaking into the fabric of space-time between Earth Alpha and Earth Beta, eating it away. Any more than what's already been leaked, and we are looking at a TFC—a total fabric collapse of our two universes."

"A what?"

"Everybody dies."

"Unless the engine is destroyed first," said Iver. "Which is why the Baron and I assembled this group of individuals. The Griffins—your Earth Beta counterparts—were a part of this plan from the beginning. To our deepest regret, they disappeared on the very mission that would have turned the tables on Von Strife." He paused and cast a sympathetic eye to the others in the room. "They were our friends. We must not let their sacrifice be in vain. We need your help, Max. We need the Griffins. Your unique talents—and your past friendship with Von Strife—may just tip the balance in our favor."

"If you destroy the Paragon Engine, what happens to the other Griffins?" asked Max.

The Baron nodded. "Monti thinks there may be a way to get the Griffins out of the Paragon Engine in time. All our hopes are with him. But yes, there are risks. We must accept them. The time to act is now. What do you have to say? Will you help us?"

Max felt overpowered by all the adults staring down at him. His stomach was in knots. He wished the other Griffins were with him. Natalia would know the right questions to ask. Ernie would know the right things to worry about. And Harley would know the right thing to do.

"It's pretty simple, Grasshopper," said Logan. "If you do nothing, everyone dies. Help, and there's a chance everyone can live."

250

Max took in a deep breath and nodded. "You can count on the Grey Griffins."

"Good. I'll inform our friends in the Templar Navy," said Logan with a nod to the Baron. He pulled a phone from his jacket and dialed. "Challenge code: Bravo eight oh seven." His steely eyes locked on Max as he spoke into the phone. "We're a go. Initiate the Omega Option. Repeat. Initiate Omega Option."

THE EXPLODING
SANDWICH

It had been decided that the Griffins would remain at the Lundgren mansion in preparation for the attack on the Paragon Engine. As far as an explanation went, the school and parents had been informed that the Griffins, along with Raven, were off on a monster-hunting mission. Of course, Von Strife would have seen through it in an instant. But he was hardly of the mind to care. His daughter had collapsed into a coma.

Within the sprawling mansion, where rooms could appear and disappear like shadows under shifting clouds, the labyrinthine hallways bustled with men in Templar uniforms, and the war room, as the Baron's office had become known, was lit with activity day and night. Except for the Griffins and Brooke, no one seemed to sleep. The Omega Option had kicked into high gear. But just what the Omega Option was still eluded Max.

"Max," said Natalia as she, Max, and Ernie walked through the garden labyrinth a few days later. The air was fresh and warm, but their hearts were stormy. "Are you sure the Baron is doing everything he can for Harley and Raven?" Max shrugged. Natalia's eyes fell as she sighed. "Even if they do find them, there's still a big problem with this plan of theirs. Let's say we manage to rescue the other Griffins. What then? Well, I'll tell you. You, me, Ernie, and Harley get erased. There can't be more than one of us in each world, and we're the ones who don't belong."

"You don't know that...." replied Max quietly.

"You heard Von Strife. Look, I'm all about keeping our promise to Raven, but this wasn't exactly what I had in mind."

"It's them or us," Ernie agreed.

"But there could still be a chance for us to get back," said Max.

"Of course there's a chance. A chance to blow up the multiverse and everything in it," Ernie said. "They'd never allow us to use the Paragon Engine. You should have thought about that before signing us up, that's all."

"The other Griffins would save us," replied Max. He believed it.

"You don't know that," argued Ernie.

"I know enough to know that being a hero isn't about saving your own skin," Max said. Ernie recoiled. "Anyway, all I said was that we'd try. Okay?"

"If it looks like there's a chance we can save them," said Natalia, "then you remember what Ernie said. It's them or us."

"What do you expect me to do with that?" asked Max. "It's an impossible situation."

Natalia sighed. "I know. I know. There has to be another way...."

Harley opened his eyes. It was dark in the cell. Three days had passed, maybe. He couldn't be sure. His and Raven's only companions were a rusty R-28 clockwork that provided the moldy food and the Slayer lying outside their cell, watching them with its remaining clockwork eye. Max had hurt the monster with his Skyfire. Harley hoped to finish the job. But it wouldn't be easy.

The monster continually snapped at them, and when the clockwork placed the food tray on the ground, Harley had only about two seconds to pull it inside his cell before the monster tried to tear off his arm. The attacks had been alarming at first. Then they became a sick game between Harley and the Slayer. Then, on the second day, Harley began to form a plan.

The tottering clockwork appeared right on time, gripping the food tray in its pincers. It was an older model, dented, grimy, and probably a throwaway from someone's house. It limped along, beeping to itself. Harley moved toward the food slot, dropped to his knees, and readied his hands. Just behind the clockwork, the Slayer licked its jaws, ready to spring.

The tray was down! Harley's hands bolted out, even as the Slayer shoved past the clockwork, sending it skittering into the wall. Harley gripped the tray with his fingertips and pulled. The Slayer was faster, slamming the tray down with its claws. With the tray immobile, Harley changed tactics and scooped as much food through the slot as he dared while avoiding the Slayer's snapping teeth. He didn't get much. Just a nasty old sandwich. But that would be enough.

A moment later, the R-28 clockwork teetered out the door.

Raven was on her feet, eyes closed as she sensed the air currents. "Okay," she said. "It'll be out of range in three minutes. We have an hour before it comes back. If you're gonna do this, you better do it now."

Harley unwrapped the tuna sandwich, long past its expiration. He then held up his right hand to the meager light. His Templar ring. He'd bought it at a garage sale from a Freemason's widow. It had been with him in every battle and had never let him down. The iron from which it was made was deadly to faeries. One punch from

Harley's ringed fist was enough to lay out any ordinary faerie. Unfortunately, a Slayer was far from typical. Still, there might still be a chance.

"Are you sure you want to do this?" said Raven, studying Harley. "You'll never get it back, you know."

"What I want is to get you out of here," replied Harley as he opened up the sandwich and stuffed his ring inside. He squeezed the sandwich into a ball.

"Gee," she said. "And here I thought you liked hanging out with me."

Harley paused. "I guess if I had to be trapped in a dungeon with a man-eating monster outside my door…" He blushed through his bruises. He was covered in them, as well as cuts, scratches, and everything else, after Blackstone's attack. He hadn't gone down without a fight. "So, uh, I guess let's do this. The clockwork out of range yet?"

Raven checked. "All clear."

Harley kicked at the bars to get the monster's attention. The Slayer leaped at him with gnashing teeth. Harley backed up, threw back his football arm, and launched. "Come and get it, Sparky!"

As the meal sailed through the bars, the Slayer pounced on it, wolfing it down in a single bite. Then it froze. For a moment, it just stood there. Then it turned its head toward Harley and began to growl menacingly.

"*Mon Dieu!*" exclaimed Raven. "It knows what you did."

256

The monster leaped at the bars in a frothing frenzy, bashing them over and over until the concrete joints rained down in clouds of dust. Harley pulled Raven into the farthest corner as the first of the bars snapped. Then another. Those that didn't break were being pried apart.

"It's making a hole!" shouted Harley as the Slayer leaped up into the jagged opening and began to wrench its body through.

"Stay down!" Harley yelled as Raven tried to squirm away.

"Why? So you can die first?" she yelled back. She took a broken bar and jabbed at the monster's face. It was a solid hit, but the Slayer's skull was unbreakable. The Slayer snatched at the bar, yanking it from Raven so violently that she reeled into the wall. Harley was there in a moment, leading her back to the safety of the far corner. The monster was nearly through.

"This isn't going very well!" she yelled over the howling.

"How about a little optimism?" Harley said.

"Sorry, I'm fresh out."

The bars crashed down, and the Slayer was through. Then it froze in its tracks. A curl of crimson smoke rose from its mouth and eye sockets. It let out a gurgling cry and fell to the floor in a convulsive seizure. Its stomach began to expand like a balloon.

"Close your eyes!" Harley shouted. He threw himself over Raven.

The monster gave a final gasp, then burst apart, painting the walls with its guts. As its last bits dripped down from the ceiling, Harley slowly rose, his back hammered with welts.

"This is so gross!" exclaimed Raven, trying not to step in anything.

"On the bright side," said Harley, motioning toward the demolished jail cell and its broken door, "I guess we won't need to pick the lock."

Raven smirked. "Nice one. Had it planned all along, did you?"

"You wouldn't have been impressed if I'd made it seem easy."

"True."

"Now, how about you find a way out of here?"

Raven stepped over the grim remains of the Slayer's spine. "Way ahead of you."

ANOTHER EARTH

Brooke sat with Max, Ernie, and Natalia in a quiet corner of the billiard room. Great heads of game animals and monsters gazed down from the trophy-lined walls, and a sleepy fireplace crackled nearby. The kids picked at their leftovers as they talked about their missing friends, Harley and Raven.

"Our worlds are a lot alike," said Brooke. "But little changes can make a big difference later on. You said your Harley was Monti's apprentice, and he took MERLIN Tech classes? On this Earth, MERLIN Tech isn't taught until college. I don't even know if Harley knew what it was."

Ernie whistled. "That is so weird to think we all have doubles out there somewhere. So...what about me? Any big differences?" He stood up, straightened his Agent Thunderbolt costume, and made several heroic poses for effect. "I bet he doesn't have threads like these, huh?"

"I think our Ernie had a bigger nose."

Ernie quickly wrapped his hand over his nose. "Well, at least someone does."

Brooke's eyes suddenly clouded over.

"Brooke, you okay?" asked Max. She didn't answer.

"Is something wrong?" asked Natalia.

Brooke suddenly clutched Max's arm. "Oh no, Max. She's dead! She's dead."

"What? Who's dead? Raven?"

"Sophia! Von Strife's daughter. She's dead! I've got to warn them." Brooke bolted out of the room, crying out for her dad.

"Wait a second." Raven pulled Harley back into the dingy hallway.

"Is someone coming?"

She ran her hand along the wall. "There's a secret room behind here. I want to check it out."

"Sightseeing probably isn't a good idea."

"Then you'll just have to rescue me again." She led him to a dark closet. "In we go."

Harley hesitated. "Are you sure we have time for this?"

"You more afraid of the dark or of me?" She took his sleeve and pulled him inside. After she closed the door behind them, she pulled a hidden lever. "It's an elevator," she explained. The walls rattled like an old mine cart as they dove underground. "Let's just hope it's not Blackstone's laundry chute. I don't want to see any dirty underwear."

The elevator halted a few moments later. The door squeaked open. Harley and Raven stepped out to find a steam-choked room of clanking gears, hissing pipes, and the *thump-thump* of hydraulic pistons. Heat rolled off the steam-powered engines in waves, and Harley had to shield his eyes as they ducked and dodged their way through the maze.

"We're not alone," Harley warned as he spied the first of nearly a dozen mechanical worker robots shambling nearby.

"Steam-bots," Raven explained. "No eyes. No ears. Talk all you want."

"What are they doing here?"

"This is the heart of Avalon," Raven explained. "The power plant. The steam-bots run it—have for practically ever." She closed her eyes, sensing the room, then headed through a narrow squeeze of pipes. "Hey, hero. Try to keep up."

Raven stopped at the base of an old control tower.

She quickly moved up the ladder rungs, and soon Harley found himself standing in the last place he'd expected. An apartment, complete with a leather couch, a television, a messy kitchen, and a computer workstation. The broad-brimmed hat of Father Blackstone hung on a peg. Its owner seemed to be away.

"We shouldn't be here," Harley said. "If he corners us in here, it's a long drop."

"Well, this is interesting!" she exclaimed, pulling a picture from the wall. It was a photo of a city. New York. Beneath it was a caption: EARTH GAMMA. Raven pulled the picture from the wall, folded it up, and put it in her pocket.

"Are you sure we should be taking that?"

"Oh, I'm sorry. I didn't know we were trying to make a good impression."

There was a sudden bloodcurdling howl from somewhere above them. "Big, Bad, and Ugly is back!" Raven exclaimed as she took her hand from the wall. The two friends raced down the ladder as fast as their feet would carry them.

THE WEREWOLF

"Von Strife's daughter died an hour ago," announced the Baron. Brooke was at his side. Besides the Griffins, nearly twenty of their allies were gathered in the Baron's office. "According to our sources, he has again activated the Paragon Engine — no doubt to search the multiverse for an Earth where his daughter yet lives. The moment the first probe goes through, the fabric collapse will begin."

Max looked around the room. Faces were solemn, jaws set, brows furrowed. Logan was there, as was Monti. Ms. Merical, however, was nowhere in sight.

"How did she die?" asked Natalia. "A virus, like Von Strife thought?"

Brooke stepped forward. "She was murdered."

"Murdered?" Natalia exclaimed. "But who..."

"Someone close to her. I could sense it in her dying thoughts. She knew. She knew who the murderer was all along."

Natalia hesitated, then lifted her hand. "It wasn't by any chance poison that killed her?" Brooke nodded. "I knew it! The little creep poisoned his own sister. Can you believe that?" She shared with the others all about the Wormwood-6, and how Sprig had run afoul of Smoke. "So that's why he was so determined for us not to find out. The other Griffins must have known...."

"This is beside the point, I am afraid," said the Baron. "At this moment, we have but one task: to stop Von Strife before he uses the Paragon Engine. This is our only focus. Our only hope. We do this, or we die." The Baron walked out from behind his expansive desk, signaling to several of the shadowed members to step into the light.

"The Omega Option has entered the final phase," he continued, turning his face to the others in the room. "Our attack will begin in the next twenty-four hours. Each of us knows our task. Captain Hecht will lead the Templar Naval forces against Von Strife's Tria base — neutralizing the enemy fleet before it even gets off the ground. At the same time, Montifer McGuiness will release the Gearz worm, an insidious virus that will knock out Von Strife's clockwork army. With his fleet destroyed and his army off-line, the Paragon Engine is vulnerable. All we need is to find it, destroy it, and get out."

The Baron pointed at a map on the wall. "The Paragon Engine is in an unknown location, accessible only by a single portal mirror. That mirror happens to be sitting in Von Strife's office at Iron Bridge Academy." He turned to Logan. "You and Strike Team Alpha must enter the school as quietly as possible and locate the mirror. You will program it using the codes provided by Montifer, and it will deliver you to the Paragon Engine. Save our Griffins if you can. Then destroy the engine. Timing is critical."

Max raised his hand. "What's our role? You never told us, except that we're going with Logan."

The Baron nodded. "If we fail and Von Strife reaches the Paragon Engine before we do, he'll use it—and in so doing, destroy the multiverse and everyone in it. This is where the Griffins come in. He cares for you like his own children. He won't let harm come to you. In fact, Iver and I believe he'll attempt to bring you with him to the next world. If he does and you do get a chance to see him face-to-face, you must do everything to reason with him." The Baron handed Max a packet of documents. "Give him these, as it will not be easy to convince him. If he chooses to listen, we will call off our attack immediately. He has my word."

"What about the changelings?" asked Natalia. "I know about Naomi, but what about all the changelings he supposedly brought here from other worlds? The Gearz worm won't stop them."

"We simply don't know. I advise caution."

"And how do we save the other Griffins?" asked Max.

Monti stepped forward. "The trick seems to be in cross-linking the quantum stabilizers. It's not going to be easy. One mistake could activate the engine. And if that happens, don't bother running. It won't matter." He pulled out a notebook and handed it to Logan. "I just wish I could go with you... or Harley—"

"Your job is managing the Gearz worm," interrupted the Baron. "You can't do that if you are not at your lab. As for Harley"—the Baron turned to the Griffins—"we have news. Ms. Merical has located your friends and has begun the rescue."

"Ms. Merical? But she's no match for Blackstone!" exclaimed Natalia. The Baron seemed surprised. His eyes moved to Iver, then back again. Natalia knew they had a secret, but the Baron didn't seem interested in sharing. "We should go with her at least. She'll need our help."

Iver shook his head. "The rescue is already under way, Ms. Romanov. Let Elaine Merical do her work. She will bring them home. We have to trust her."

"Leaving so soon?" Father Blackstone said with a sneer. His eyes shone like spears. His remaining Slayer was at his side.

"What do you want?" said Raven as several steam-bots loped past her, oblivious to the showdown.

"Good behavior, for one," Blackstone replied. "However, killing someone's pet was not a very promising start."

"Couldn't get any dogs to like you?" said Harley.

Blackstone smiled condescendingly. "Absolutely charming. It's no wonder your father left you back in your own world." Harley's eyes narrowed. "Yes, I know all about you dysfunctional little twerps and your pathetic secret. You see, I've met the other Griffins. You are sad substitutes. Conniving. Weak."

"I didn't know we had so much in common with you," Harley snapped.

"Enough!" Blackstone hissed, clenching his fist and hitting a steam-bot so hard that the little clockwork's head sailed across the room. "I only need you as a hostage. I don't need your girlfriend. Maybe feeding her to my pet would teach you some respect." The Slayer growled menacingly at Raven, its forked tongue lolling from its jaws.

"If you even touch her…" Harley warned.

"And what do you intend to do about it, boy?" replied Blackstone as he threw his gloves to the ground. Back in Harley's world, Blackstone had been an assassin for the Black Wolf Society with a special interest in killing kids. This version seemed a chip off the same block.

Harley stumbled backward as he watched Blackstone's shoulders suddenly broaden, claws shoot from his fingertips, and black, heartless eyes glare back at him from behind black fur. Blackstone had transformed into a werewolf, nearly seven feet tall. His fangs glinted eerily in the dim light of the steam engines.

"Wow, that's quite an overbite you've got there." Raven clenched her fists, ready for anything. "Did you ever think about braces?"

"All the better to eat you with, my dear," snarled Blackstone. He dropped the Slayer's leash. "Sic her!"

Harley threw himself in the monster's path. He might as well have tackled a train. "Raven! Run!"

But Raven didn't run, even as the beast plowed through a squad of steam-bots, knocking them over like bowling pins. The Slayer roared as it leaped into the air. Steely-eyed, the changeling girl brought out a steam hose she'd been hiding behind her back. She jammed it into the monster's jaws as it reached her, then threw herself clear.

The Slayer halted, confused. Then it began to feel the pain. All at once, it began thrashing violently, frantically tearing at the hose of death while superheated steam poured from its mouth and nose slits. The monster wailed and kicked. The lenses of its clockwork eyes fogged, then cracked, then finally exploded. Within seconds, the monster had collapsed, its insides completely evaporated. All that was left was a sack of skin and a ribbon of mist coming up from its jaws.

No one said a word as the opponents eyed each other across the foggy battlefield. As for the steam-bots, without eyes to see or ears to hear what had happened, they continued to pursue their primary programming to keep the steam engines running.

Together, Harley and Raven faced down the werewolf. "You seem to have bad luck with pets," Harley said, wiping away a trickle of blood from his mouth. Tackling the Slayer had been a bad idea.

Blackstone snarled, licking his teeth. "There is one more monster left in this room. And you seem to be all out of fancy rings and steam hoses."

Just at that moment, there was a knock at the door and in stepped Ms. Merical. She looked around the room, quickly taking in the dead Slayer and Blackstone's transformation. She took off her white silk gloves and walked up to the scene with brisk steps. "Ah, Diamonte Blackstone." She smiled kindly. "So this is where you've been spending your time. I can't say I fully grasp your taste in decor, but I am very thankful to see you've taken such care of my students." As she spoke, her eyes lit with that same glittering glow that Harley had seen in the police station when they'd first arrived in this world.

Though the werewolf towered over her, Blackstone didn't lift a finger. "I should have known they'd send you, Elaine." His voice was a low growl as his eyes studied her.

"Even the Baron needs to have luck on his side from time to time," she replied as she checked Raven for bruises. "And luck is my specialty, as you know. Without it, how could I possibly have found your quaint little home?" She cast a disapproving glance at the surroundings. "But you might have picked a more hospitable residence. With all this steam down here, you could catch your death of pneumonia."

Harley watched his teacher in wonder. Ms. Merical's power was luck? He wasn't even sure what that meant. But evidently Blackstone sure did.

The werewolf eyed the fog suspiciously. "I've survived you before. I can do it again."

"I am afraid your luck has just run out, Diamonte," she said. Her smile faded to stern resolution.

Blackstone squirmed. "So what will it be? A heart attack? I slip and break my neck? I choke on a dinner roll? What lucky little event do you have planned for me?" His teeth were bared as Ms. Merical regarded him with pity. He shook with indecision. Should he wait and let the unlucky event happen, or should he act now before the bad luck caught up with him? Of course, waiting wasn't his thing. With a roar, Blackstone lunged at Harley. "If I'm going down, I'm taking you with me."

Harley dove behind a small, wobbly steam-bot. It wasn't much of a shield, but Blackstone hadn't expected it. Stumbling over the fragile clockwork, Blackstone crashed to the ground in a clatter of metal. Embarrassed, he slowly rose to his feet. He sneered at Ms. Merical. "Really, Elaine? Tripping me? That's all you've got?" Then he paused and looked down. His chest was bleeding. The clockwork's spindly arm was embedded in him. As he plucked it out, his eyes caught the familiar glint of silver. In fact, the entire clockwork had been plated with silver to keep its innards rust-free from all the steam. But the plating had been so tarnished by the decades of work underground that Blackstone had never noticed that he'd been living side by side with Kryptonite: silver was fatal to werewolves.

He looked up at Ms. Merical. "So this is how you planned it all along...." His voice was dry. He fell to his knees.

Ms. Merical shook her head sadly. "Luck isn't planned, Diamonte. It just happens." As she finished, Blackstone watched in horror as the wound in his chest began to shine a brilliant blue and his flesh and clothes around it to blacken and bake like charcoal.

As the burns spread down his legs and arms, he cried out, "You can't let this happen to me, Elaine. Please, I'll do anything you ask. Just don't...just please don't... don't let it end like this!" The smoldering fire beneath his skin had by now swept over his shoulders, up his

271

neck, and consumed all that was left, leaving his face frozen in a silent scream. Only his eyes remained alive, and only long enough to see his body burst apart in a flash of blue fire. When the cloud of ash cleared, Blackstone was no more.

Harley stood up and found Ms. Merical standing next to them. She meticulously cleaned an ashy smudge from her cheek with a powder puff and compact mirror. After a moment, she looked back down at Harley and Raven, her face perfect. "Well, I believe it's nine o'clock. As you know, that's past my bedtime. Let's not have any pumpkins." A portal opened up behind her. Without answering Harley's look of astonishment, she promptly herded both children through.

INVADERS

"And so that's the end of Blackstone?" Natalia asked an hour later. She sat at the kitchen table with Ernie, Max, Harley, and Raven as they munched on leftovers. Mostly turkey and potatoes. Natalia quietly noted Raven sitting closer than usual to Harley.

"Ms. Merical's a superhero," Ernie said, astonished by the revelation. "The power of luck? I mean, that's got to be right up there with, I don't know, Superman or something. How can you fight luck?" He was almost as relieved to have Blackstone out of the picture as he was to see Harley back safe. "Do you think she's a changeling? I totally bet she is."

"She ain't a changeling," said Logan as the Scotsman entered the kitchen. He was washed, shaven, and dressed in his Templar leather jacket. "She's not human, either. As for who she is, those in power call her Lady Luck. Things always go her way. Let's just be glad she's on our side." He paused. "At any rate, we've got a job ahead of us. Raven, I think it's time you showed Natalia what you nicked from Blackstone's lair."

As Raven pulled out the folded paper, Max regarded the Goth girl, who didn't look quite so Goth with her hair smelling like Brooke's lilac shampoo and her eyes scrubbed free of black eyeliner. And unlike her caustic double in Max's world, this Raven was kind of nice to hang out with, if you didn't mind the occasional kick in the head.

Natalia scanned the paper closely, then nodded. "Well, I think that explains just about everything."

"What do you mean?" asked Ernie.

"This is all about Smoke, that's what. Everything! Don't you see? He hates this place, and everyone here. He wants his own Earth where he can be a big shot." She set Raven's paper on the table. "See that? It says Earth Gamma. See the Latin next to it: *Veneficus Absentis*. It means there's no magic on Earth Gamma. Smoke could set himself up as king. That what he's been up to all along. He just needed to keep anyone from getting in his way. He kept Von Strife away by poisoning his sister. He keeps us busy by hiring Blackstone. Meanwhile, he's taught himself to use the Paragon Engine somehow. . . . I guess I have to give him credit for that one."

"But why would the picture be in Blackstone's place if Smoke was the one going to Earth Gamma?" asked Ernie.

"Maybe he promised to take Blackstone with him. A werewolf would do pretty well in a place like Earth Gamma."

"I don't think Blackstone will be going anywhere anytime soon," Harley said with a laugh.

Logan gripped Harley's shoulder and gave it a friendly squeeze. "Good to see you again, kid. Heard you gave one of those Slayers a case of indigestion. And Raven here steam-cleaned another. Nice work."

Harley grinned. "Lost a good ring, though."

"I'll get you another. Now, grab a drumstick and go see Monti. There's a chance we could save the other Griffins, and it may be up to you to make it happen."

"What?" Harley nearly choked. "I only just started learning about Paragon Engines."

"Get!" Logan ordered. Harley excused himself and disappeared down the hall. "Now," continued Logan as he turned back to Raven, "you sure you're up to joining us? We're asking a lot from you, and you've already been through a battle of your own."

Raven nodded coolly. "You need someone with brains on the team."

Logan nodded. "All right. Things are moving fast. Go time is oh four hundred. That means you lot have a few hours of sleep you'll be wanting. When the alarm sounds, you better be on your feet."

Harley found Monti laboring over a DE Tablet, feverishly coding something in with an occasional cross-check from his notebook. He started at Harley's knock, then rolled his chair back and smiled weakly at him. "So I hear you took out a Slayer with your bare hands."

Harley shrugged as he looked at Monti's screen. "Wow, you're doing some heavy-duty work here. What is it?"

"Oh this?" Monti perked up. "It's called the Gearz worm. A little something I've been working on to remotely shut down Von Strife's army of clockworks. It should work. I think. In theory, anyway." He paused, then looked up at Harley. "Sorry I was such a jerk at first. I just, well, I didn't know you, even though you knew me. With all this coming to an end, I'm sitting here regretting that I didn't talk to you more. Spend more time, learning about whatever it is that you like to do. What you've done. I procrastinated, I guess. I always do that. Then it's too late to change things."

Harley smiled. "Hey, don't worry about it. Parallel worlds are crazy things."

"Yes, they are," said Monti with a sigh. "I'm not really good at talking, you know. I don't get many visitors at the lab. But, well, anyway, Natalia said you never knew your real dad. Had to be weird to see him in this world."

Harley sat down next to Monti and picked up an interesting-looking gadget. He examined it absently. "I've fought monsters. Zombies. Werewolves. Even met a vampire once—pretty cool guy, by the way. But being alone with Henry was the most scared I've ever been."

"I know what you mean. I was raised in an orphanage until I was twelve. Then out of nowhere, my mom reappears. She yanks me out of the only place I've ever known and moves me into her apartment on Cheap Side. I was so freaked out I didn't leave my room for a week. She used to shove tiny sandwiches under the door." He scratched his head thoughtfully. "You ever think about looking up your real dad?"

"Henry seems like a pretty cool guy. If my dad is still out there somewhere, I think I'd like to meet him." Harley paused. "Just don't tell Natalia."

Monti laughed. "All right. Fair enough. But for what it's worth, Natalia is quite the little detective. If anyone could find your father, she could."

"And she'd never let me forget the favor." He laughed to himself, then turned his eyes back to the gadget. "Say, what is this thing, anyway?"

"It's an X500 Take-Down. A little weapon I developed last year for Logan. It's an air gun powered by

MERLIN Tech. It can shoot a small neural inhibitor at high velocity. If it hits a changeling, their powers go out like a light."

Harley nodded in admiration. "I've seen these before, back on my world. Pretty awesome."

"Take it," offered Monti. "You might need it where you're going."

Harley grinned as he attached the X500 to his belt. "I'll give it back to you when..." He paused. He didn't even know if he would be coming back.

"Don't worry," said Monti, catching the worry in Harley's eyes. "The Baron's plans never go wrong. Which reminds me. We have some Griffins we need to get out of a bind. You ready to take some notes?"

Harley pulled up his chair. "Lay it on me, maestro."

"You're not coming with us?" Max asked Brooke as the two of them lingered by the foot of the stairs. The others had already returned to their rooms. The house was quiet. The lull before the storm.

"I have to stay here. To help Dad." She paused. "You know, it's weird to think that you're about to invade our school."

"I know." Max had thought about it a lot. Iron Bridge wasn't just a school. It was a fortress. If the Omega Option failed, Strike Team Alpha would be in big trouble. "I'm glad I met you," said Max after a long silence. "It's weird, but it's like we've always known each other, you know?"

"In a way, I guess we have," she replied softly. "And we always will. Even if it's not us, there will always be a Max and a Brooke out there in some parallel universe. And for them, maybe tonight isn't the end. It might only be the beginning."

"Sounds like a nice place to live." Max sighed.

She laid her head on his shoulder. "Come back alive, Max...."

Max awoke a few hours later. He stumbled into the shower, then dragged himself downstairs. The place was a beehive of activity. Max ducked under arms, dodged around elbows, and jumped over furniture to finally reach the kitchen, where his friends were gulping down cold oatmeal. Harley looked up at Max, then turned at the sound of his name.

It was Monti. There were gadgets stuffed into his vest pockets, an old keyboard under his arm, and dark circles under his eyes. "I gotta go, Harley. Please tell me you'll remember everything I told you about the Paragon Engine. You have to do it just the way I said. Got it?"

"Don't worry," said Harley. "And good luck on the Gearz worm. It's brilliant."

Monti smiled self-consciously. "Well, I guess we'll find out." His wristwatch beeped. "Oops. Sorry. Gotta go. Okay, then...well, it was, ah...good knowing you." He rushed out through the front door.

"Good knowing us?" Ernie repeated nervously. "I thought this plan was foolproof?"

Raven laughed darkly to herself but said nothing. Next to her stood Natalia, decked out like a super spy. Black leather from head to toe, with plenty of buckles and belts. Aside from Agent Thunderbolt, the other Griffins were similarly dressed. But Natalia accessorized with a climbing harness, night-vision goggles, and earrings that doubled as encrypted wireless communicators.

A light suddenly streamed through the lakeside windows in a blaze of shimmering green. The Griffins watched breathlessly as the water of Lake Avalon exploded upward. The ghostly form of a Templar super-carrier, no longer hidden by cloaking shields, rose into the sky. Nearly a thousand feet long, it was still hard to describe at such a distance; but Max recalled the pictures of the ship at school: satin black hulls of meteoric iron, six massive MERLIN Tech aerial propulsion screws, and a crew of skeletal clockwork sailors. It had enough firepower to blow the moon out of the sky.

Acting as its escort were six grim battleships bristling with steam-driven pulse cannons and grinder missiles. Max watched in awe as Captain Hecht's fleet prepared their jump drives. Then, with another flash, they were gone and halfway around the world. Von Strife's fleet, stationed at the Tria facility in Italy, was about to be blasted into oblivion.

Monti's Gearz worm would come next, knocking out the clockwork army. And then...

"All right, team," said Logan, checking his watch. "Iron Bridge is waiting." Through countless corridors and winding staircases, Strike Team Alpha moved into the bowels of the mansion. They came to a halt in front of an iron door. Logan swiped his badge across a security pad. The door rolled away. They filed into a massive concrete bunker, complete with rumbling generators, flashing red lights, catwalks, and, more important, a submarine. It was a fantastical machine resembling some ghastly mechanical whale whose head had been lopped off and replaced by a globe of glass wrapped in an iron lattice. The glass was polished to a mirror shine, but the shadows of busy workers could be glimpsed within.

"There's our ride," said Logan as the submarine's engines shook the walls of the bunker.

Max mounted the sub, then led the Griffins down the iron-riveted hatch. He followed a narrow corridor to the glass-globed bridge, where the command crew readied for their departure. Water lapped at the sides and would, Max knew, soon slip over their heads when they set off. But what a view! This would be like floating through the sea in a magical bubble—a bubble with steam engines and torpedo bays.

With everyone aboard, the submarine shot out of the channel and disappeared into the inky blackness of Lake Avalon. Next stop: Iron Bridge Academy.

"Cutting over to Merlin Drive," announced a man. "Steam and diesels off-line. Initiating the cloaking system." There was a series of three beeps, and a thud. A red light went on. They were now cloaked—completely invisible to any outside eyes. But to Max, nothing seemed to change. He could see everything just as before. The view was glorious. As they slipped through the lake waters, he could almost hear the rush of water past his ears. The Griffins and their hosts seemed to be floating in a world of shimmering green.

Dark, monstrous shapes slipped through the waters around them, oblivious to their passage. Were it not for the cloaking device, the creatures that lurked in the icy depths of the lake would have made a meal of them. As it was, Logan's team had to constantly correct their course to avoid hitting a slithering behemoth or a school of bony fish the size of a city bus. It was terrifyingly beautiful.

Next to the Griffins, Logan rummaged through a weapons pack, taking inventory of all they'd need. "'Course, we shouldn't need much," he said, regarding a sonic grenade in his hand, "if everything goes according to plan."

"Logan," said Ernie, looking out into the lake, "what happens if we save the other Griffins? What happens to me? Von Strife said that there's some rule. And to fix things, one of us will disappear."

Logan zipped up the bag. "Not my area."

"I don't want to disappear. . . . I like being me."

Logan cleared his throat. "Our duty today is to save lives. I'd stay focused on that and leave the science stuff to the others."

Natalia threw her arm around Ernie and pulled him close to her and Max. "We'll stick by each other, Ernie. Just like always. This is just one more adventure." She noticed her other hand was trembling and bit it self-consciously. Dying in battle was one thing. But walking freely into oblivion? That was horrifying.

The door to the bridge opened, and Iver stepped inside, his great height forcing him to lower his head under the iron bulkhead. He hadn't boarded with everyone else, so he must have teleported onto the submarine. He was dressed like a Victorian gentleman from the boots up. But the seriousness of his mission was clear judging by the well-oiled, five-barreled revolver that hung just inside his worn and weathered trench coat. He turned to Logan. "Well, so far so good. I just heard from Captain Hecht. His ships are in position, awaiting the signal to begin the bombardment."

"And Monti?" asked Logan.

"He should be releasing the Gearz worm in" — Iver brought his pocket watch to the meager light — "about eight minutes. Let's hope for clear sailing." He spoke too soon. Just at that moment, a deafening explosion rang out. The alarms sounded.

Logan was on his feet. "Status?"

"All systems operational, sir," said a man. The computer screens were blazing with activity. "We weren't hit. But something big just struck the water."

"Take us to periscope depth," Logan ordered. They ascended while Logan adjusted the lenses of the periscope. "Can't see a thing. Switching view to spectral." Logan peered again. As he did, his shoulders slumped. He sighed angrily, then spun the periscope away with a growl.

"What is it?" Max asked. "What do you see?"

Logan lowered the periscope and motioned for Max to take a look.

Just ahead towered a wall of emerald flames that reached into the heavens. So powerful was the magical fire that the lake itself had begun to boil. And beyond that wall, waiting for them on the other side, Max could make out figures, hundreds of them, hovering in the air.

"Changelings…" Max said. "Von Strife has a whole changeling army waiting for us."

Iver set his hand on Logan's shoulder. "This could complicate things, my old friend."

THE LOST SOULS

Alarm bells rang, and the submarine dove. Men ran around the bridge and down the corridors, barking orders and shouting replies. Iver took the spotlight now, sitting down in the captain's chair, in the very center of the globe, and closing his eyes. The wall of green fire loomed before them.

"It's a class-eight Wall of Will," Iver said, his eyes remaining shut. Max only knew of these within Round Table. But of course, that's what Round Table was all about: preparing for the real thing. "Correction, make that class nine." The whole of the globe filled with flickering light green flames.

"Iver, are you up to this?" shouted Logan. The ship was moving too fast to stop.

"We are about to find out," Iver replied. A surge of blue energy rolled off Iver's fingers, down the chair, and into the vessel itself. The Griffins tightened their seat belts as the wall loomed closer. And then, with a grinding boom, the ship struck the wall!

The ship heaved, and screens exploded. But Iver's eyes remained shut as he waged his invisible battle against Von Strife. Max didn't know what was behind Iver's mysterious powers, and as he studied the blue energy coming from Iver's fingers, he couldn't help but wonder if it was like his own.

Iver let out a sudden cry, as if he'd been struck. Max could feel that he was losing the battle. Iver needed help. Before he knew it, Max's hand shot out and gripped Iver's wrist. His Skyfire flooded into Iver's body. There was a flash of light, and Iver's eyes shot open, flickering like orbs of lightning. Max's eyes burned as well. He and Iver were linked like two supercharged batteries.

With a rush, the submarine plunged ahead. The iron hull shuddered, and then the globe cracked, as if some invisible hand was desperately squeezing the submarine. Then, with an explosion that sent the submarine rolling on its side, the Wall of Will was broken. They'd made it through!

The alarm silenced. Iver let out a breath and turned

286

his face toward Max. For several moments, they floated in the still water. No one said anything, eyeing one another in disbelief. Iver offered an exhausted smile. "That was close, was it not, Master Sumner? You see, our enemy is more powerful than you'd imagined. Had you not come to my aid, our story might have been over before it even began." Iver slowly rose from his chair and announced to the others, "The first of our trials is over."

"Full ahead," Logan barked. "Shields maximum. How's the cloaking device?"

"Batteries are down twenty percent, sir!"

Max didn't have to time to figure out what had just happened between him and Iver. Without the cloaking device, the sea monsters would become a bigger problem than Von Strife's forces.

"Max said there are changelings up there, in the sky," Ernie said as Iver sat down beside them. "I don't want to fight my friends...."

"Those are not your friends," Iver replied. "Those are the Lost Souls. Von Strife was unable to save all the children he brought with him into this world. Those who didn't die outright had their souls scooped out and placed into genetically engineered clones, programmed to do whatever he commands. We'd wondered where he was keeping them. This is not how I wanted to find out, however."

"How many are there?" asked Natalia in horror.

"Too many. Far too many."

The alarm sounded again, rattling Max's head. "Bogeys in the water. Two. Three. Five of them. Life-forms. Humanoid. Coming up from behind."

"Changelings," Logan spat out as he fell into the captain's chair. "What do we have, Søren?"

A man in a black mask walked over to a computer screen and punched in a command. "Two water-based changelings. An air elemental. The fourth is a shape-shifter, currently in shark form. The last... I can't quite read. Could be an electrical-based changeling, judging from the interference. Confirmed. Electrical, class two. Attempting to overload our sensors."

Logan sat back. "Fire up the EELS."

"The eels?" Ernie mouthed. Slithery fish defending the submarine didn't sound very practical, no matter how nasty and slimy they were.

"EELS, Master Tweeny," explained Iver. "The Elementary Erg-particle Laser System."

The room flashed red, and there was an explosion somewhere out in the darkness of the water.

"We got two," confirmed Søren. "But the others are..."

At that moment, the face of a changeling kid could be seen looking back at them through the glass of the bridge. He was surrounded by a pocket of air, which propelled him around as fast as any fish. As he moved to get a closer look, Ernie let out a gasp. This was no ordinary boy. Half of his face had been replaced with clockwork components. The left eye blinked like a targeting system. Before the boy could attack the submarine again, a shadow fell over him. He let out a frantic cry, and then he was snapped up in the jaws of a black-skinned dinosaur fish. He was gone in a single gulp.

"The air elemental is down," said a sailor. "Taking damage from the electrical changeling now. Shields at sixty percent and dropping. Fifty-five percent." Again, the ship was struck. Lights dimmed. Bulbs burst.

Max was on his feet. His energy was rippling up and down his arms and sparking from his fingertips. He'd never felt more powerful—something about the link between him and Iver. "Let me try my Skyfire."

"Not a chance," said Logan, pushing Max back into his seat. "This boat's shielded. Without Iver's focus, you'd fry us up like eggs. Keep your power to yourself until we're on dry land."

The submarine was suddenly struck broadside, heaving dangerously to port. Max was on his back, strapped to his chair. He heard the EELS fire again and again. The sub righted itself.

"Cloaking device off-line, sir! The changeling is sapping the batteries."

"Someone take that electrical kid out!" Logan barked as he warily eyed a sea monster that had just turned toward the sub. "And launch a concussion missile to star-board. I'm not interested in being eaten." There was a bone-jarring explosion outside. A solid hit. But the wounded animal drew unhealthy interest from bigger creatures below. "Iver! We're gonna be swimming if you don't do something fast!"

Max looked over to find Iver's eyes closed again. They soon fluttered open. "The cavalry are on their way," he said.

"How long do I need to hold this bucket of bolts together?"

"As long as you can."

The Griffins gritted their teeth as the submarine absorbed blow after crunching blow. The command globe held, but they were taking water. Steam hissed through the shattered pipes. All the while, the crew of the submarine continued the rat-a-tat of the EELS. Max heard shouts and screams from the aft. The fire alarm rattled as smoke began to choke the main corridor.

"Almost there!" Iver shouted.

"Can you tell them to move a little faster?" Logan yelled back.

Suddenly, it went peculiarly quiet. The attacks had stopped. Max heard the sailors shouting in the engine room and the sound of fire extinguishers. The cloaking device was soon repaired. Not a moment too soon, judg-ing by the gigantic shadows moving toward them from below.

"We can't stay submerged any longer," said Logan, checking the oxygen levels. "I don't know what's topside, but we're coming up one way or the other." Max felt a lurch as the ballasts were blown, and the ship's nose rocketed toward the surface.

INTO THE
IMPOSSIBLE

The submarine blasted to the surface, hung in the air for a moment, then crashed down onto the water. The crew members were covered in cuts and bruises, but they'd survived. So far.

Max gazed up through the glass to see a sky exploding with fire. Everywhere he looked, the changeling army was locked in brutal combat with the Templar, who had arrived on the scene with jet packs, sky cycles, and armored gunships. Unfortunately, the Wall of Will had devastated most of the Templar forces. Those who survived were vastly outnumbered by the host of fire elementals, telepaths, and countless others with even greater powers.

Ernie shook his head. "It's like every super-villain who ever lived is up there!"

"How long can they last against those changelings?" asked Harley.

Iver shook his head soberly. "I suggest we keep moving." The diesel engines reengaged, and soon the submarine was slicing through the water beneath the fireworks of life and death. While they made good time, their arrival was hardly a secret. Cloaking device or not, it was hard to conceal the wake of the boat as they closed in on the island. As they neared the dock, they saw several Grimbots waiting for them with their clockwork skeletons, broad chests, and multibarreled blasters. Behind them, more clockwork infantry were taking position.

"What about the Gearz worm?" asked Natalia.

"Just what I was thinking," replied Logan. "Søren, what's taking Monti so long?"

Søren pulled off his headset and let it fall on the table. "We have a problem."

"You don't say."

"Seems Von Strife is on to the worm and is in the process of uploading a new operating system to his clockworks. Monti is trying to adapt. He needs time."

"And Captain Hecht?"

"Success! Three of Von Strife's carriers have been

destroyed, two battleships, a frigate. And...it appears the main facility has sustained heavy damage. Von Strife's air squadrons were not able to launch in time."

"At least one thing went right," said Logan. "Still, without Monti's Gearz worm taking down the enemy clockworks, landing this boat is gonna be a problem." He checked the ship's speed, his stopwatch, then the battle in the sky. He ran a gloved hand over his short cropped hair, growling to himself. He was going to make a decision. A very ugly one. "All right, team," he said finally. "Looks like we're going to have to cowboy this." He turned to his bridge crew and barked, "Full ahead! All right, lock it in. Good. Get ready to seal the doors. Everyone, to the back of the boat! On the double." As they cleared the bridge, Logan slammed the hatch down behind him. "That should hold."

"Hold what? What are we doing?" asked Ernie.

"We're ramming the dock," Natalia explained as she pulled Ernie down the corridor after her.

The Grimbots opened fire the instant they realized their situation. But it was too late. With a thunderous roar, the submarine plowed into the dock. Everything turned upside down. The lights blew out. Then things went eerily silent.

"Everyone okay?" Logan flipped on a pen light and swung the beam around. Everyone was there. Still in one piece. He ordered them topside and out before the fires in the engine compartment could sweep into the bridge.

The Templar soldiers were out first. There were a few bursts of scattered gunfire. Max followed as the last of the Grimbots sank into the water. As for the sub's glass-and-iron bridge, it had been obliterated. The submarine was a wreck: a headless whale beached upon rocky shores. But it had done the job.

"Follow me," said Logan. He handed out the packs and led them into the woods. Above, the battle in the skies still raged. When they came to a sewer entrance, the soldiers sliced through the grate with torches. Max quickly lowered himself into the darkness.

Max was having flashbacks. Hadn't he just done this? Just before coming to this world? Dark tunnels, sentry clockworks. It was all the same. And just like last time, everything had gone horribly wrong. Von Strife had known they were coming all the time.

"Keep your head straight, Grasshopper," Logan reminded him. They were moving toward a dim light. "Von Strife doesn't know about this tunnel."

"How can you be so sure?" asked Raven.

"Call me an optimist," Logan said with a smirk. His pulse rifle was slung under one arm, and a grenade satchel was under the other. "You're the structural empath," he said to Raven. "Why don't you make yourself useful?"

"So that's what her power is called!" said Ernie. "It's been killing me. It's not in any of the books, you know." He looked over at Harley, who didn't seem impressed. "What, are you saying you knew?"

"She told me."

Ernie rolled his eyes. "Great. Now you two have secrets. How adorable."

"The school security system is still armed," Raven said as she pulled her hand away from the slimy wall. "There's no way to turn it off. Not from down here."

"I suggest we take the Bearing Corridor," said Natalia, who'd memorized a map of the school's hidden passages while in the Baron's library. "I don't think the security system monitors it, and maybe Von Strife doesn't even know about the secret door?" Raven agreed to check it out, moved down a narrow passage, found the door, and soon talked it into opening up. She called for the rest of them.

She motioned for them to follow her inside. "We only have about three minutes before the security drones make another sweep. *Envoye!*" Max was glad to have the changeling on the team. She would have made a great Griffin.

They emerged from the secret passage into a scullery. Over the next few minutes, they slid from one hall to the next, stepping behind doors and slipping into secret passages at just the right moment. It worked well, so far. "But when we get to the main floor, we're up against environmental sensors," said Raven. "Unless we're ghosts, we're gonna stand out like spoons in a knife drawer."

As they filed into the boiler room, Logan produced a familiar device. An IPA. It would turn them into ghosts just long enough to get past the environmental sensors Raven had been concerned about. The only trouble was that Von Strife knew about IPAs. He had given one to Ernie back on Earth Alpha.

"Each one has its own channel," explained Logan, typing a code into the gadget. "Von Strife's quick, but I don't think even he will be able to unscramble the encryption in less than five minutes. And that should be all we need."

"Better move fast," said Raven. "The Grimbot parade is on its way."

As the clockwork killers clanked into the boiler room, Strike Team Alpha faded from view. They were virtually undetectable now—invisible and silent ghosts capable of walking through walls.

Logan signaled to his men to get ready. "Von Strife's office is directly above us."

"Sixty feet, three inches," confirmed Søren.

The men, nearly a dozen, pulled out strange-looking guns—loaded grappling hooks. They took aim and fired. The hooks, ghosted by the IPA, phased right through the ceilings, one floor after the other. At just the right altitude, they solidified and caught hold of the rafters. Fine cables were attached to the utility belts of each team member. With an explosion of compressed air, they all launched upward like ghostly spiders, passing through floors, walls, and furniture. It was an odd feeling to travel this way, with only the flickering darkness to indicate passage through solid objects. A moment later, they were standing in a copy room, directly below Von Strife's office.

"Why did we stop here?" asked Ernie.

"His office is shielded from IPAs. So from here, we'll use the stairs like everyone else," said Logan. "Everyone drop your packs. Bring only what you can carry."

Max and the other Griffins looked around the room. Because of the phase adjustment of the IPA, the normally dark walls appeared ghostly, as if they were made of clouds that had been nailed in place. Max had been in the administration building many times. They all had. But now it was different. Now they were invaders. And upstairs was someone who would not be particularly happy to see them.

CLOCKWORK JUNGLE

As they stepped into the hallway, Logan let out a grunt, dropping the IPA to the ground. A field of fiery sparks shot out from the device as it disintegrated before Max's eyes. It didn't help that nearly a dozen Grimbot eyes were there to see it. The clockwork super-soldiers were vaguely humanoid, but they had broad chests of steel, shoulder-mounted cannons and blazing red eyes that burned through the slits in their skull-like faces. There was an awkward silence as the surprised enemies regarded each other. Then the metal monsters opened fire.

Logan tackled the Griffins in his thick arms, shielding

them with his own body. Behind them, the hallway was a storm of hellfire and pulse cannons. Grimbots' arms were blown off, men fell, and the air filled with chalk and plaster dust. It had happened so fast that there was no way to recover and regroup. Something drastic had to be done.

Iver dodged a swinging fist and placed his hand on a Grimbot's chest. When Iver pulled his hand away, Max saw a small black box affixed to the machine. It was blinking. "Magneto Collapse!" Iver shouted. "Everyone down!"

All at once, the air seemed to bend. Max felt his teeth rattle. And then he saw the iron railing rip off the wall and shoot through the air. Covering his head, Max peered up at a hurricane of metal objects: nails, hinges, doorknobs, and Grimbot debris. They were being sucked toward the hapless Grimbot, which was clawing desperately at the black box Iver had left behind.

The Magneto Collapse kicked into high gear. First a gun. A cannon. Anything loose. Then a few bolts sheared clean from a nearby Grimbot's leg as it tried to scramble away from the magnetic garbage disposal. Its body buckled, and it tumbled backward into the vortex of metal. The more the vortex ate, the more powerful it seemed to become. Another Grimbot lost its footing. Two more followed. Any clockwork standing was sucked off its feet, and those that clung to the stone were stripped bit by bit until there was nothing left. With a flash, it was over, and all that remained of the clockwork force was a tangled sphere of shredded metal in the corner.

Max tasted blood in his mouth. Ernie's chin was damp with red. "What happened?"

"Your fillings," said Logan. He looked over at Iver, brows furrowed in disapproval. "A Magneto Collapse isn't exactly an indoor weapon."

"Our equipment was shielded," said Iver. "Theirs wasn't. It was our only advantage."

"The shrapnel could have killed the kids."

"I'd never have let that happen. We need to move on. Now."

The hallway was secured. Iver dusted off his hands and took inventory. Two men down, four others wounded but able to walk. Logan checked the Griffins for bumps and bruises, then shouted up at Iver, "If the gunfire didn't wake up Von Strife, your Magneto Collapse sure did. We need to move fast."

"Where's Raven?" shouted Harley. The last time he'd seen her was on the ground floor, putting on her grappling harness.

"She never made it up," Iver answered darkly.

"What do you mean?" exclaimed Harley.

"Her grappling hook is here, Harley, but she is not. She is somewhere below."

Harley raced toward the stairs, but Logan caught him

by the collar. "Don't even think about it. If she's down there, she knows how to hide herself. Believe me, it's more dangerous where we are. She's safer."

"We can't leave her!" Harley shouted.

"No time. We're going up, and that's an order."

Max heard the rumble of clockwork feet marching above them. "It's not gonna be pretty up there."

Logan handed weapons to each of the Griffins. "That it ain't. Get your *Codex* ready. The main attraction is about to begin."

"Looks like it already has," said Iver, pointing at the ceiling plaster, which suddenly exploded downward. A squad of Grimbots dropped from above, weapons blazing.

Positioning themselves behind fallen statuary, the Templar returned fire with their upgraded MVX pulse rifles. In a torrent of blaster fire, the Grimbots began to lose ground. Their armor pulverized. Arms shattered. Legs flew through the air.

"Use the EM grenades!" Logan called as he dodged an incoming energy bolt. "Finish them off before they rebuild themselves."

But it was too late. The damaged Grimbots were already rebuilding themselves. Heads were snapped back into place, arms screwed on, guns realigned. With a metallic roar, they jumped back into the fray, smarter and meaner than before. Max knew the Templar wouldn't be able to keep up this one-sided battle for long. Already, two of Logan's men had been vaporized.

Max turned to Ernie. "Do you think you can keep them from rebuilding?"

"What? How?"

"I don't know. If a body part hits the floor, scoop it up and throw it out the window?"

Ernie nodded and was soon playing a game of keep-away with a Grimbot head. Yet no sooner had he thrown it out the window than he heard it plink off something outside. Something metal. Something big. Then Max saw a massive shadow looming just outside the window.

"Everyone down!" shouted Logan just as the outside wall was peeled away. Peering through the hole was the giant itself: a Juggernaut clockwork. The ultimate battle machine. Powered by a changeling mind, adaptive, fast, and loaded down with firepower. It was a battleship with legs.

Max whirled and raised his *Codex* gauntlet, letting go a blast of blue Skyfire that struck at the metallic monster's face. Its invisible shields now flickered into view, deflecting Max's attack easily.

"We need an exit!" Max heard Logan growl. The Juggernaut's shoulder-mounted rocket launcher pivoted around, its barrel pointed directly at Logan and Max. Any escape was blocked by smoldering rubble. Neither would be able to scramble out in time. A missile launched.

"Incoming!" Logan shouted. Max felt two strong arms pick him up. "Out you go, Grasshopper!" In a moment of inexplicable strength, the Scotsman hurled

Max into the air. He sailed over the rubble and landed nearly twenty feet away with a thud. As he looked back, he could see the place where he'd been standing had turned into an apocalyptic firestorm.

"Logan!" Max shouted in horror. He sprang toward the destruction. Iver caught him.

"No time!" Iver shouted. "We've got to get you upstairs! To the mirror!"

"But Logan!" Max cried. "He didn't make it out! He's the only one who knows how to use the Omega Option." Iver was already barking orders to the two remaining soldiers. As the Griffins were herded down a service corridor, Max prayed that Logan had made it out alive. He looked over to see Harley, scraped and bruised. Max realized that they still didn't know what had happened to Raven.

They located a set of stairs and raced up. Gunfire erupted near the top, and several spy drones plummeted down the stairwell. But the drones had taken their toll. By the time the Griffins neared the top level, Søren was the only remaining Templar soldier still on his feet.

"The final stairs!" Iver called, dragging Max by the arm. "Hurry! We're running out of time."

"Holy smokes!" Harley shouted as they emerged into the upstairs hallway. Nearly half the building had been torn away by the Juggernaut. To get to Von Strife's office, the Griffins would have to pass right in front of that killing machine.

"Leave the Juggernaut to me!" shouted Søren. He slung the plasma launcher from his back and checked the charges. It was a massive weapon, built specifically for taking down big clocks.

"You can't use something like that in here!" exclaimed Natalia. The recoil fire would burn them all to cinders. "Wait...oh no. You don't mean you're going to..."

"Wish me luck," said Søren. He took off at a run and leaped out into the emptiness, the plasma launcher's barrel glowing an electric purple. There was a crash and a crunch of gears, followed by an explosion.

Iver wasn't about to wait to see what happened. He pushed the Griffins down the hall, through the smoke and fire, toward Von Strife's office. As they moved, Max looked over his shoulder to the destruction behind them. So many of their allies had been wounded or killed. Logan was missing. And now Søren...

"Flakbots!" Natalia called. Metal beasts with barrel breastplates and shoulder-mounted cannons took position between the Griffins and Von Strife's office. The Griffins looked around for cover. There was none. "We are so dead...."

Yet, even as the walking artillery took aim, the Flakbots suddenly collapsed into a heap of metal bits and steam pistons. Behind them stood Ernie in thick rubber gloves, holding a wrench.

"For goodness sake, Ernie!" cried Natalia. "Why didn't you do that before?"

"Flakbots don't armor up like Grimbots," explained Harley. "All their bolts are exposed." As he spoke, a shadow loomed over him. A Grimbot was about to take off Harley's head.

"Look out, Harley!" Natalia screamed.

But it wasn't Natalia who acted, nor was it Agent Thunderbolt who raced to the rescue. It was Raven. Having bolted up five flights of stairs, she reemerged, breathless, just as Natalia cried out. The Goth girl swung around, a Disintegrator Revolver in each hand. She pulled the triggers quickly and furiously. Whether through some unspoken training or just plain luck, her blaster bolts blew out the clockwork's knee. It stumbled backward, tripped over the rubble, and tumbled out into the night.

Harley's heart pounded. They stood there for a breathless moment. Harley and Raven stared at each other.

"I owe you one," Harley said finally.

"I collect," she replied with steely gleam.

"Your hair is a mess."

"You like it that way, so shut up."

THE FIRE GIRL

Logan was missing, his team obliterated. Everyone had taken damage, including Iver. They'd fought their way through the school—Max's school!—and now stood outside Von Strife's office. Nothing now separated them from the object of their mission.

"This will be your greatest moment, my Griffins," Iver said as he placed his hand upon the ornately inscribed doorknob. "What lies on the other side of this door will define who you are and who you will become. No matter what else you do, do the right thing. Always."

Max smiled. "It's good to have you back, Iver. We couldn't have done it without you."

"And I've missed you four very much as well," said Iver, placing his other hand on Max's shoulder. Then he pushed open the door and stepped inside as casually as if it were a doctor's office. There was a flash of red flame, brighter than the sun. Searing heat forced the Griffins to scramble for cover. Their lungs burned. Their eyes watered.

It was over in an instant. As Max struggled to the door, he found a smoking hole in the floor where Iver had been. Its edges were smoldering.

"Iver!" screamed Natalia, racing up to the edge and nearly slipping over the side. Then her eyes raised skyward to see a girl, about sixteen years old, hovering in a miasma of flames. Wind whipped her fiery hair, and the wreckage of the school's roof sizzled beneath her.

"Oh my god," Natalia gasped, stumbling backward out of the heat. Indeed, the changeling did look like a fiery deity. Electrifying power rolled down from her in searing waves.

"My friends just call me Naomi," said the changeling.

Max's gauntlet blazed with Skyfire, and his eyes narrowed. "You're going to pay for what you did to Iver."

"You're brave, kid," Naomi replied. "Maybe in a few years, you'll be a contender." She smirked, and with a wave of her hand, Max's Skyfire dissipated. He staggered as his only defense was wiped away like rain on a windshield. "But today you're playing in the big leagues."

Raven drew her Disintegrator Revolver, aimed it at

Naomi, and squeezed the trigger. *Click!* "Oh, you have to be kidding me," Raven growled.

"Nice try," Naomi said with a smirk. "But this room is programmed to disable energy weapons."

"Then maybe you should try this on for size," said Harley, whipping a small air gun from his belt. Taking aim, he squeezed the trigger. The next thing Max knew, Naomi clutched her neck. With a cry, she dropped to the floor, unconscious. Her fire extinguished.

Max looked at Naomi in amazement, then over at Harley. "Dude, what was that?"

Harley patted the air gun. "An X500 Take-Down. Basically a MERLIN Tech–powered tranquilizer gun for changelings. Monti gave it to me, just in case." He nudged Naomi's form with his foot, flipping her over onto her back. "She'll be out for hours. Long enough for the Baron to find her."

Natalia returned to the smoking hole where Iver had once stood. "He's dead. I can't believe it. Not again… not again…" Max found himself on his knees next to her, holding her hand. The other Griffins joined them.

"This can't be the way it ends for Iver…." Ernie's voice cracked.

"I am afraid it does," said a familiar voice as Von Strife emerged from a side door. Harley spun around, air gun raised. But with a wave of Von Strife's hand, the weapon clattered to the ground. "Now then," Von Strife said as he moved across the charred floor, "I suppose you are wondering why I called you all here?"

"I didn't see an invitation in the mailbox," said Max, wiping the char and ash from his face.

"Yet here you are." Von Strife smiled weakly. But he was far from weak. Max could sense the currents of some monstrous power within him. Something that eclipsed even Naomi. "As you know, I have failed. Again. Sophia is dead. I am alone. And perhaps that was the way it was always supposed to be. But"—he scanned the Griffins intently—"I have you, my friends from the old world. The only people in all the worlds who understand. I'd like you to be with me, in these final moments."

"Iver isn't dead," Natalia spat out, almost believing her own words. "He'll come back. Wait and see. And then you will be sorry."

"In the grand scheme, it hardly matters. My wife is dead. Now my daughter. And soon, I will join them. In fact, it is to my death that I have invited you." A dozen clockwork soldiers appeared, sleeker and more refined than the Grimbots. "Please, join me," said Von Strife as he walked over to his portal mirror—the very mirror they had come to find. He entered his security code and stepped through. The Griffins and Raven followed, blaster barrels at their backs. There was a flash, and they were gone.

THE PARAGON
ENGINE

The Paragon Engine lay within a massive cavern somewhere deep underground—large enough, in fact, to
swallow up a city. Or two. But the engine itself was identical to the one the Griffins had seen in their own world:
a colossal ringlike machine that was more of an elaborate
collection of millions of smaller machines, all ticking
away with clockwork precision. Within the engine's interior roiled a surface of blue fire, the doorway through
which Smoke had sent the other Griffins. They were still
in there. Somewhere.

The floor of the cavern was damp and smelled faintly
of oil, the very same wet-dog smell that had permeated

the *Wormwood-6* scrap of paper, as well as Smoke's footprints in the girls' bathroom. This room was where everything came together for Natalia's case, though she was a little too distracted at the moment to enjoy her achievement.

The Griffins were marched past a sobering line of Grimbots, Flakbots, Iron Mongers, Dreadnaughts, and even a few Juggernauts. And then there were the changelings, flying, threatening, and glowering at the Griffins. There were nearly as many here as there had been back in the skies above Iron Bridge. But at least here the Griffins could get a better look at them. All the changelings had been modified, surgically altered or enhanced with clockwork machinery. These were the Lost Souls, and their blank stares were all Max needed to know that they'd live and die for Von Strife without hesitation.

"Yes," said Von Strife, catching Max's gaze. "The Lost Souls, as the Templar like to call them. They were, once upon a time, all like you, Ernie." Von Strife motioned toward a winged changeling who passed overhead. "Many were from Earth Alpha, cursed with powers that would ultimately destroy them. If I hadn't brought them to this world, they'd be dead by now. So, as you can imagine, they are fiercely loyal."

Ernie watched the changelings in both loathing and fascination. They reminded him of the Agents of Justice, except for the fact that they were on the wrong side. He wondered if there were any speedsters here. He'd never fought another changeling like himself.

The underground compound buzzed with activity as Von Strife and his captives approached the Paragon Engine, which towered above a multilevel platform that served as its control center. "And so our journey begins," said Von Strife. He climbed the stairs and settled into a leather chair, the likes of which the Griffins had never seen. It could recline flat, and along the polished brass frame were dials, toggles, and cylinders filled with bubbling liquid. Above it hovered a clockwork robot with a dozen spidery arms that seemed to flex and twitch apprehensively. What it would do to the chair's occupant, Max had no idea. But he knew one thing: this was the chair of a mad scientist.

"Max, the letter," Natalia prompted. "The one the Baron gave to you. In case we were caught, remember?"

Max frantically dug in his pockets. With a sigh of relief, he pulled out the letter and waved it in the direction of Von Strife. "I was supposed to give this to you," he called.

The letter was snatched away by a clockwork, and Von Strife scanned its contents. He discarded it carelessly a moment later. "The Templar," explained Von Strife, "think I know nothing of the danger the Paragon Engine poses to our two universes. Balderdash! Not only was I aware, I designed it that way. Earth Beta was my last hope. If I didn't succeed here, I had no hope of succeeding anywhere."

"Then what are you doing?" called Max with a gun barrel against his back.

"I am programming the Paragon Engine's self-destruct sequence, which will set off a cataclysmic chain reaction, obliterating this world, as well as our own."

"You're going to destroy us all?" cried Natalia. "This is crazy."

"Crazy would be me moving on to another Earth—another Sophia—expecting another outcome. My daughter, a child so perfect that my heart ached just to watch her breathe, was meant to die. And if that's true, then existence itself is fatally flawed. This is not a crime. I am committing a long-overdue justice."

Max shook his head. "Back in your office, you said something about calling us here. Why bother? I mean, why not just let Naomi finish us off instead of bringing us down here?"

Von Strife smiled warmly. The same smile he shared with them as their old friend, Obadiah Strange. "Ah. Well, when the end comes, we all want to be surrounded by those we love. And while you may not think well of me at this moment, I still care for you four. Very much." He reclined the chair, and dozens of snakelike coils shot down from the spider-bot, attaching themselves to Von Strife's skull. "Please pardon me for a few moments while I calibrate the Paragon Engine."

"We can't let you do this, Von Strife!" Max shouted, but his voice died among the ringing of hydraulics and steam pistons as the Paragon Engine fired up.

"Max," Natalia whispered, "you're the only one who can stop him."

Max's heart raced. He glanced over his shoulder at the army of clockworks and changelings, then back at the Paragon Engine. He'd have one shot at this. All his power. He'd throw everything he had at the machine. Then, well, he wasn't sure. What was certain was that if Von Strife wasn't stopped, the Paragon Engine would kill everyone and everything, including themselves. "If I do this, I won't be able to protect you...." he said to Natalia.

"We can take care of ourselves," said Raven. "Besides"—she pointed to her holster—"he didn't disarm us before bringing us down here. Big mistake."

"What's a Disintegrator Revolver going to do?" asked Ernie. "Von Strife is immortal."

"But his friends aren't," Natalia replied, unsnapping her own holster.

Ernie looked at his companions, then took a deep breath and faked his best steely-eyed determination. "Well, not every hero has a chance to go out in a blaze of glory, right?" He knew as well as they did that this wasn't a fight they could win. Not by themselves. But he knew they had to try.

"For Logan, and Iver," Max said, clenching his fist.

"For the Griffins," said Natalia. She glanced over at Raven. "Of both worlds."

Max took another a deep breath and quarterbacked. "Harley, Raven, and Natalia, I'd stick to the changelings. Keep them busy—and take out the flying ones first." He turned to Ernie. "I need your help with the clocks. Look for some way to disable them or their weapons, like you did with the Flakbots back in the hallway. And in your spare time—because you are the only one here who will have any—keep an eye on the rest of us. Just in case there are any sneak attacks or whatever."

Ernie saluted resolutely. "Agent Thunderbolt is on the job."

"Well, I guess that's it, then. I just wanted to say that you're the best friends anyone could ever have. With my parents' divorce and all, well, you're the only family I have left."

"Don't you even make me cry," Natalia warned. "I have some serious business ahead of me, thank you very much."

They put their hands in a pile, Raven's on top. They were all smiling. "Go, Griffins!"

Ernie was gone in a blast of wind. Raven, Harley, and Natalia stood back to back, triggers snapping as fast as they could pull. It was Max's turn.

316

Max raised his gauntlet, and a surge of blue fire swept out from his fingertips, blowing away the Grimbots between him and the Paragon Engine. Gear bits zinged and zoomed in every direction as the massive wave of Skyfire swept up the platform, and struck at the engine itself. However, like the Juggernaut before, Von Strife knew a thing or two about the limits of Max's power. The Skyfire roared, but it couldn't touch the machine. An invisible barrier protected it.

Max groaned as Von Strife's forces regrouped and launched an attack of their own, putting the Griffins on the defense. The air snapped and sizzled with phaser blasts, organic electricity, and cries of alarm on both sides. The changelings were one thing, but the clockworks just picked themselves back up after being blown away.

"This is getting nasty," Raven said as her blaster bolt ricocheted off a clockwork and nearly struck her ear.

"Blasters are no good against bots," Max called back. "Stay on the changelings."

"Hit the electrical kid!" Natalia shouted. "He's the biggest threat." The flying changeling, realizing he was the new target, dove for cover, but the second he touched down, he got a bang on the head from Agent Thunderbolt's fist of fury. The flying changeling fell over cold. Ernie grinned, then disappeared again to hammer away at the remaining Flakbots. They were the easy ones. After that, he'd need a bigger wrench.

"Keep it up!" Harley cried. He, Raven, and Natalia were backing toward the wall as the clockworks and changelings charged. More than one blaster bolt had nearly ended it all. But Ernie kept nudging the bolts out of the way just in time. Meanwhile, the three of them kept squeezing their triggers.

Seven changelings down, and Max had blown away an additional twenty clockworks, slinging his Skyfire like a cowboy at a shooting gallery. But the Griffins were outnumbered, and neither the guns nor Max's Skyfire would last forever. Every blast had to count.

"We need some help!" Max shouted. He pointed to his gauntlet. "I'm going to summon something."

"Do it fast!" Natalia rang back as she blew the wings off a fireball changeling. The Lost Soul hit the ground with a thud, rolling nose over tail.

Max's Skyfire formed a blue flickering shield to protect himself while he figured things out. While he reached into the quiet of his mind, a steam-driven missile hammered into his shield. The shield wavered for a moment, but Max was quick to repair it. He just needed a few moments. The *Codex Spiritus* was more than just a gauntlet. More than a ring. It was first and most importantly a mystical prison for monsters. Of course, it was a dangerous business to summon a monster into the real world. With the wrong monster, Max could easily get himself killed. His mind raced for just the right one, then locked on. Max spoke the words of release. "Kienasara!"

A class-three Metal Biter, easily twenty feet tall, emerged from Max's *Codex* gauntlet and raced toward the Grimbots. The mountainous troll had a sweet tooth for iron and steel. Sensing their danger, the clockworks scattered — but not before three of them were snatched up and eaten. Every clockwork's weapon was turned on the Metal Biter. The monster shrugged off the missiles, picked up a Flakbot by the leg, and began batting practice. Heads, arms, and wire guts flew in all directions.

Max turned his attention to his friends. They were pinned down, surrounded by a wall of ice.

"Take out those frost changelings, Ernie!" Max called. Before he could finish the words, Ernie had swept through the changelings, wrapping them up in Grimbot guts and pulling them along after him. Max leveled the icy wall with his Skyfire, but quickly found himself the target of a fire changeling, who shot blasts of hissing magma toward him in a steady rain of death. Max staggered. Then his enemy hit the ground with a crunch, thanks to a deadeye shot from Harley's pea-pod 7000 blaster.

"Nice shot," said Raven, pushing back her hair.

"I wondered what it would take to impress you." Harley grinned at her. She grinned back.

"Max, the Metal Biter!" Natalia called. Max turned to see the Goliath go down under a hundred pounding metal fists. There was a horrible, monstrous scream, then silence. A moment later, the clockworks were back after the Griffins. This time they brought reinforcements. The Juggernauts had joined the fight. Max could see them powering up. Lights flickered across their shells, and pistons pumped. Steam rolled out from their vents. The metallic monsters, immune to Max's Skyfire, bore down on the Griffins like roaring steam locomotives.

"Um, anyone got a bigger gun?" asked Raven.

Max gritted his teeth and gave it all he had. Everything went blue again as the fire spread through every cell of his body, leaping from his fingertips, his eyes — even his mouth. He was mentally exhausted, but he just kept pouring it on, wave after wave.

The cavern burned in the brilliant crush of magical energy. Changelings were knocked out of the air. Grimbots exploded. Drones evaporated. Dreadnaughts were swept away. But when the tidal force of Max's Skyfire receded, three Juggernauts remained standing over the Griffins, unimpressed.

"Dibs on the big ugly one," said Raven. No one laughed. Their weapons were useless. Their lungs burned. Even Ernie stood beside them now, unable to do anything other than die beside his friends.

Without so much as a "Prepare to die," the Juggernauts snapped their rocket launchers forward, took aim at the Griffins, and pulled the triggers.

WHERE IT ALL UNRAVELS

Max opened one eye. Then the other. The missiles hadn't fired, and the Juggernauts were slumped on their sides, as if they had fallen asleep. All the machines were. Every clockwork killer in the cavern—with the exception of the largest machine, the Paragon Engine.

"The Gearz worm!" Harley exclaimed, patting Max on the back. "I knew Monti would pull through." Monti had done it, all right. Yet there was still so much to do, and so little time. As the five kids stole between the lifeless clockwork giants, they found a familiar face waiting for them on the other side.

"I should have killed you a long time ago," said Smoke. His blond hair was swept up into menacing spikes. In his fist twitched the tail of a small catlike creature. Sprig. He tossed her toward Max, where she hit the cold floor, fur matted and eyes glazed. She wasn't moving. "Miss your little Bounder? She's so cute. Well, not so much now. Sorry about that. You know what they say about curiosity and the cat...." He smiled an evil grin.

Max frantically scooped up his Bounder. She was alive, thank goodness, but she needed help. Max's eyes rose to meet Smoke's. His anger flared, but his Skyfire was gone. He'd need to sleep a week before he'd be up to taking on Smoke.

"Smoke, you're way out of your league," said Ernie, stepping toward him. "And it's time you and I settled things once and for all." Smoke laughed.

"This ought to be fun, Thundertwerp," said Smoke. "Catch me if you can." He was gone in a swirl of mist. But so was Ernie. A moment later, Smoke reappeared with Ernie only a few microseconds behind. Smoke looked over his shoulder and instantly vanished. For the next frantic moments, the two changelings ran a dizzying race from one side of the cavern to the other, but Ernie narrowed the gap with every step. Smoke grunted as Ernie finally tackled him to the ground, wrapping him in a headlock. Smoke coughed, but he was still smirking. "Okay, kid. You're faster. Thing about it is you're not very bright." There was an electrical zap from Smoke's hand. Ernie let out a cry, then rolled to the floor with a grunt, passing out.

Harley leaped at Smoke, but the changeling vanished. When he reappeared farther away, his smirk had crept up his face.

Max raised his *Codex* threateningly. "You're finished, Smoke." It was a bluff. A big one.

"Oh, your Skyfire. Right." Smoke laughed. "That's the problem with you, Mr. Hero. You are always thinking by the rules. Me? Not so much."

In a flash, he was gone.

Max heard a scream.

"Raven!" Natalia shouted, pointing up. Nearly twenty feet above them dangled Raven, caught in Smoke's arms. Her legs kicked at the empty air as Smoke kept them both suspended by a constant pulse of teleporting.

Harley's eyes smoldered with rage. "Smoke, you set her back down, nice and easy."

"Geez, Harley," Smoke said. "I don't know about that. What's in it for me?"

"Your teeth."

Smoke rolled his eyes. Raven looked like she was considering biting his arm, but after glancing down, she thought better of it.

"What do you want from us?" Max said, seething.

"I want you dead," Smoke replied. "What, is that some big revelation? Am I the only one here who can see it? The Paragon Engine is the greatest invention of all time. And you want to destroy it, just like the other Griffins. You want to destroy it because you don't understand it. You're afraid of it."

"Maybe you missed it," Max said, "but when Von Strife powers that baby up, it's going to rip apart the multiverse—killing all of us!"

"Blah blah blah. I've heard it before. The other Griffins went through, and guess what? The universe is still here."

"Went through?" Natalia said. "You mean, pushed through."

"If that's all it took, you'd be in there already. You have to program the machine just right."

"You don't have the brains to pull it off!" shouted Harley.

"I guess genius runs in the family." Smoke glanced over at Von Strife, who was still working on the Paragon Engine, seemingly unconcerned with the destruction around him.

"You're adopted," Harley said, stabbing at Smoke with the only weakness he could think of.

Smoke glared at Harley, then let go. Raven screamed as she plummeted. The Griffins raced toward her. But before crashing down, she was teleported back up into the air. "The next time, I drop her for real," Smoke warned.

"Just tell us what you want!" called Max frantically as he kept Sprig close. She still hadn't moved.

"That's what I thought," Smoke said, gloating. He then sniffed Raven's hair. "Huh. Lilacs. Smells pretty."

"I am so going to kill you," she said as she struggled to get her breath.

Smoke grinned. "You know, I have to say I'm impressed you guys even made it this far."

"What, Blackstone didn't work out so well?" said Natalia.

"Well, he worked cheap."

"If you call Earth Gamma cheap."

"What?" Smoke snorted. "Oh yeah. The deal. I wasn't planning to take him with me anyway. Kind of a creep, you know?"

"You won't be going, either,"said Max. "Your dad's about the blow us to kingdom come."

Smoke paused suddenly, his eyes flitting to the Paragon Engine and back. He grinned nervously. "Nice try… I almost bought it. But you guys don't know him like I do. He'd never do anything to hurt Sophia. No matter how crazy he got."

"Sophia's dead, Smoke," Natalia said. "She died last night, thanks to your poison. Didn't you know?"

As the words left her mouth, Smoke's face lost its color. "No…no, that's impossible. The Wormwood isn't that strong. I only used enough to keep Von Strife busy.…I…wait…wait! You guys are trying to mess with me." He seemed to be struggling with the news, then abruptly disappeared, taking Raven with him. A moment

325

later he reappeared, his face as white as ash. For several moments, Smoke hung there in the air, looking like he was going to be sick.

"You went to see Sophia, didn't you?" asked Natalia grimly. "Well, now you know we were telling the truth. How's it feel?"

Smoke said nothing.

Natalia stepped forward. "We already know everything, Smoke. We know about your deal with Blackstone, how you lied to your dad, and your big escape plan to Earth Gamma. And yes, we know all about how you slowly poisoned your sister with Wormwood-6."

Smoke's mouth fell open.

"I have to admit, it was pretty sneaky how you used Monti's portal mirrors to sneak into her bedroom and poison her food—and poison Sprig. But not sneaky enough." Natalia was guessing now, but she knew she wasn't far from the truth. Smoke's horrified eyes confirmed it. "Sure, you didn't expect to kill her. But she died anyway. Your own sister. That's pretty low, Smoke. Even for you."

"The only thing I don't get," said Harley as he helped Ernie back to his feet, "is how a creep like you figured out how to operate a Paragon Engine."

"That would be my doing," said the haggard voice of Von Strife. They turned to find the evil genius standing nearby, unhooked from the Paragon Engine's nervous system. The news of Smoke's betrayal had roused him from his work, delaying the end of the universe. "I needed someone to keep the gateway open long enough for me to do my work on Earth Alpha and get back again. I trained him myself. And...as a result, I orchestrated the death of my own daughter." He turned his eyes upward to Smoke, and the power of that gaze struck the boy like an icy dagger.

Smoke was as pale as a breathless fish. His muscles gave, and Raven slipped from his arms. Harley was there in a moment to catch her. The two of them went down in a tumble but were soon back on their feet.

Von Strife looked up at Smoke and shook his head. "I have been so blind...." With a wave of Von Strife's hand, Smoke's teleporting was over. He was lowered to the ground next to Raven. For many long moments, nothing was said. Max braced himself for the worst.

"Smoke," Von Strife said, "I saved you from a life of misery. Brought you into my house. You were given a sister. You were given a future. And this is how you repay me?" Smoke looked away. "You have driven a stake through my heart."

Smoke turned back, his eyes blazing. "You killed Sophia by not loving me. If you'd have cared even a little, I wouldn't have tried so hard to leave this rotten place."

Von Strife staggered. His hands shook. "Smoke, you have abandoned your humanity."

"Humanity?" Smoke spat. "We're changelings. We're not like them. We have the power to change the world—

rule new worlds if we wanted. But instead you wasted your time trying to save a girl who never wanted to be saved."

"Never wanted..." Von Strife's hands trembled. "You know what she wanted, Smoke? You know her last words? Were they about me? Her dead mother? They were about you. She asked me to forgive you. But I didn't know why, until now. Yes, she knew you were poisoning her. And she loved you anyway."

Smoke's face drained of color. "She couldn't have known. She couldn't. She was asleep...."

"She knew...." replied Von Strife, his voice rising. "And she let you kill her anyway—afraid that if I found out what you were up to, I'd never forgive you. She covered for you, like she's done since the day you came under my roof. You killed my little girl, without knowing she was your only friend."

"No, that's impossible!" Smoke's wild blue eyes locked on the roiling ring of the Paragon Engine. As his eyes remained locked on the machine, he gritted his teeth. "I hate this place. I hate everything. And more than anything"—he turned to Von Strife—"I hate you!" Smoke bolted up the stairs to the Paragon Engine.

"He's going to jump through!" Natalia shouted to Ernie, but he was still too dazed to even stand.

"Wait!" Von Strife shouted. "It's not calibrated yet. Smoke, stop!" It was too late. Smoke leaped through the Paragon Engine and disappeared in a flicker of light.

Von Strife was a statue for several minutes, dark and brooding. His eyes never once left the Paragon Engine, his face lit in ghostly blue. "In my quest of save Sophia, I've become a monster," he said finally. "Perhaps Sophia couldn't see it. But Smoke did. My own insanity infected him like a virus, turning him into the very weapon that would destroy the last of the goodness left to me: Sophia. He didn't kill her. I did...." He took in a ragged breath, then turned to the Griffins. "It is over." He rolled up a sleeve, revealing a wristband of polished chrome and etched gears. He tapped a sequence of pearl-inlaid keys.

"What are you doing?" asked Natalia, eyeing the gadget with suspicion. "You're still going to blow us all up?"

"No, Ms. Romanov. There's been enough death today, I think." He looked regretfully at the Paragon Engine, the final resting place of his adopted son. He passed his hand over his grief-stricken eyes. "More than I ever could have imagined. I am surrendering Iron Bridge. Its defense systems are off-line now. There is nothing to prevent the Baron and his allies from sweeping up whatever remains of my legacy."

"You've made the right decision," said the soft voice of Ms. Merical as she emerged from the same portal through which the Griffins had come. There was a second flash. Monti and the Baron appeared. Behind them stood the tall figures of some of the most powerful men and women the world would ever know. Brooke was there, too. Spotting the wounded spriggan in Max's arms, she rushed over.

"Is it bad?" asked Max as Brooke took Sprig into her arms. A warm golden glow moved across Sprig's matted fur. Max's Bounder suddenly twitched a whisker, then an eyelash. She raised her eyes to Max. Smiled. Took in a deep breath. Then nestled farther down into Brooke's safe arms. She was going to be just fine.

Otto Von Strife's face clouded as he regarded his erstwhile enemies. He sighed, then slowly turned and approached the Paragon Engine. "Please, allow me the honor of deactivating it. It is, after all, my creation. My greatest creation...apart from my daughter. And it is the final resting place of...my son." With a shaky hand, he pulled a lever, and a stream of clicking gears set to work, spitting out a feed of symbols across a screen. "Wait..." mumbled Von Strife, as he stepped closer to the machine and scrutinized the data. "This isn't right."

"What is it?" asked the Baron.

"Something is preventing me from powering down the engine." His voice rose in agitation. "I can't seem to stop the self-destruct!"

Harley and Monti were beside Von Strife in an instant, reviewing the readout. "It's the buffer!" Harley exclaimed. "I knew it! Monti, the buffer. The Griffins are still in there!"

"My Harley is still in there!" Raven shouted. "I knew it!"

Von Strife paused. "What? In the buffer? Impossible. Their particles would have lost coherency long ago."

"Not necessarily," said Monti, pointing at a strange sequence of symbols. "Look here.... How would you explain this background scatter in the buffer? Now let me match it up against the bioprints.... Yes! Do you see now? They're in there. And we have a plan to get them out."

Von Strife listened to Monti's plan, then studied the screen with bloodshot eyes. "If you are right, if they are in there, they are doomed. Your plan is a reasonable one, if only these bioprints hadn't been exposed to the electrical currents for so long. We can't rebuild the Griffins — not without killing them."

"If we can't get them out," said the Baron, "how can we stop the Paragon Engine from destroying itself and our universe along with it?"

In a fury of discussion, interjections, and heated debate, the three minds — Von Strife, Monti, and Harley — set to work on the problem. At first Harley only listened, but soon he added his own ideas. They argued, but Harley stood his ground. While the conversation was on a topic far beyond Max's comprehension, he could see plainly where this was going: a very painful choice.

Within a few moments, the debate closed and Von Strife turned to the crowd of Templar leaders. His eyes were stones. "To stop the deadly chain reaction, the Griffins must be removed. To do so, there are two options, both of which are ghastly. The first and most straightforward solution is simply to demagnetize the pattern buffer. In effect, erasing the Griffins." He paused. "To save billions of lives, it is a mathematically reasonable sacrifice."

"You slimy, murdering..." Raven said as she made for the platform. Natalia caught Raven's sleeve, just enough to slow her assault and ask a question of her own.

"And the other option?" she asked.

Harley stepped forward. "We take their place." Ernie nearly fainted again.

"Harley is essentially correct," said Von Strife. "To get the others out alive, we need valid bioprints. As fate would have it, you Griffins are an exact match." He sighed. "Give me a week, and we could resolve this more elegantly. However, given that our life expectancy is considerably shorter than that, a more radical approach is required: to bring the other Griffins out safely, you must go in."

"You want to erase us, instead of them?" Ernie shouted. "You might as well tell us to jump off a building!"

Von Strife shook his head. "Perhaps I misspoke. I don't mean to send you in. I mean to send you through. Back to Earth Alpha. As you pass through, your bioprints will briefly come into contact with those of the other Griffins. In that moment—the smallest sliver of an instant—lies our hope of restoring the stability to the Paragon Engine."

"What are the odds of it working?" asked Max.

"Less than one in seven hundred," admitted Monti with a groan.

"If it doesn't work?"

"You will be caught in the pattern buffer as well," said Von Strife. "And to save our two universes, there would be no choice but to erase you. All of you. Eight Griffins, rather than just four." Von Strife turned to the Baron. "As I mentioned, the only option I feel confident in is the first: erasing the pattern buffer. A repugnant choice, but there it is."

"Eight minutes and counting," said Monti apologetically. "We have to do something, and soon."

"There's no alternative?" asked the Baron. "You realize what you are asking the Griffins to do...."

Von Strife nodded. "Billions of lives are in the balance. A decision must be made." He turned to the Griffins. "I am sorry, but no one can make this decision except you. And once the decision is made, there is no going back. You four mean more to me than you know. Outside of my own family, no one has a greater share of my heart. But that is why I must also be brutally honest with you. Your choice is to go through, knowing that you may well die, or to remain and allow the other Griffins to be erased. There is no other option. No alternative. I am sorry...."

Max looked at Ms. Merical, hoping there might be some other way. Some lucky chance. But she only shook her head.

Ernie squirmed. Natalia bit her lip. Raven was too horrified to say anything at all. Harley slowly stepped down to join his friends, his face apologetic. Meanwhile, Max looked from face to face. Precious time was ticking down, and he knew that those in the room agreed: the Grey Griffins were the ones to make the final decision.

Max glanced up at the Paragon Engine, studying it. He wondered if the other Griffins — somewhere inside — could hear what was being said and the choice that was being made. He wondered what they would say, if their situations were reversed. Would they even hesitate? With that thought, Max felt a creeping shame. There was no first option. Not to a Griffin. If there was a chance, no matter how small, hadn't they always put their lives on the line for others? And if they failed, at least they'd know they'd done their best.

Harley thought of Henry and Candi Eisenstein. He never had a chance to say good-bye. Never had a chance to explain why he'd acted so distant. They deserved an answer. Now they'd never get one. He'd made a mistake. He'd made a big mistake.

Natalia's mind shuffled through the scrapbook of her life on Earth Beta. She'd been happy. Happier than she'd been in a long time. She loved her new family. Even her new sister, and the sneaky ways Kat would steal Natalia's things. Everything had been so perfect. But looking up at the Paragon Engine made her suddenly aware of how much she missed the little things of her own life: her diary, her pillow, her favorite pair of shoes, the way her mom bargain-shopped, her father's hugs.... This world had been wonderful. But it wasn't home.

Meanwhile, Ernie was a miserable wreck. It wasn't so much the possibility of losing his powers once he got home, or even dying before he got there. It was that he'd never had the chance to say good-bye to anyone. His new friends. His family. What about Robert? Now he'd never get a chance to fix things. It all felt so disappointing. Yet as he pulled down the chin strap of his helmet—the helmet of the superhero known as Agent Thunderbolt—he knew, as the others did, that there was only one choice. Ernie lowered his brass goggles. "Let's do it."

The Griffins nodded in agreement. Max turned to Von Strife. "We're going through." There was a murmur among the adults.

Von Strife nodded back. His eyes looked heavy, and his hands shook. He'd been through a lot. "If you'll give me a moment, I will make the necessary calculations for what is to be, regretfully, a one-way trip, for both you and me."

"You're coming with us?" asked Max incredulously.

"I am afraid not."

"But you said this was a one-way trip for you. I don't understand."

"In order to improve the odds of your survival, I will need to take a more direct hand. It will require a vast amount of concentration and energy. Everything I have, to be precise."

"It will kill him," translated Harley. "And every version of him across the multiverse. There will be nothing left of him."

"Ironic, yes?" Von Strife said. "In the end, I am the Omega Option." He glanced over at Ms. Merical, who offered a sad smile in return. "Perhaps I was all along?"

GOOD-BYE

"We don't have much time," warned Von Strife. "Please step up on the platform."

"I want to wish you good luck," said Ms. Merical as she moved next to Max.

"Can I borrow some of yours?" Max asked.

She laughed and gave him a hug. "My power can't follow you through. But something tells me you carry all the luck you need inside of you. All you need is to believe in yourself." Then she held out her hand, in which lay a small furry shape that purred when it saw Max. "You have one more passenger," she said gently. "And she seems to be feeling up for a ride."

Max's stomach sank. He couldn't ask Sprig to come along on this mission.

"Sprig goes where Max goes," said the spriggan as she curled around his neck, taking her natural shape for the first time in a very long time. "New adventures. Wait and see. Wait and see."

Max nodded, his lip trembling. "Yeah, sure, Sprig. New adventures for all of us." He kissed the spriggan but kept his eyes locked on the swirling Paragon Engine.

Monti set his hand on Harley's shoulder. "Maybe this isn't the end, you know?"

"You're the scientist," Harley replied grimly. "Our chances aren't good."

Monti shuffled his feet. "Well, I don't know about that. I just wish you could have stayed longer. I have so many questions about the other Monti, the projects he was working on, how different our science is over here.... And then there's you, Harley. Our Harley isn't even aware of his potential. You are light-years ahead. I wish you could talk to him...help him understand what he's capable of."

"You tell him," said Harley with a smile. "And trust me, he'll listen to you."

The Griffins were placed next to the Paragon Engine.

"Well, I have to go," said Brooke, squeezing Max's hand. Her eyes were soft, uncertain—but hopeful. "I'll see you soon, okay? One Max. One Brooke. On both worlds."

338

"Let's hope so," said Max. He gave her a hug and watched her move down the stairs. He'd give anything to be following her.

"You, too, Raven," said the Baron.

Raven stiffened, realizing she had instinctively followed Harley onto the platform. Looking down, she saw she was holding his hand like a vice. Blushing, she pulled away. "Well, I guess this is good-bye, then."

"Guess so." He watched her intently. Her magenta-streaked black hair shimmered under the shine of the Paragon Engine. Her face was sooty from weapons fire and debris, but her cheeks were flushed with sadness rather than fright.

They stared at each other for several quiet moments. With a silent rush, Raven hugged Harley so ferociously that he thought his neck might break. Then, after an awkward moment, she pushed away. "Well, don't get all sappy or anything," she said. A tear escaped her dark lashes. She turned away.

"You may step through," said Von Strife. "And go with my regrets and my grandest wishes." The greatest scientist the multiverse had ever known plugged himself into his engine one final time. Blue energy coiled down from the spider-bot directly into Von Strife's flesh, fusing him permanently to the machine. His eyes clouded.

With Sprig safely wrapped about his neck, Max reached out for Natalia's hand. Natalia took Harley's. Ernie linked them together. With a quiet look at one another, and a nostalgic, longing look back at the world and friends they were leaving behind, they stepped into the swirling gateway, knowing they were doing the right thing. And that made all the difference.

REFLECTIONS

Max recalled nothing of the journey. No bright lights. No chasm of darkness. Just an expanse of grey as he violently returned to consciousness, gasping like a fish that had been washed ashore.

He felt several hands on him. Turning him over. There were voices.

"Max, are you all right? Can you speak?"

Max's eyes fluttered. His blurred vision focused. Staring down at him was the face of Iver. Max blinked, then rubbed his eyes. He sat up unsteadily and looked around. Sprig lay on his lap, guarding him from whatever this new world had in store for them. Natalia, Harley, and

Ernie lay nearby, looking terrible but otherwise unharmed. A Templar medic checked their vitals.

"Where am I?" Max croaked. He coughed, then took a drink of water. "Man, I thought I was dead...." Brooke was there in a moment, channeling her healing powers into him.

"I knew you'd be back." She smiled and gave him a quick hug before moving on to help the others. She was different somehow. Then Max remembered. If Von Strife's plan had worked, this should be Earth Alpha. The Griffins were home! Or were they?

"Yes, Master Sumner," Iver said, reading Max's thoughts. "And a welcome home it is."

"But how, Iver?" Max stumbled over the words. "I saw you die...."

"Von Strife would never have led you to the Paragon Engine if I were with you. No, it was time for me to return to this world. While you were fighting the changelings, I was hurtling across the dimensions toward Earth Alpha."

"But I still don't understand how you can do that without a Paragon Engine."

"Dimensional travel has always been possible. It's not easy. And it's not for everyone. Von Strife, however, wasn't interested in limits. He needed to move armies, not just himself. And so he built the Paragon Engine. Although there was not quite as much time as I would

342

have liked. After all, you've only been gone a couple of weeks."

"Weeks?" said Max, sitting up.

Iver wiped Max's forehead with a rag, pulling away a red, gritty smear. "Each universe has its own laws, which include time. What seems like months on Earth Beta was nothing more than a few weeks here on Earth Alpha." Max slowly rose to his feet. The world spun around him. He moved a few unsteady steps toward Natalia and stumbled.

"Take it slow, Grasshopper," advised a decidedly familiar Scottish voice. A strong, leather-clad arm steadied Max as he looked up to see Logan. There was no patch over his eye. "Things will take some getting used to."

"But..." Max's head began to clear again. "What about the Griffins from Earth Beta? The ones trapped inside the Paragon Engine? Did they...were they...?"

"They are alive and well," Iver answered, pulling a pipe from his pocket and inspecting its innards. "And quite happy to be back. Your mission, Master Sumner, was a resounding success."

"And Von Strife?" asked Natalia as she pushed away the medic and joined Max. "Did he...?"

"He paid his debt," Iver answered. "A tragic story. But through his final sacrifice to bring you home, he has now embarked upon a journey into the great unknown.

343

And who is to say that upon those far shores he did not find someone waiting for him? A little girl, I fancy. And very relieved to see him."

"But how could you know what happened to him or any of the others if you weren't there?" asked Ernie as he and Harley approached them.

Iver waved toward the swirling Paragon Engine. "Thanks to Monti—our Monti, that is—we were able to tune the engine in such a way as to watch the events unfold in Earth Beta. How else could we prepare for your arrival?"

"You guys were amazing," said Brooke as she healed a nasty gash on Harley's face. "The way you fooled everyone into thinking you were someone else, solved the mystery of Sophia's poisoning, and then how you marched into the Paragon Engine, knowing you'd probably die. It's unbelievable!"

"You saw everything?" asked Ernie, blushing and hoping there hadn't been any cameras in his bathroom.

"Everything that mattered. And I wasn't the only one." She gave a meaningful glance at Harley, then nodded toward an approaching figure.

Harley turned to discover Raven next to him, watching him intently. If he thought leaving the other Raven had been difficult, seeing this Raven was a shock he hadn't imagined. His heart was pounding, his hand trembled. "Raven, I, uh…"

"Don't ruin this with talking," she interrupted, and

blushed. "I don't need anything. Except, maybe, to talk. But not now. I'm just... glad you're alive."

Harley moved toward her, then stopped, glancing cautiously back at Ernie.

"Go on," said Ernie with a wink. "She's waiting for you. Besides, this world is about to meet the new, improved, interdimensional-traveling Agent Thunderbolt. Look out, ladies."

Max's eyes turned to see several clockworks—Monti's creations—approach the great Paragon Engine, and with a pull of a great iron lever, it was deactivated for the final time. Then, piece by piece, the engine was dismantled. Max watched as the world he'd left behind grew farther and farther away. It had been a great place. His parents together. His place on top of the Round Table charts—everything had been so perfect. Just the way he'd always wanted them to be. It was gone now. Already like a dream. Yet he couldn't help but think that he'd brought something of it back with him. Different choices, maybe. Different outcomes. He'd start, he promised himself, by calling his mom. He'd ask her to give up the Hamptons and move back home. Bring Hannah. Even without a dad, they could still be a family. After all, Harley had managed it for years.

Natalia's head fell on Max's shoulder a few hours later. The Griffins were snugly fit into a helicopter. On his other side was Ernie, snoring like a warthog. Max's eyes moved across the compartment to see Harley. The boy smiled back at Max and nodded toward the sleeping Raven next to him. Max could read Harley's thought in his eyes: *Things are going to be okay.* As the helicopter chased the setting sun, he knew things would be different, because the Griffins were no longer the same.

Spring arrived in a burst of flowers and sunshine. Avalon's parks filled with laughing children. Down its sidewalks paraded the local folk, in their plaid shirts and blue jeans, tipping their hats to one another, and passing along gossip, recipes, and advice. The return of the Griffins had hardly been noticed, because few, if any, had known they'd been gone at all—or even that their whole world had come so close to a conclusion.

But, it was better that they didn't, Max thought as he pedaled his bicycle along Main Street in the early morning sun. It wasn't yet seven o'clock, but there was one door that would always be open. Max hit his brakes and popped over the curb in front of the Shoppe of Antiquities. The door rang with the familiar chime of Iver's bell. Max took in the scent of tobacco and moved briskly through the eclectic store and its shelves of knucklebones, unicorn statuettes, and leather-bound books. He raced up the creaky stairs and pushed through the door at the top. Inside sat Ernie, Natalia, and Harley. Iver stood over them, chewing on the stem of his pipe.

"I apologize for the early appointment," began Iver with a broad smile, "but I wanted my best friends with me for the official reopening of the Shoppe of Antiquities."

Natalia pushed away a wisp of red hair from her sun-freckled face. "We wouldn't have missed it for the world, Iver." As she went on, Max regarded her thoughtfully. She was a different Natalia now. Her stay in the other world had changed her. She was a bit taller now, a bit softer, and a bit more patient with others, especially the girls at Iron Bridge Academy. She wasn't quite the icon of cool she'd been on Earth Beta. So she'd made changes. It started with Brooke, because Brooke was decidedly safe. Then she'd approached Katie, hoping for the best. Soon, Brittany and Gwen were carefully added as friends. As for Natalia's sense of fashion, well, she saw no reason to hide her goggles, corsets, and lugboot-style from the world beyond Iron Bridge any longer. Not Avalon. Not anywhere. She was who she was. And she liked it.

Ernie set his Agent Thunderbolt helmet on the table and tapped his fingers thoughtfully. "You know, I'm even faster than I was back on Earth Beta. Monti clocked me at 372 miles per hour the other day. I think it's time to start up a new superhero team."

"Are you keeping the name Agents of Justice?" asked Natalia.

"Nah. I'm retiring it. With Von Strife gone, we'll need a new mission. And that means a new name. And a new team."

"I thought we were your superhero team," Harley said, laughing and kicking back lazily in his chair. His T-shirt was frayed and stained. He wore a new ring on his finger — a silver one with a familiar black bird on it. No one had asked him where he got it, but they had an idea. As for tracking down his father, Harley had finally broken down and talked to Natalia. She'd begun work immediately. No leads yet. But if anyone could find Henry Eisenstein, she could.

Ernie shook his head at Harley. "You? Superheroes? You guys don't look the part. I'm talking logos, spandex, the whole enchilada."

Max laughed. "You can keep your spandex. Jeans are good enough for me." And yet, Max's clothes had changed as well. Although not as bold as Natalia's fashion, his jeans were darker and he'd taken to wearing a leather jacket similar to the one Logan had worn in Earth Beta. Max never knew what became of that Logan. But he had a hunch. A tiny clockwork ladybug had flown in through his bedroom window one day and settled upon his ring. It sat there, quietly regarding Max, as if to say it would be keeping an eye on him. Max blinked. And it was gone.

The Griffins and Iver talked briskly about their past adventures, laughing at times, sighing at others, until the clock struck eight. Then they descended and moved to the front door. Iver winked at them, paused dramatically, then flipped the CLOSED sign to OPEN. He flicked on the lights, and the bell immediately chimed. Several customers bustled in, nodding their hellos, then disappeared into the maze of aisles.

The Griffins soaked up the scene, meandering down the aisles, lost in the memories of all their adventures, their wins, their sacrifices. Time seemed to stand still as the sun climbed higher into the sky, filling the shop with a cheery glow. They wished it could stay like this forever. They wanted to stay there, locked in that happy moment for as long as they could. But they had places to go. And people to see. And they couldn't put it off forever. They finally filed toward the front door, where Iver waited for them.

"And the world goes on...." Iver smiled at the Griffins. "And it is now time to say good-bye."

"But we'll be back later," assured Ernie.

"No, Ernie. I mean we must say good-bye to the past. You're older now, my friends. Wiser. You four have had extraordinary adventures. You've lived life at its best, and at its very worst. Life is not perfect. But you've overcome this with the choices you've made, large and small. And oftentimes, it is the littlest decisions that matter most. So make the most of them. Yes, the Grey Griffins have always turned hardship into something good. Something special. I am very proud of you."

As Iver opened the door for them, Max paused and gave a last look at the Shoppe of Antiquities, the place where their adventures had all begun. "So what comes next?"

"Next, my Griffins?" Iver looked at them with a sparkle in his eye. "When you step outside this door, you leave your childhood behind. Look out to the horizon. There lies the dizzy heights of a world you have only dreamed possible. Your greatest adventures are yet to come. Yes, my friends. I have high hopes for you. High hopes."